PRAISE FOR FINDING FOREVERMORE

Kelly Jo Wilson is one of my new favorite authors. In *Finding Forevermore*, she spins a realistic adventure of two lifelong friends coming together to put the pieces of their lives back together. I loved the tenderness of the romance and the spiritual journey. I encourage you to pick up a copy and enjoy the read.

-**Tracie Peterson**, award winning, ECPA and USA Today best-selling author of over 140 novels including the Hope of Cheyenne series.

Kelly Jo Wilson's debut novel is one full of faith and second chances. As the two friends go on a road trip to find some needed answers, they're forced to confront their feelings in all the areas they've been hiding. Fans of Melissa Tagg and Becky Wade will love the way Kelly Jo merges faith and romance.

-**Toni Shiloh**, Christy award winning author

I will be forevermore enchanted by this book! Once I began reading, I put my life on hold until I reached the final page. This is a lovely story of personal growth and reflection, sweet romance, and a beautiful reminder that friends are family. I cannot wait for the continuation of this series.

-**Holly Varni**, Author of the Moonberry Lake series

Raven Cunningham's search for answers about her father leads her to Army Ranger Cole Walker—still carrying battlefield scars and the very secret she longs to uncover. But Raven is also the one who once slipped away from him, making their reunion as tender as it is complicated. A moving, page-turning story of second chances and the healing power of truth.

-**Suzanne Woods Fisher**, bestselling author of *Capture the Moment*

Finding Forevermore

A Renewed hearts Novel

Finding Forevermore

A Renewed Hearts Novel

Kelly Jo Wilson

Grace Tree
Media

To Jesus Christ, my Lord and Savior, to You be all the glory and praise. You are the author and finisher of my faith. I trust in You with all my heart.

To my husband, you are my absolute favorite person to do life with and I love you more than you know. Forever and ever, Babe.

To my boys, you are living proof of God's grace. I love you no end to no end.

ROAD TRIP MAP

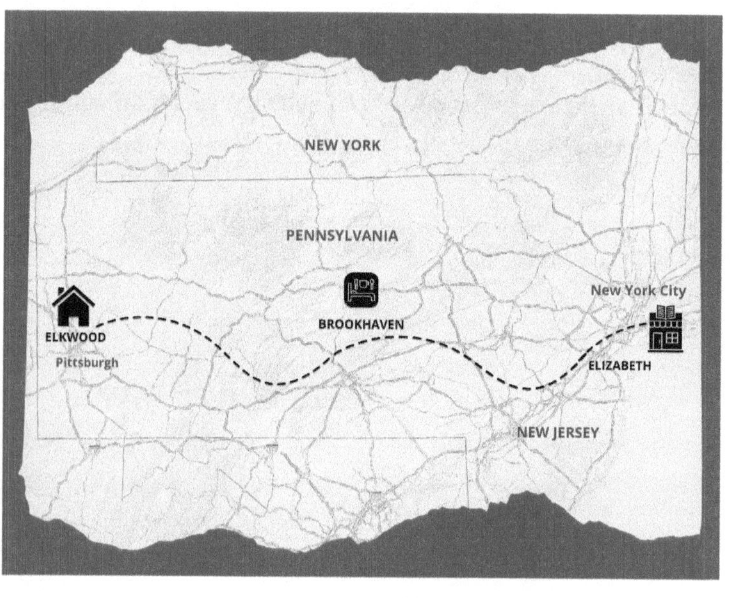

PROLOGUE

My dearest Raven,

The doctors told me the cancer has spread to my bones and lungs. But don't you worry about me. I'm going home to be with your grandfather and my Lord and Savior, Jesus.

I'm writing this for two reasons. The first is to remind you how cherished you are. You are kind, creative, and brave. Never apologize for who you are. God crafted you with purpose, and when life feels messy, He's still writing your story. You must know how deeply I love you. You've been the light of my life since the moment your mother brought you to my home. Our life wasn't always easy, but every decision I made was out of love and a fierce need to protect you.

The second reason is harder for me to put into words. You deserve the truth, and I've kept it from you for far too long. I pray you'll forgive me. Your father wrote to you. He tried to stay in your life. When I asked your mother about it, she claimed she was trying to work things out and didn't want to confuse you. I wanted to believe her, but later learned the truth. I was afraid she'd take you from me, so I stayed silent.

I managed to save one letter from him. I kept it for you, tucked away all these years. The weight of my silence will come with me to my grave. But I need you to know, I never stopped hoping you'd find the truth. Remember, people don't always show up the way we expect, but we can still hold on to hope. I'm so sorry, Raven. I pray you'll forgive me.

Love always,
Gram

CHAPTER 1

THREE MONTHS AND FOUR days since Gram had been gone.

Gone.

Raven still couldn't bring herself to say *died*. Words like that were too final, too heavy.

She should be writing Chapter Three of *The Pet Whisperer's Guide to Fixing the Humans: How to Rehabilitate Your Abused Pet (Without Losing Your Mind)*. She had a deadline. A client expecting her to deliver. But instead of knocking out the section on understanding boundaries with an anxious rescue dog, she was staring at a blank page, her fingers frozen over the keyboard.

Her coffee had already cooled. Her brain felt about the same.

She was supposed to channel emotions into her writing—wasn't that what a good writer did?

Ghostwriting *The Pet Whisperer* books was probably as far as her writing career would ever go. Usually, she could churn out a step-by-step guide to reading a German Shepherd's body language without breaking a sweat. But nothing surged forward.

She hadn't touched her own novel in weeks. Writing about the lie her heroine believes and why she can't open her heart? Crickets. Yeah. Sure. Raven Cunningham, mystery romance novelist. Who was she kidding?

The cursor blinked at her, mocking her inability to summon a sentence. This time of day used to be her favorite—sipping her breakfast blend as ideas poured out of her. But now? The quiet of the morning had a way of stirring thoughts she'd rather bury. She rubbed her hands over her face, exhaling hard.

Come on, focus.

She needed to finish this chapter. Or at least get past the opening paragraph. Something.

But all she could think about was the one person who used to believe in her when she didn't believe in herself. Gram.

And her funeral.

How Raven stood by the casket long after people left, staring at Gram's hands folded over her chest. Her hands were too still, too pale. Too not-Gram. Those hands had baked peanut butter cookies every Friday after school. And tended prize-winning roses in the western Pennsylvania frost eight years in a row, no easy feat.

Parts blurred, but she remembered Mom showing up hours late to pay respects to her own mother. Typical. She'd swept in wearing sunglasses big enough to be a windshield for a compact car. The beer on her breath mixed with the smell of funeral lilies. Her apology sounded more like a weather report, flat and devoid of emotion. "Sorry I missed the service. Traffic was murder. You know how it is."

Mom had declared herself in charge of everything Gram left behind, despite having barely spoken to her mother for the last ten years. Less than a day after the funeral, there she was, strutting around Gram's house with her arms full of clothing and knick-knacks, muttering things like, "This'll fetch a decent price at the pawnshop," or "Bet someone'll want this tacky lamp." That lamp wasn't tacky, it was Gram's reading lamp. That lamp glowed over hundreds of romance novels and dog-eared gardening guides.

Raven grabbed her coffee mug and crossed to the kitchen for a refill.

How was she supposed to move on?

Gram had been the only real family she'd ever had. The only one who stayed. The ache of her absence hadn't dulled. If anything, it felt sharper in moments like this—quiet mornings with no one to share coffee with. No warm encouragement nudging her forward.

Raven shoved the thought aside and walked back to her desk. She sat in front of the laptop, willing words to emerge. But they wouldn't come.

Her fingers curled against the keyboard. She wasn't a kid anymore, tiptoeing around shattered glass and slurred words. She had worked too hard to build a life outside of that. And yet, without Gram, it all felt like a house of cards.

Raven inhaled.

Focus. One paragraph. One sentence. Anything.

Still, nothing came.

She slammed the laptop shut and ventured to the couch. The silence in her apartment thickened, almost palpable. It pressed against her skin and settled deep. The urge to hear Gram's voice tightened.

Deep breath.

After listening to the news for a little while, Raven sauntered to the bathroom to get ready for work. She stared at her reflection in the mirror. Dark circles ringed her eyes, and her face seemed gaunter than before. She traced a finger along her cheekbone. Concealer hid the evidence of sleepless nights. She dressed for a morning shift at the bookshop, pulling her dark hair into a messy bun. She grabbed her bag and keys, casting one last glance at the photo of her and Gram on her dresser.

As Raven stepped into the crisp morning air, the streets of Elkwood, Pennsylvania stirred with life. Rain came in soft sheets, misting the windshield. She parked her old Subaru in the small lot next to Main Street. The bookshop, Belles Pages, was still the only place she felt halfway normal since she was a teenager. Its familiar scent of worn pages and vanilla candles greeted her as she turned on the lights. She could breathe there, if only a little. It helped to be surrounded by stories, even if her own words were stuck somewhere she couldn't reach.

A few customers trickled in throughout the morning, but Wednesdays gave her a chance to catch up on her reading. The rain didn't let up most of the day. Nina stopped at about ten o'clock to check in a delivery. After lunch, while Raven shelved a new mystery series, her phone buzzed.

Zoe: Don't forget about tonight. You promised.

Raven set the phone face down on the counter. Tonight?

Oh, right, the investor meeting.

Her stomach twisted.

Zoe needed her as a backup. But the effort required to feign enthusiasm for the night out sounded exhausting. Energy would be better spent trying to will words from her limbs for Chapter Three. The last thing she needed was another call from Jo, The Pet Whisperer herself.

As Raven headed toward the back room, the bell above the door chimed. In dashed a young girl with blazing red hair, wet and stuck to her forehead. She clutched her father's hand, dragging him to the children's nook.

"Daddy, look!" The girl's voice bounced with excitement, pointing toward the Nancy Drew Mysteries.

Raven smiled. "Can I help you find something?"

"I love mysteries! I need one for a book report, but we get to pick whatever we want." The girl traced her finger along the book spines. "I just finished *Werewolf in a Winter Wonderland*. Do you have any other books like those?"

Raven pulled out *Whispering Pines*, the first in the Shadows of Hawthorn series. "I used to love these books when I was about your age. They have mystery but some magic, too." Seeing that familiar lettering took her back to what seemed like a lifetime ago.

The antsy redhead pointed to the cover with a girl wearing yellow shoes. "Wow! Daddy, look at the girl on the front."

Her father flashed a smile.

"There's a map too." Raven opened the book to show her.

"Cool! I want this one, Daddy. Please?" The girl clutched the book to her chest, then accidentally dropped it in her excitement. Raven stooped to pick it up, her fingers brushing the open pages. The dedication caught her eye:

To the whispered echo in the shadows of my heart,
To the lone voice that sings in worlds torn apart,
In the quiet moments, when the night's silent core, Whispers
    softly . . . Nevermore.
Know that with each beat, each lore,
Dad loves you, forevermore

Breath caught in Raven's throat. A sense of connection stirred inside her, but she wasn't sure why. Probably because she'd read that book a thousand times.

"You've made her day. We'll take it."

Raven scrambled up and led them to the counter. The father corrected his daughter to stop wiggling more books from the shelves beneath the register. She chuckled at the girl smitten by books—reminding her of herself at that age. Raven handed her a free bookmark, and the girl's eyes grew big as saucers.

The girl and her dad ran to their car in the rain, the warmth of their bond lingering like a bittersweet perfume. The way the father knelt to speak to his daughter, so gentle and present, it stirred something in Raven.

Don't think about it.

The last hours of her shift passed in a daze. By the time she got home, a little after five o'clock, the rain had slowed to a drizzle. She tossed her keys on the table, collapsed on the couch, and stared at her closed laptop on the desk. She gripped a throw pillow to her chest and shut her eyes. Just for a minute . . .

A knock on her door made her jump. Zoe's unmistakable yell followed. "Rae, open up! Don't even think about bailing on me."

"Just a minute." Raven hustled to the door while smoothing down her hair. She loosened the deadbolt and opened the door.

Zoe barged in past her. "You'd think I was trying to make you give an acceptance speech by the way you're avoiding me. I called and texted like ten times." Zoe stepped back, eyeing Raven from head to toe. "Is that what you're wearing? Wait, were you sleeping?"

Raven rubbed her eyes. "I just laid down for a second."

"It doesn't matter." Zoe marched to Raven's closet.

"Where are we going, Zo? You still haven't told me."

"The Timber." Hangers screeched as Zoe sifted through Raven's clothes. "Don't you have anything that isn't black?"

"Black is my signature color." Raven chuckled to herself and walked into the bathroom to brush her teeth. After rinsing, she leaned against the bedroom doorframe, crossing her arms.

Zoe investigated Raven's closet with exaggerated horror. Her perfectly manicured fingers picked up Raven's favorite oversized sweatshirt off the bed. She held it up like it was evidence of a crime.

"Please tell me you weren't planning on wearing this tonight." Zoe's own designer blazer and sleek boots were as polished as ever—a sharp contrast to Raven's faded jeans and lived-in sweatshirt.

Raven rolled her eyes. "What's wrong with being comfy?"

Zoe arched an eyebrow, unimpressed. "Everything. Tonight, you're going for hot professional not work from home. Put this on." She tossed a satin green blouse Raven had worn once, to last year's Christmas party.

Raven spit in the sink and wiped her face. "Seriously? That's absurd for the Timber."

"Just put it on. We have to hurry. I told Luke we'd meet them at seven."

"Them? You told me you needed a wingman in case he asked for the shop's sales numbers."

Zoe flashed a sly grin. "Okay, maybe I wasn't entirely honest. Luke's brother just moved back from London and he's tagging along."

Raven groaned. "You really didn't learn from the last time."

"This is an opportunity to meet someone new . . . and handsome . . . and well-traveled. It's about time for you to get over he-who-shall-not-be-named."

"Fine. But if he eats half of my burger and licks the ketchup off his fingers one by one like that last guy, I'm taking my wings to go."

"When are you going to get over that? It was like a year ago."

Raven slipped into the green blouse, smoothing it down over her black jeans. She had to admit it looked good, even if it wasn't her usual style. It felt snugger than she remembered, probably because of her recent diet of Lays potato chips and Marionberry Pie ice cream from the glorious geniuses behind Tillamook.

As they stepped outside, a flicker of hope mixed with dread. Maybe tonight would be different. Or maybe it'd be another reminder of why she should've been under her covers reading or scrolling cat videos on TikTok.

Cole shoved open the door, the morning chill clinging to his skin. He dropped his gym bag with a thud, rolling his right shoulder out of habit. He ran a hand through his damp hair, the ends spiking. Sweat darkened his collar, and his arms ached in that satisfying way, as if finally getting somewhere. Bit by bit, he was piecing himself back together. Better to be home, without the docs watching his every move. Today's workout had been solid—probably his best since the injury.

Thirty-six days left.

Plenty of time to get back in shape, if he kept pushing. Plenty of time to prove to the Physical Evaluation Board he was ready to work. He just had to keep going and stick to the plan: intense cardio, boost endurance, and power through "feelings therapy". His body had to be ready, no excuses. No setbacks.

But first, he had a fence to fix.

He dropped his keys on the entryway table. Lemon air freshener overpowered him as he walked toward the kitchen. Radar, his parent's golden retriever, bounded towards him with a husky bark.

"Hey bud." Cole scratched behind his ears. The old pup still had spring in him, shaking his entire backside, loving the attention.

The house hadn't been his home in over ten years, and with all of Pop's renovations, it hardly looked the same. Though he'd been back for a few days, he still felt out of place. The seventies ranch house he grew up in now had pale blue walls and crisp white trim. Pop spared no expense to give Mom her dream kitchen. Farmhouse sink. Stainless steel appliances. Black-and-white checked every-thing.

Sticky notes hung on every surface, scribbled with Mom's instructions, from feeding Radar to where she'd hidden the spare keys. Apparently, she thought he was eight years old. He grabbed an apple from the counter, scanning the note next to the fruit bowl. His parents took a two-day trip to Lake Arthur, and the furnace filters needed changed? Mom had a healthy sense of humor.

Cole checked his phone as he bit into the apple. Missed call from Sergeant Johnson. He'd call him back later. Not in the mood for another lecture. The waiting clawed at him. He needed to be useful again. Stronger. Ready.

He stepped onto the back porch. Radar pushed himself under Cole's arm as he sat on the steps, crunching another bite. The trees blazed in reds and yellows, their colors sharp in the crisp fall air. A memory stirred—apple picking in the orchard as a kid, back when life had been simpler. Different time, different him.

He tossed the apple core into the woods and pushed to his feet. Enough sitting around. Radar padded behind him as he walked to the garage. Inside, Cole grabbed a hammer and a box of galvanized nails. Simple task. Get it done.

He lined up the first nail, raised the hammer—

His right hand trembled.

The hammer slipped, clattering to the concrete floor like a gunshot.

His jaw locked. He squeezed his right fist open and closed, willing the shaking to stop.

He slammed both fists onto the workbench, nails scattering like shrapnel.

Radar watched him with a tilted head.

Cole rubbed his right arm, trying to sooth the burn. "What?"

The dog nudged against his calf.

Cole knelt on the ground, gathering nails as Radar kept nudging, forcing his nose under Cole's arm.

"All right, all right." Cole laughed as Radar licked his face, drenching him with sloppy affection. "You got me, boy."

Cole wrapped his right arm around the dog, opening and squeezing his fist. The burning faded, but the sting lingered. The Army doctors had nothing for him except pushing narcs. Sure, the nerve pain was pretty much constant, but he'd take the burn and numbness over the fog. Narcs made him fidgety and unsettled. Worse, they clouded his mind, dulling everything he needed sharp.

Radar barked, and his whole body wagged. Cole jumped to his feet. A black Honda pulled into the driveway, kicking up gravel. He walked toward the driveway as his sister Emily stepped out of the car.

"Hey creep." She shut the car door.

Radar rushed over, almost knocking her down.

Cole followed, reaching his arm out for a hug. "I thought you were staying at camp until Friday. Where's Greg?"

Emily shook her head. "Long story. Let's just say his family's got enough drama to fill a soap opera. I bailed early. His crazy cousin joined in the festivities after having too much wine, which made her tongue loose. It was like one of those celebrity roasts, except without all the laughing and witty banter."

"Sounds fun."

"Right. Greg had to stay back and clean up after the fight."

"Fight? As in blows?"

"Yes. Don't ask. His mom is a wreck over it."

Cole grabbed her bag and followed her inside. He dropped it on the couch and slid onto the stool at the kitchen island.

"I'm sure Greg's loving all that."

"Exactly. My appointment got moved to tomorrow, so he told me to take the car. He's driving back with his dad in the morning."

She snagged a jar of peanut butter from the cabinet and grabbed the loaf of bread.

"Were you alright to drive? What about—"

"I'm perfectly fine." She pushed the fridge door shut.

Cole tilted his head back, looking at her.

"Stop it. I know that look."

"Make sure you're taking it easy," Cole said.

"Don't worry so much. My gosh, you're worse than Mom and Dad. I know my limits."

"How did your blood tests look?"

"Good. My hemoglobin was a little low, but that's normal for me." She clinked the knife around the grape jelly.

"How low?"

Emily sighed. "Not low enough to be grilled about it the second I walk in! You're not at work right now, Mr. Army Medic. Or should I say, Doc."

"Just checking on my baby sister, is that so bad?"

"Baby sister? I'm twenty-two years old. But to answer what you're really asking, the oncologist said he's happy to keep annual check-ups." She took another bite.

Cole nodded. "You're still taking kitchen bites, huh?"

Emily finished chewing. "I must test the sandwich. Make sure it has a good ratio of peanut butter to jelly."

They shared a quick laugh.

"You want one?" Emily held up her sandwich.

Cole shook his head. He'd kept in touch with Emily during his deployment, but it had been over a year since he'd been home to visit. Seeing her in person was much better than over video calls, but he'd never tell her that. His little sister had grown so much. Still barely a flyweight, but looked healthy.

"So?" Emily stuffed another bite into her mouth. "How long are you going to be home?"

"Not sure yet."

She narrowed her eyes. "What does that mean? Are you still being evaluated?"

He shrugged. "Something like that."

"So, they haven't decided?"

His jaw tightened. "It's a process."

Her eyes flicked over him. "Right. A process."

Cole could feel her watching him, waiting for him to fill in the gaps.

Emily wasn't stupid. She probably knew something was off. But as long as she didn't ask outright, he didn't have to lie.

She sighed. "You'd tell me if something was wrong, right?"

Cole forced a smirk. "Since when have I ever done that?"

Emily's brows arched, but the worry didn't leave her face. "You're taking it easy on workouts, right? Not pushing your heart too hard like that doctor said."

"I'm fine. What is this?"

"Why are you acting like your last tour never happened? I mean you were in the hospital for three weeks. When your heart stopped we—"

"That has nothing to do with it."

Emily put down her sandwich and wiped her mouth. "What do you mean? That has everything to do with it." Her voice quivered. "We thought you were gonna die."

"Come on, Em. Don't do that."

"Hearing you talk like it's no big deal scares me."

"You're getting more sensitive as you get older, you know that?" Cole hoped to lighten things up. He flashed a quick grin.

"Oh please, talk about aging. Are those gray hairs on your chin?" She pointed at him.

"Whatever." Cole crossed his arms over his chest. A small chip on the edge of the butcher block island top caught his eye.

"Guess who Mom saw the other day?" Emily said.

"Who?" He'd probably be able to patch it. Surprise Mom by sanding her new island. Or, just put a sticky note over it.

"Raven. She still works at that little bookshop in town."

He straightened and leaned forward. "How is she?"

"Yeah, I figured that'd get your attention. She's hanging in there. Her grandmother passed away a few months ago, so Mom—"

"What? Why didn't anyone tell me?"

"You'd just gotten out of the hospital. We didn't want to add more stress. Plus, how were you supposed to make it up here for the funeral, in a wheelchair?"

"I would've figured it out." He rubbed a hand over his face, frustration simmering. "She must be devastated. She and her grandma were so close."

Emily nodded, studying him. "Maybe you could call her. Tell her you're back."

Cole clenched his jaw. "Yeah, maybe."

She folded her arms. "Wow."

"What?"

"You still get that 'one that got away' look."

"Give it a rest. We were just friends." But the words rang hollow, even to him.

"Uh-huh. You were too much of a chicken to make a move." Emily put her empty plate in the sink. "Oh, before I forget, Greg wants you to check out my car. It's making this horrible noise in reverse. Like a dying walrus or something."

Cole chuckled. "A dying walrus? And you drove two hours home like that?"

"Not in reverse." She winked.

Cole shook his head, half amused.

But a familiar knot twisted in his stomach, tugging him back to that last time seeing Raven—the things left unsaid, the apology he owed her.

He'd told himself he'd made peace with it. But now, with her losing her grandma?

He had to see her.

CHAPTER 2

As Raven waited for her order at the coffee shop, her mind drifted to last night. For a brief minute, Zoe had almost convinced her to date again. But the awkward silences and stilted small talk reminded her why she preferred solo nights with a book.

Why did dating have to be so hard?

Weird rules about who calls who, uncomfortable silences, odd conversations talking about hobbies.

And when did guys become so pushy? That guy last night practically asked her to go back to his hotel—right before she'd launched into a whole tangent about how the London Underground map is a masterpiece of design but wildly inaccurate in terms of real-world geography. Not exactly flirty banter.

She groaned, pressing her hands to her face.

He had *not* been impressed.

She recalled another random fact she fired off. "Did you know Covent Garden and Leicester Square look far apart on the map but are actually a five-minute walk? People take the Tube one stop when they could—oh, you're ordering another drink. Cool, cool."

Ugh. Why couldn't she be normal?

And yet, despite that, he had still assumed she'd be interested in *his* "late-night cultural exchange."

Even if a few dates went well, it was a matter of time before the situation got messy. Ethan, or he-who-shall-not-be-named as

Zoe calls him, convinced her they had a future together. Until Zoe spotted him ring shopping, just not for Raven.

She refused to make that mistake again. Except—

It doesn't matter. Who cared if she was still single at twenty-nine years old? There were plenty of things to—

"Order up." The barista called before a swift drop off at the end of the counter.

"Thank you," Raven said.

He gave a quick nod and hurried back to his station. She placed the four coffees into a carrier. Zoe never turned down a double shot caramel macchiato and Nina loved her café au lait. Raven balanced the carrier in her right hand, thanking a customer for holding the door as she walked outside.

The coffee shop was only a block away from the bookshop on Third Street. Raven didn't mind working a couple days a week to help Nina. Not only was she Zoe's mom, but since Raven was sixteen, working there after school, Nina hadn't been just a boss, more like family. Plus, Raven had endless access to books.

Raven grabbed a coffee for old man Lou on Thursday mornings too. He liked his coffee "black and bitter." He usually met his son at the bench next to the bus stop, and they'd go to the cigar shop. Although he kept most people at bay, Raven didn't mind his dark sense of humor. Beneath his unshaven face and coarse voice was a teddy bear—shouting profanities about sports and politics.

As Raven crossed the street, she saw Lou on the bench, paper in hand.

"Hey." Raven called from a few yards away.

Lou did a quick head nod. His face scrunched, and his eyebrows slanted, looking gruffer than usual. She sat on the bench next to him, holding the carrier.

"Do you believe this?" He swatted his hand at the paper. "Look at what these politicians are doing with our tax money!" He shoved the paper in Raven's face. The headline read: *Modernizing Public Spaces: Taxpayer Funds Fueling Office Renovation Project.*

Raven set the tray of coffee on the ground, taking Lou's cup out first. "Here, maybe this will soothe your fury."

Lou grabbed it with a grunt that might have passed for thanks. He sipped and scowled deeper. "I don't like the idea of my money going to fancy office swivel chairs."

"Maybe it'll mean more jobs for the area." Raven pulled out her own latte.

"Doubt it. Just another excuse for more red tape."

She shook her head, hiding a grin by raising her cup to her lips.

"So, how was the night owl's date?" He grinned over the rim of his cup while stretching his left arm.

"How did you know?"

He gestured toward the bookshop.

"Nina." Raven nodded. "About as enjoyable as reading your paper."

"Back in my day we at least pretended to be gentlemen."

"Well, chivalry is dead these days." Raven sipped her coffee.

Lou stared at the paper, shaking his head. "Look at this. Ridiculous. They want big fancy offices for themselves and try to label it 'renovation.' I should call—" Lou clutched his chest.

"Lou? What's wrong?" Raven set her coffee on the pavement and put her hand on his back.

His face winced as if someone lassoed a rope around him and kept squeezing. He grunted. He moved his lips, but no words came out.

"Lou?" She steadied him from swaying. The heaviness of his body was becoming too much to hold. He curled his body inward and lurched forward, tumbling to the ground. She crouched next to him holding onto his arm.

"Help, someone, please! Lou, tell me what's going on. Talk to me." She tapped his arm to get his attention, raising her voice.

A woman darted toward them. "What happened?"

"I don't know. We were just talking, and he grabbed his chest." Raven's heart pounded fast.

Lou moaned and winced in pain. His eyes circled back and forth like he might pass out.

"Call 911!" Raven directed the woman. "Stay with me Lou. We're going to get you help, okay?" She pleaded with him to hold on while he writhed on the ground.

Lou's grip on her arm slackened, and his breath came in sharp, uneven gasps. Raven's mind raced. Her fingers trembled as she brushed his hair back from his forehead.

"Hang in there."

The woman who had called for help knelt beside them, her eyes wide and anxious. She asked Raven questions about him, echoing the answers into the phone.

Raven shook her head. "Just stay with us, Lou."

A small crowd gathered. She wanted to scream, but she stayed calm for him. His son dashed through the crowd and crouched on the other side of him.

"Ambulance is on its way." The woman rested a hand on his son's shoulder.

Lou's eyes fluttered open. He tried to speak, but only a garbled sound emerged. His face looked pale.

"Dad, it's going to be okay. Just hang on."

Lou gripped Raven's hand, and she stayed by him.

A man burst through the crowd and knelt next to her. Lou's eyes struggled to stay open.

"Sir, can you hear me?"

Raven snapped her head up. She'd recognize that deep voice anywhere. "Cole?"

Cole turned to her. "What's his name?"

"Lou. His name's Lou." A well-groomed beard partially obscured Cole's face, but those piercing blue eyes still made her heart skip.

"Try to keep him awake, okay?" Cole put two fingers on Lou's neck. "Talk to him. Keep saying his name."

Lou's son did as Cole instructed. Raven squeezed Lou's left hand.

Cole pulled off Lou's coat and ripped open his buttoned-up flannel. Lou's eyelids grew heavier by the second.

"What's this scar here?" Cole tapped on Lou's chest, then looked at his son. "Did he have heart surgery?"

"Yes. Um, two years ago. He had a stent placed."

Cole ran his hands across Lou's wrists and examined a red and white bracelet. "Does he carry meds with him?"

"I, I think so. I don't know for sure." A flicker of panic darted through Lou's son's eyes.

Cole scavenged Lou's pockets. Calm and collected—as if he'd done this a thousand times.

Raven's heart raced watching the scene unfold. She clenched her jaw and squeezed Lou's hand again. Everything inside her wanted to burst.

"Yes!" Cole held up a small, brown pill bottle. He turned to Raven. "I need your help, okay? I'll talk you through it."

Raven gave a quick nod. The lump in her throat rose.

"Take out one pill from that bottle."

Her hands shook as she opened the bottle.

"Careful, they're small." The drum of Cole's deep voice steadied her nerves.

She poured the bottle and one flat white pill landed in her palm. Cole moved to Lou's right side.

"Great, now I'm going to lift him up a bit. When I tell you, put that pill under his tongue."

With a deep breath, she steadied her hand open, the pill in the center.

Cole lifted Lou's torso as if he were made of feathers.

Lou let out a quick groan.

"Okay, all you have to do is push that under his tongue. It'll dissolve in a few seconds."

Despite her shaking hands, Cole's guidance gave Raven a sense of control. She squeezed Lou's cheeks to open his mouth, noticing his complexion going paler.

"Now. You can do it." Cole propped up Lou's limp body.

Raven slid the pill under Lou's tongue. His eyelids fluttered, letting out a short moan. Cole eased him to the ground and checked his neck again. Lou's son tried keeping Lou awake. After a few minutes, Lou's color started coming back, but he was still groggy.

Cole hovered over him, inches from her. "Get out another pill. We're going to do the same thing again." Raven's breath hitched as she locked onto those blue eyes. For a fleeting second, he held her gaze before shifting his focus back to Lou. Cole lifted him, and she put another pill under his tongue.

Sirens wailed from a distance, growing louder.

"You'll feel much better soon, Lou." Cole stood up and walked to the edge of the curb, flagging down the ambulance as it pulled up.

Raven squeezed Lou's hand while his son talked to him.

Lou propped his head up. His eyes swept back and forth. "I feel like I was hit by a truck," he said in a low, raspy voice.

The ball in Raven's chest floated down.

Everyone parted to allow for the EMT's to get through. They arrived in a blur, swarming around Lou. Cole rattled off medical jargon.

They transferred Lou onto a stretcher and lifted him into the ambulance.

"These guys will take care of you. Stay strong," Cole said.

Lou gave short answers to the EMT. He turned to Raven and flashed a crooked smile.

"I can't thank you both enough." Lou's son climbed into the back of the ambulance.

Raven gave a small wave to Lou and his son as they closed the doors. The crowd dispersed and Raven watched as they drove away. Her pulse finally regulated to a normal speed.

"You did great." Cole turned toward her. There went her pulse again.

"Really? I thought I was going to be sick. I can't believe that just happened."

"No one would have guessed that. You were steady as a rock."

"Is he going to be okay?" She stepped closer to him.

Cole nodded. "I think so. Once they get to the hospital they'll check his heart. He's in good hands now."

"But what about those pills? They helped, right?"

"Yeah, nitroglycerin. Probably for heart disease. Fast-acting. They did what they were supposed to. Could've dropped his blood pressure some, but it gave his heart a fighting chance."

She looked at the ground, then back at Cole. Five months since she'd last seen him. He was hooked up to wires and tubes, barely conscious in that hospital bed.

"Wow, it's good to see you." He stepped forward and hugged her. His strong arms wrapped around her. A faint scent of his cologne caught her nose, and her knees nearly gave out.

She stepped back as they pulled apart. He had that unnerving way of looking at her without saying anything. Was he trying to read her mind? Knowing him, he waited for her to fill the silence.

Raven's heart kicked up, and she crossed her arms, like that would somehow make her immune to his gravitational pull. "I didn't know you were coming home."

"It was a quick decision, kinda last minute." He shifted on his feet, rubbing the back of his neck.

"How do you stay so calm?"

He shrugged. "I guess it comes with years of being shot at."

"That'll do it." Raven let out a small laugh. "I don't know what would've happened if you didn't step in like that."

"Training kicked in. Muscle memory, I guess. Anyone else would've done the same."

"I don't think so." Raven glanced up, meeting his eyes.

Cole nodded, letting a wry grin through. "Guess it's a good thing I know how to rummage through someone's pockets, huh?"

She let out a nervous laugh. "What are you doing here? I mean—do you need to be somewhere?" What a stupid question.

The words hung between them, heavier than she wanted them to.

"Rae . . . I came to see you." His voice softened, like he wanted to say more, but he stopped himself. "How have you been?"

"Fine. Good, you know. Really good." She avoided his eyes, focusing instead on the crack in the pavement. Did he just say he came to see her? No. She couldn't get caught up in that again.

"That's great. I'm happy to hear that." He shoved his hands in his pockets and rocked back on his heels.

The silence stretched, awkward and suffocating. She twisted her ring around her finger. Raven wasn't sure what shocked her more, witnessing Lou having a heart attack or the fact that she was actually having a conversation with Cole in person. The air buzzed with leftover adrenaline, but time slowed around them. Cars passed by and people returned to their routines.

And here she stood, in front of Cole Walker on a random Thursday morning. Her eyes traced the edges of his familiar silhouette, noting how time had altered him in subtle ways. His shoulders seemed broader, his hair a shade darker. A scruffy charm to his beard that wasn't there before.

Why was he *really* home?

Cole shifted his gaze to the street, trying to still his pulse. Seeing Raven after all this time, standing there with that same spark in her eyes was a balm and a burden all at once. Her dark hair caught the sunlight. It framed her face with an effortless grace she seemed blinded to. He didn't want to lie to her, but the truth tangled in knots he wasn't ready to share.

"Are you still writing?" He tried to sound casual.

She nodded, tucking a stray hair behind her ear. "Yep."

"How are you feel—"

"Do you—"

They both stopped and stared at each other, wide-eyed.

"Sorry, you go." Cole said.

"How are you feeling?" She looked up at him with those big brown eyes. "But you don't have to talk about it if you don't want to. I just didn't expect you to come home."

A subtle tension melted in his chest. She had a way of granting him grace he hadn't deserved.

"It's been a journey, that's for sure." He shifted his stance. "Still rebuilding. Some days are better than others."

She nodded, eyes locked on his face, as if trying to read between his words. "You're looking good, considering."

He grinned. "Considering?"

Raven smiled back, the corners of her eyes crinkling. "Well, considering you're supposed to be out saving the world and all that hero stuff."

"Ah." Cole chuckled. "I'm not some old man."

They stood in the embrace of shared laughter, a sound that he could get used to.

Traffic hummed in the background, breaking the silence. Raven shifted her weight, shying away from looking him in the eyes.

"Well, I have to get to work." She motioned to the bookshop behind them.

"Right, I won't keep you."

Raven glanced at the bookshop, then back at him. "Good to see you, Cole."

As she took a few steps toward the building, something compelled him to stop her. "Are you busy tonight?"

Raven paused mid-step, turning back to face him. "No, why?"

"Maybe we could have dinner? Catch up properly without the street corner noise."

"Dinner?" She raised a brow.

"Yeah." He hoped he didn't sound as nervous as he felt. "You know, just two old friends having a meal."

Her smile widened. "Sure, as long as you're not cooking."

Relief washed over him. "Hey, I make a mean ramen."

Raven shook her head and laughed.

"Is that a yes, then?"

She nodded.

"How about I meet you at The Smoke Pit at seven?"

"Okay. See you then." She turned back toward the bookshop.

He waited as she went inside. An inkling of hope dug into his chest. Maybe he hadn't ruined their friendship, at least not entirely. He'd realized how much he'd missed her, missed this feeling of normalcy that only existed with her.

He climbed in his truck. His fingers curled around the steering wheel, knuckles tight. The Army had already made their decision. He needed the PEB to see they were wrong.

Because if he wasn't a soldier, then what was he?

As he drove the streets of Elkwood, he couldn't shake the look in Raven's eyes—sweet but miles away. He should've said something about her grandmother, told her he was sorry for not being there. Instead, he stood there, silent and useless. Same as—well it didn't matter. Too many unspoken words. His foot pressed a little harder on the gas as if distance could clear his mind.

He tightened his grip on the steering wheel, turning onto a familiar gravel road that led to the outskirts of town. He needed space to think. The clearing opened up on Oak Hollow Road, the towering oak branches arching like old bones. This part of Elkwood always brought him a strange sense of calm. He killed the engine and sat back.

He couldn't help but remember Preach egging him on.

"You might have a shot with her."

Cole huffed a laugh. "Yeah, if I don't screw it up first."

"Just tell her the truth, Doc. Leave it to God, my brother."

Cole didn't have Preach's knack for blurting out what was on his mind without filter or fear. Raven deserved more than his half-baked humor and guarded silences. She deserved someone who wasn't stuck in a holding pattern.

He's a Ranger—meant for the field, not for counting therapy sessions or taking orders from medical boards in some tight office. He fired up the engine and headed home.

CHAPTER 3

RAVEN STEPPED INTO THE bookshop and exhaled, ready to put the morning behind her. She needed to work. To shelve books. To focus. If she could do that, maybe the sight of Cole standing over poor Lou wouldn't keep replaying in her head.

Nina greeted her with a knowing look. "Quite the event this morning. How are you holding up?"

"Fine." She carried the coffees over to the counter. Nina followed. After dropping her coat and bag, Raven grabbed a stack of trade paperbacks before Nina could dig deeper.

Nina raised a skeptical brow. "So, do you want to talk about your hero friend?"

"What do you mean?"

"Don't play dumb with me."

"He's an old friend. No big deal." Raven inspected the paperbacks—the new release by Willa Ashcroft, a historical romance. She ran her thumb along the smooth, colorful covers, dodging Nina's probing stare.

"Well, I saw the way he looked at you, that's all I'm saying." She winked then greeted a customer.

As Raven finished stacking the books on the display at the end of the counter, the bells above the door jingled. In barged Zoe with sunglasses perched on her nose, clutching a massive water bottle.

"Only a half hour late today. That's a new record." Nina poked as Zoe made her way toward the stockroom door.

"Ha, ha. Very funny Mom. I was out last night trying to talk Luke into getting those marketing materials you wanted for the book show. It's only a week away."

Zoe popped back out of the stockroom sunglasses on her head, chugging the water bottle. Zoe plopped down on a stool behind the counter, groaning as she massaged her temples. "I need eight hours or my head feels like it's in a vice."

"That's what you get for scheduling a weeknight business meeting and trying to play matchmaker." Raven chuckled, handing Zoe her double caramel macchiato.

"You are a Godsend." Zoe sipped her coffee and let out a sigh. "Good thing you were there. Just having you next to me helped break through the pitch. Luke kept looking at me like I was speaking in Morse code."

Raven straightened the book stack. "Yeah, but you didn't mind his company."

Zoe eyed the ceiling. "Okay, maybe he wasn't too bad. It's just that every time he said 'synergy,' I felt my soul leave my body."

Raven laughed. "Synergy. The buzzword for people who want to sound like the smartest person in the room."

Zoe leaned on the counter. "But can we talk about his brother?"

"Ugh, do we have to?"

Zoe set her coffee down. "What did you think? He was kinda cute, right?"

Raven slammed one of the books, making a loud thud on top of the pile. "No."

She recalled his overbearing laugh, drawing unwelcome attention from everyone at the Timber. "I don't think I've ever heard anyone brag so much about their gym routine."

"Yeah, he was getting a little carried away. What was with the arm-wrestling challenges with those guys playing darts? That was weird. Even Luke thought so."

"No idea. But just another reason I prefer an evening with Mr. Darcy or Mr. Rochester. At least they come with plot twists I can see coming. Besides, a book boyfriend doesn't leave you wondering if he'll call."

"Where's the fun in that? At least you got back out there. Anyone is better than he-who-shall-not-be-named. Plus, it beats taking calls from The Pet Whisperer about how to clean anal glands."

Raven glanced sideways, caught between a laugh and a groan. She grabbed the stack of books and moved to the nearby shelf to display them.

Nina walked behind the counter with a smirk. "Did Raven tell you about all the action this morning?"

Zoe's eyes widened. "Action? What kind of action?"

"Nope." Raven wedged a book into the shelf. "Not discussing it."

"Oh, but we are." Zoe wiggled her eyebrows.

Raven turned and shoved another book onto the shelf. "Let it go."

"No chance. Spill."

"Old man Lou had some kind of episode. The paramedics came and took him to the hospital. But I think he'll be okay . . . because of Raven and her handsome friend." Nina nudged Raven's shoulder.

"I'm not surprised. You always know what to do." Zoe took another gulp and inched closer to Raven. "But who's this handsome friend? Did Luke's brother stop by after the catastrophe last night? Now that's just stalker material."

Raven snapped around, facing her. "No!"

If she said Cole's name, she'd get the third degree.

"You better give me details." Zoe leaned closer.

Raven grabbed a stack of books and walked to the end of the counter. "Let it go."

"Rae? Why are you being weird?"

"I'm not being weird. It was a lot to handle at nine in the morning. I felt so bad for Lou. And you should've seen the look on his son's face . . ."

Raven shoved the last book onto the shelf. She realized how much worse the situation could've been if Cole hadn't been there. And Lou's son had the same look she'd had when the doctors told her Gram's cancer had spread. That helpless, maddening moment when screaming was futile.

She shook her head. "If Cole hadn't been there—"

"Cole? As in *Cole Walker*?"

You and your big mouth, Raven.

"I freaked out and some woman called for help and he ran over out of nowhere."

Nina popped behind the counter. "*That* was Cole? I thought he was stationed in Georgia. He looks different since the last time I saw him."

"Mom, stop." Zoe planted her elbows on the counter and cupped her face in her hands. "So, he, like, saved Lou's life?"

"Yeah, I think so. I don't know. He knew what to do. He figured out what was going on. He had me give Lou some kind of medicine." Raven realized how amazing it was as she heard the words out loud.

"Wow. That sounds crazy." Zoe took another sip of coffee. "Who would've thought the old curmudgeon Lou would need saving. By Cole Walker nonetheless, who's supposed to be fighting terrorists on the other side of the world. Best friend—turned crush—turned total ghost—Cole Walker. What a morning."

"Um, that's not a super accurate summary." Raven laughed, shaking her head at Zoe.

"Does he still have that scruffy beard and those steel-blue eyes, locked and lethal? Just curious."

"Zoe!" Raven's cheeks flushed.

"What? Those are *your* words, not mine."

Raven returned to organizing books on the shelf she'd just finished. But part of her couldn't erase the image of Cole, standing there so confident and capable. Who cares if he looked better than ever. So what if he's quite possibly the most handsome man she's ever seen, besides Chris Hemsworth.

"It was nice seeing him," Raven said. "But honestly, it's complicated."

Nina snorted from behind the register. "Darling, when is romance not complicated?"

"Who said anything about romance?" Raven wanted to crawl into the supply closet and hide.

"Please." Nina shushed with a wave of her hand. She nodded toward a new customer entering the shop while lowering her voice. "Even if you're not looking for love it might be looking for you. That's what happened to me."

"Mom, please." Zoe rubbed her temples. "So, did you talk after or did he run away again?"

Raven looked her in the eye. "You just don't stop, do you?"

Zoe and Nina exchanged a glance. They looked like hungry wolves about to lunge at a baby deer as they waited for her to answer.

"He wants to have dinner and catch up." A sly grin formed, and she couldn't peel it off.

"When?" Zoe said.

Raven walked past Zoe to grab a stack of board books. "Tonight. Now are you done with the questions? I'm trying to work."

Zoe clapped. "Like a date?"

Raven hesitated. Then squared her shoulders. "Like two old friends eating food."

Zoe chased after her. "Eating food after the sun goes down is a date, but whatever. What are you going to wear?"

"I have no clue." Raven glanced down at her rumpled sweater and faded jeans. She squatted next to a shelf, pretending to adjust a row of picture books.

Nina strolled over and leaned on the nearby display, wearing an all-knowing expression. "I vote for that nice red dress. Ooh and the shimmery white scarf."

"Mom's right." Zoe chimed in. "Not that he deserves you dressing up for him."

Raven shot her a look.

Zoe huffed. "What? I'm happy you're getting out there, really. But let's not forget that this man vanished faster than a half off Gucci bag on Black Friday. Now he waltzes back into your life?" She crossed her arms. "Don't let him think for a second he's got you all figured out."

Raven sighed, shifting the T. rex plush in her hands like a shield. "It's not a date. We've been friends pretty much my whole life."

Zoe blinked slow. "Right. And if he tries to pull any stunts, I'll rage-text him until the wee hours of the morning."

Nina patted Zoe's arm. "Let's try to channel our emotions in a positive way, dear."

"Fine. But if he does something stupid, I fully intend to hold a grudge."

Raven set the dinosaur back in its spot with deliberate care.

As the day progressed, she thought about Cole. Worried, more like it. If he wanted to catch up with her, why didn't he call or text? A familiarity fluttered in her stomach, but she couldn't get ahead of herself. They were old friends, nothing more, nothing less.

Later that evening, after plenty of deep breaths, Raven arrived at The Smoke Pit. She hesitated before entering, tugging at the bottom of the same emerald blouse Zoe had forced her to wear the night before.

Ugh, why did she listen to her? She should've worn a hoodie. This was a barbecue place. He'd think it's weird. The last time they ate here together, she'd worn gray sweatpants and a Harry Potter T-shirt.

Okay, deep breath. This is not a date.

Raven scanned the restaurant, searching for any sign of Cole. He was nowhere in sight. A quick check of her phone showed 7:02 p.m.

She headed to the bar, hoping he might be waiting there instead, but still no sign of him. The scent of pork ribs and barbecue sauce wafted through the air, making her stomach growl. What was she thinking wearing a scratchy Christmas blouse and white scarf to eat ribs? She was going to seem desperate, or ridiculous with barbecue sauce all over herself.

She checked her phone again. 7:07 p.m.

Was he ghosting her again?

She had to go. She clutched her purse and rushed to the door.

"Raven." His deep voice stopped her in her tracks.

She turned, heart pounding.

There he was, Cole Walker, moving through the crowded restaurant with that unmistakable stride of his. He wore snug jeans and a crisp black shirt under a black pea coat, looking like he'd walked straight out of a catalog.

"Hi, um . . ." She adjusted the strap of her purse. "I thought I left my headlights on."

"You're still a terrible liar, huh?" A smile played on his lips as he stepped back. "Wow, you look—"

"Ridiculous? I know. Who wears a white scarf to a rib place?" She yanked the scarf off and stuffed it in her purse.

"I was going to say beautiful." His eyes softened, meeting hers, and for a moment, the noise of the restaurant faded. "I'm sorry I'm a few minutes late, I parked my truck at the far end of the lot."

She wondered how long before she witnessed that boy-next-door charm. The noxious charm that had wooed her into thinking they could be more than friends.

"It's okay. And the scarf was an impulse decision. Like when you bought that neon-orange fishing hat back in high school." Oh my gosh, did she just say that?

"Hey, it had personality." He turned to the hostess. "Table for two please."

Led by the hostess, she followed Cole through the maze of tables. She settled across from him at a corner booth. The familiar warmth of his presence seeped into her bones.

It had been too long.

She'd hoped he wouldn't bring up the hospital fiasco. The last thing she wanted to do was replay the entire situation again, or why he disappeared afterwards. She knew better than to hope for anything different.

Or at least, she should.

The Smoke Pit hadn't changed at all, except for the flat screen TVs lined around the bar. The familiar scent of grilled meat and wood smoke reeled Cole right back home. Sitting across from Raven at the same worn wooden table by the window stirred memories from every angle. Here, they'd shared countless meals and jokes. Talking about everything and nothing at the same time.

Cole shifted in his seat, gripping the menu like it was a mission briefing. This was his shot to make things right. To apologize for not being there. No overthinking, no backing out.

Today had been the first he'd seen her in person since the hospital. That little crease between her eyes still darkened when she got nervous. Her order used to be ribs with extra sauce and a side of mashed potatoes. He wondered if it had changed, if *she* had changed.

"I—" he started, but the server appeared with a notebook in hand, ready to take their order. Cole found himself almost grateful for the interruption.

"I'll have a half-rack of ribs, extra sauce, please. And a side of mashed potatoes." Raven gave him a half smile.

Some things hadn't changed.

"The same for me, a full rack though please." Cole handed back the menus.

As they waited for their food, she traced her finger around the top of her water glass. He wanted to say so much, but—

"When did you get back?"

"Just a few days ago." He tried keeping his tone light. "Figured it was time to come back and see what Elkwood's been up to without me."

Raven nodded, but her eyes searched his face for more. She saw through his brush off. He missed that about her, but it chewed at him.

"Elkwood's still the same, mostly." Her eyes met his again.

He exhaled one slow breath and leaned in. "Well, I heard they finally fixed the pothole on Main Street. Had to see it with my own eyes."

Raven's lips curving into that reluctant smirk of hers. "Oh yeah, can't miss such monumental town improvements."

"I have my priorities." He ran a hand through his hair. "Okay, truth. World-class fishing tournament, and I needed my lucky orange hat."

She laughed, finally. "My goodness." She sipped her water. "So, how have you been?"

"Good. Training hard."

She put her glass down slow. "I meant with everything, you know, since Preach."

His fingers flexed around his sweet tea. Not the question he was expecting.

"Fine." He took a quick sip.

She hesitated. "What about his family. They—"

"They're getting by."

The air filled with things neither of them said. He didn't look up, didn't meet her eyes, because he knew he'd see questions in them he couldn't answer right now.

He took another drink. If he wanted to mend anything, he'd have to step it up.

"I want to hear about you. What's new in Raven's world of ghostwriting and mysterious adventures?"

"Mysterious adventures? Not sure I've had one of those in a while. Oh, I won a scratch-off recently, so there's something."

"For how much?"

"Ten dollars. But it's still a win, right?"

"Dinner's on you then, lucky." He flashed a smile and warmth settled in his chest when she laughed again. A sound he forgot he needed.

As their small talk continued, Raven started to loosen up. He waited for a break to ask about her grandmother, but didn't want to kill the mood. He'd wondered if she forgave him. Not that she should.

When their food arrived, the rich smell of barbecue sauce and mashed potatoes made his mouth water. Raven unfolded her napkin in her lap. Then she picked up her fork and butter knife, poking around the ribs, trying to pull off the meat.

"How's the book coming along?" Cole grabbed an end bone and the meat fell off. The bark melted in his mouth after a slight crunch. It was more delicious than he remembered.

"It's okay." She stabbed at a small piece of meat with her fork but couldn't get it.

Cole put down the bone, his fingers doused in sauce. "Did you ever end up talking to that agent?"

She shook her head. Then fumbled with her fork, trying to pick up another piece.

"Of all the times we've come here, I've never seen you eat ribs with a fork." He took another bite.

Raven put down her fork and let out a laugh. "I look stupid, don't I? I was trying to be ladylike while wearing this preposterous shirt."

"Why? Just dig in."

She smiled at him, then grabbed a bone and took a bite.

"Yes! That's how you eat Pit ribs."

A glob of sauce smeared onto her cheek.

"That's the ladylike I remember," Cole said.

They laughed together. As she grabbed another bone, a small piece of meat fell onto her lap. Together they were one big saucy mess of ribs and laughter.

Once he polished off his ribs, she got a small to-go box. He kept the conversation light, steering into safe territory like small-town happenings and updates on his family. But a comfortable stillness stretched between them.

He leaned forward. "What's going on with the book? I thought you loved writing about the case with a missing heirloom or something."

Cole caught the way she froze. She turned those brown eyes on him, soft with something he couldn't quite name. It hit him harder than he expected. The way she looked at him made him forget the weight of everything he didn't want to talk about, just for a second.

"You remember that?"

He nodded. "Of course I do. It was good, Rae."

For a moment, she said nothing. She looked down, twisting the ring on her finger. "It's been a rough few months, actually. After Gram passed . . ." Her voice trailed off. "I've been kinda stuck."

Her admission settled over them, quiet and heavy. He couldn't stand to see her carrying that weight. She'd had enough burdens, now this.

He leaned forward, waiting for her to look up. "I'm sorry, Rae."

"It's okay. I just miss her." She fidgeted with the Wet Nap packet.

For a second, he almost let the moment pass. Reaching for her would make this real. Would mean everything unspoken was finally on the table. His chest tightened, instinct telling him to stay guarded, but he ignored it. He reached across the table, laying his hand atop hers. "I should've been here. I'm so sorry."

Raven shook her head, her lips pinching. "Oh no. It's okay, really. I mean, you were dealing with so much."

"It doesn't matter." Her small hand felt so delicate within his grasp. A surge of something pushed to the surface, demanding to be said. "I never should have shut you out like I did. I was wrong.

That's why I was in front of the bookshop earlier. What I came to tell you."

Raven looked at their joined hands, her hair falling into her face. She looked up at him. "Why didn't you call? Or text, or anything? I just wanted to know you were okay."

His thumb brushed lightly over her knuckles. "I don't know."

Her eyes met his, wide and questioning. The warmth of her hand in his grounded him. But the way she looked at him, vulnerable and open, set his pulse racing. He hadn't meant to say it, hadn't meant to let the words hang there like a confession, but there it was.

Her lips parted like she might say something, but the server interrupted.

"How was everything folks? Need another refill?" The server gathered their empty plates onto his arm.

"Everything's great, thanks. But I think I'm good on the refill." Raven's voice sounded higher than usual.

He nodded in agreement, though his mind was only half on the food. The server left, and quiet returned to their small bubble. He'd come home not intending to reconnect, but maybe he had a chance.

"Thank you for that. I'm not holding a grudge about anything." Her voice was gentle, like she'd wrapped it in fleece for him. "We've always been . . . well, us."

He swallowed hard, but words lodged in his throat like thick mud. He took a deep breath and forced them down.

Raven leaned back, crossing her arms while giving a mock glare. "But I'm still mad at you for eating my chocolate chip cookie in fourth grade."

He laughed, caught a little off guard. "You mean the one you left on the counter for hours? It's not my fault you abandoned it, and it found a better home."

"Better home? It wasn't a stray puppy. My name was literally written on the napkin under it."

He smirked. "In my defense, you have terrible handwriting. It could've been anyone's name."

The tension thawed, replaced by a warmth he hadn't experienced in a long time. Conversation flowed like muscle memory, each word stabilizing the friendship he thought he had destroyed for good. For a moment, it seemed like the clock turned back.

But as Raven looked away, something crossed her face. Something she wasn't saying. Doubt clawed its way back in. He wasn't sure what he expected. Of course, there were still things between them, things he couldn't shake off with a simple apology.

Walking away wasn't an option this time. If he wanted to make things right, he'd have to earn it.

CHAPTER 4

WHEN RAVEN TURNED ONTO Maplewood Lane, a knot tightened in her stomach. The gravel driveway—shared by Gram's house and her best friend Gladys next door—looked untouched by time. Raven had been back only twice since the funeral. Gram's house came into view, with its taupe siding and red mailbox. Gladys had insisted she come early, before Raven's mom returned from Tim's house.

Fine.

She'd go into Gladys' house, sign whatever papers needed signing, and leave. No reason to linger.

Trash bags rested against Gram's house, torn open with the contents strewn across the yard. On the covered porch leaned the screen door off its hinges, a hole torn through it the size of a fist. The ladybug garden flag hung between overgrown rose bushes in the garden beds.

Her heart clenched at the sight of it. Gram would never have left the garden like that, or the house for that matter. She was out there weeding and pruning even after her first round of chemo. But Mom couldn't bother with things like that. She swooped in selling everything she could, even Gram's wedding ring. Now, a rusted blue Volvo with the backend propped onto cinder blocks took up most of Gram's driveway. Probably one of Tim's junk projects. Gram's car was gone. Mom took that, too.

Raven tightened her grip on the wheel, her pulse quickening as she pulled in beside Gladys' Cavalier. Being back felt wrong, like trying to force her foot into an old shoe that no longer fit. The last thing Raven needed was to fall apart over trash and an overgrown yard. Still, the sight of the place gnawed at her. It wasn't supposed to look like this.

She blinked hard, willing herself to stay focused—but then, out of nowhere, Cole's face slipped into her thoughts. His apology. The warmth in his voice. The sincerity in his eyes that had settled into all the cracks he'd left behind. She swallowed hard, shoving the thought away. They were friends.

Friends.

Exhaling, she turned her attention back to the task at hand. Gram's will.

Deep breath. You can do this.

Raven forced herself out of the car. Her shoes crunched on gravel and dried leaves as she walked toward the porch, trying not to look at Gram's house in her periphery.

A grapevine wreath with pumpkin accents adorned Gladys' front door, and a sign that said *It's Fall Y'all*. When Gladys opened the door, a ball rushed into Raven's throat.

"Hi sweetheart." Gladys embraced her the same delicate way Gram always had. Though Gladys had a short frame, her gentle hug kept Raven from falling apart. A few tears escaped, but in good company.

"You look beautiful. It's good to see you." Gladys reached up to run her fingers through Raven's hair. "Come inside. It's chilly out here."

Seeing Gladys without Gram nearby seemed unnatural.

When Raven stepped through the door, the smell of apple pie and berry potpourri hit her. Gladys' tabby cat Whiskers perched in a beam of sunlight atop the floral couch. Raven gave him a soft stroke as she walked past. Gladys shuffled toward the kitchen, motioning for Raven to follow.

"Have a seat, dear. I'll be right back."

A basil plant and porcelain Precious Moments figurines sat along the windowsill above the sink. Her kitchen was laid out similar to Grams—the wood paneling, accordion door to the pantry, and burnt orange GE wall oven.

As Raven took a seat at the table, she noticed a picture on Gladys' refrigerator. Gram beamed as she clutched a small, gold trophy. Gladys and a few other friends surrounded her, all grinning from ear to ear. That was a couple of years ago when Gram had won the senior dance-off at the local community center. Her moves wowed everyone. My gosh, it seemed like years without her already. Raven looked away, twisting her opal ring as she waited. The ring Gram gave her.

Gladys reappeared from the other side of the kitchen, holding a large, tan envelope. She sat across from Raven, putting on pink-rimmed glasses. She fixed her gaze on the envelope and tears welled in her eyes. With a tight-lipped smile, she placed it on the table and gently laid her hands atop Raven's.

"I promised Rosie I'd keep it together." Gladys sniffled. She grabbed a handkerchief from her robe pocket and dabbed her nose, one hand still holding Raven's.

"Now, your grandmother is—was—my best friend. More like a sister for what, forty years? I trusted her with my life. And she trusted me with hers."

Raven trembled, anticipating Gladys' next words.

"She wanted me to give this to you. She didn't want to risk your mother finding it in the house, so she put it in a safe deposit box. As the executor, I'm following her wishes. Rosie made me promise to almighty Jesus to make sure you got this and never let it get in the hands of that mother of yours." Gladys paused, taking a shaky breath.

"I know it's been a few months," Gladys said. "Do you remember what I told you at the funeral? About how the will needed to go through probate? Well, it finally got sorted. These things take time, but the lawyer Rosie chose, Mr. Whitaker, he's thorough. I couldn't give it to you 'til it was all official."

"You did mention something . . . I think. I didn't take much in that day."

"I know, sweetheart. No one expected you to. But Rosie made sure this would get to you when the time was right."

She moved her hands off Raven's and picked up the envelope. Raven stared at it. Keeping things from Mom was not abnormal. Truth was, she hadn't kept enough things from Mom. But this seemed too specific. Part of her didn't want to know what was inside.

"Now, about the house. It's all paid off, so there aren't too many hoops to jump through, but you'll still need to transfer the deed. Oh, that reminds me." Gladys got up from the table and returned with papers clipped together. "Here's a copy of the death certificate, just in case you need it. Also, Mr. Whitaker's information is in there, so you call him with questions."

"What do you mean, *the house*? Mom's living there. Wouldn't she need to do all that?"

Gladys shook her head. "No dear. Rosie wanted you to have it. Most things are taken care of, but you call that lawyer. He'll help you with the next steps."

"So, the house is mine? Just like that?"

Gladys pulled down her glasses and looked at Raven. "Your grandmother loved you, dear. She wanted to make sure you didn't have to worry about all of this. And she knew whatever you decided to do with it would be the right thing."

Raven's hands trembled as she reached for the crisp envelope. It had the words For Raven written in Gram's messy cursive. The ball in her stomach pushed up against her ribs.

"She loved you more than anything in this world. When your mother finally brought you into her life, she was convinced God sent her an angel." Gladys dabbed her nose again with the handkerchief. "You remember that, okay?" She gestured for Raven to stand and pulled her into a hug.

"Thanks Gladys. Gram was lucky to have you."

"Oh honey. I'm the lucky one." Gladys pulled away from the hug. "I miss her so much. And your grandmother thought of everything. You know how she was."

They walked to the door and Gladys clutched her robe together as she opened it.

"Sift through those papers and be careful around your mother. She has been hounding me about that paperwork since the funeral."

Raven walked out to her car. She slid into the driver's seat, the envelope clutched in her hands. She'd crossed the seatbelt over herself as questions spun in her head like an old film reel on overdrive.

"God, what am I supposed to do with this?" She looked down at the envelope as if some grand answer would appear on it.

Gram's house was nothing without her. No more sitting on the front porch drinking sun tea with Gram. Or evenings of puzzles while watching reruns of *Murder, She Wrote*. The one place she felt the most solace transformed the day Gram died—when Mom staked her claim and never looked back. The last thing Raven wanted to do was fight her for it.

She sighed and jammed her keys into the ignition. She stuffed the envelope and papers between her seat and the center console, then shifted the car in reverse.

Drive, she needed to drive.

A big part of her wanted to tuck the envelope away unopened. But, if Gram trusted her with it, she owed it to her to at least look inside.

Cole tightened his grip on the phone, staring out the kitchen window. Checking in wasn't a crime, right? Last night lingered in his mind, the way Raven's guard had slipped for a moment. He wasn't sure where they stood, but one thing was clear—he needed to show her he meant the apology.

"Hello?"

He cleared his throat. "Hey, I just wanted to thank you for joining me last night."

"Yes, uh, I had a nice time." Raven's voice sounded shaky, tentative. Not the same Raven from last night. Maybe he made a mistake.

"Is everything okay?"

She paused, and he could almost hear her weighing her words, deciding whether to let him in. "I—I've been trying to reach Zoe all morning, and I can't get a hold of her."

There was an edge to her voice.

"Is that normal? Not being able to reach her?"

"Not really. Well, early morning, yes. But after 10 a.m. she's usually good about picking up. I just . . ." She trailed off.

"Just what?"

She paused. "There's a lot happening, and I don't think I'm cut out to handle it today. I'll talk to you later, okay?"

He could let that stick. But—

"Wait, what's going on?" he said.

Raven sighed.

"Rae, you can tell me. I'm still the same guy who used to sneak into your grandma's attic to grab boxes so we could build forts."

She paused, but he heard the faintest huff of a laugh. "I went to Gladys' house today, Gram's neighbor." Raven's voice broke, and she sniffled. "She gave me my portion of Gram's will."

He stayed quiet.

"Gram left me a note . . . talking about my father."

He leaned against the counter as he clenched his right fist to pump out the tingling. "What did it say?"

"It—it said he never left. My mother took me from him after they had a falling out, but things became complicated. A mess I never knew about."

Another pause.

"She kept a letter from him—from my father. One he wrote years ago."

Cole's jaw tightened, a protective instinct flaring up. The idea of Raven being betrayed by her family again, tightened his chest.

"I don't know what to think. It's like . . . everything has been a huge lie. I feel so stupid."

"You're not stupid. People can be selfish, and it has nothing to do with you." He waited a beat. "Did you open the letter?"

"No. I don't know if I want to." She let out a small whimper.

His heart twisted. "Hey, it's a lot to take in. When the time comes to read it, you'll know."

"I can't get over the fact that Gram kept this from me, Cole. Not her."

"She was probably trying to protect you. I doubt it was to hurt you."

A thick silence from her end.

"Look, it's understandable to be upset. But don't let that stop you from finding out the truth."

"I guess you're right," she said.

His instinct was to let it go. Let her handle it on her own. That's what he'd usually do. But he couldn't ignore the ache in her voice.

"Are you home? I can swing by and pick up some cookies along the way to make up for my fourth-grade heist." He had to take a shot.

Silence stretched. Cheesy, yes, but he hoped she'd bite.

"Okay."

"Be there in a few." Cole hung up and headed to his truck. He didn't fully understand the bond she had, or wanted, with her father. She hadn't mentioned him in years. Not since second grade, when she'd first moved to Elkwood.

He couldn't show empty-handed after the makeshift promise, so he stopped at 7 Eleven and grabbed two coffees and a bag of chocolate chip cookies. By the time he pulled up to her place, the afternoon fog lifted. He climbed out and approached the door, hesitating at the entrance.

It had been a long time.

Once she opened the door, he had an insatiable urge to hold her. Shield her.

This might have been a bad idea.

The thought clung to him like the stubborn mud on his boots. He should've turned around. In her life wasn't his place anymore, not really. But there she stood, eyes red-rimmed, wearing an oversized sweatshirt that swallowed her frame. And suddenly, none of that mattered.

He held up the carrier and bag of cookies. "Hungry?"

His idiocy produced a tiny smile. As she ushered him in, he noted how little had changed in her apartment. The smell of cinnamon greeted him, reminding him how much she used to love this time of year. He noticed a picture on the bookshelf that lined the back wall. The two of them at their high school graduation. Young and naïve. Taken a few short weeks before he left for basic training.

"Here." She stopped in front of him, flashing a quick smile. "I'll take these."

She set the carrier and cookies on the coffee table. She dropped onto the couch and reached for one of the coffees.

A well-worn envelope lay in the center of the table next to a larger envelope and a few papers. Cole took a seat beside her and leaned back into the cushion. He sipped his coffee, trying to buy time. He wasn't sure what to say but figured he'd follow her lead.

Raven cradled her cup, eyes staring at the floor. "It's strange. After I re-read Gram's note, I realized something."

"Yeah?"

She met his eyes. "She didn't say it, but my mother must have threatened her. Gram worried about me being taken away. And that's why she didn't tell me right away about my father's letter." Raven pressed her lips together, as if holding in a breath. "I think you were right, she was trying to protect me."

Cole gave a slow nod. It made sense. Her grandmother had been that way her whole life, even overprotective. But with Raven's mom in the mix, she had to be.

He leaned forward, elbows on his knees. "She loved you. I wouldn't question that."

"But that also tells me that my mother probably knew about the letter." Raven let out a long sigh and crossed her arms.

Cole reached for the bag of cookies. He opened it and held it out to her.

She flashed a tiny smile and reached in. For a moment, the silence eased the tension.

Cole motioned to the envelope he assumed was her father's letter. "You don't have to read it today if you're not ready. We can stuff our faces like old times."

She shook her head, huffing out a small breath. "No, I think I do." Her voice firmed up, and she stiffened her posture. "I need to know what he wanted to say."

She picked up the envelope, tracing the edges. She slipped a finger under the flap, then hesitated, looking up at him with those big doe eyes. "Thank you for being here."

"Whatever is in there, you can handle it," he said.

Breaking the seal with a slow slide of her finger, she removed the folded paper inside. She unfolded it, pinching her lips together as she read.

Stillness filled the room as she read her father's words. Cole couldn't shake that sense of duty ingrained in him. Raven needed someone to lean on. Someone who could be there for her. A realization crept in causing a hollow void inside him.

He wasn't the one.

He could be here now, but what about tomorrow? What about when she needed more than cookies and small talk? He wasn't the guy for that—not anymore. Maybe he never was. His life remained stuck in a holding pattern, and he refused to drag her into it. He shifted himself away from her, just an inch, but it felt like a mile.

Chapter 5

To My Little Bird,

May this letter find its way to you, even if my presence cannot. I understand you don't want to see me, and though it tears at my heart, I have to respect your wishes. Perhaps seeing me would only add shadows to a path that's already winding. I have made countless mistakes, but none more grievous than the years spent apart from you.

Today, you turn thirteen. In my mind, I see you clearly with your yellow shoes and sticky fingers, looking for clues that only you and I could ever see. Those moments are my treasures, memories woven into my soul.

Know this, Little Bird: distance does not diminish love. My heart holds you always, with a wish that your life is filled with wonder, joy, and light. Time can be a strange companion, softening wounds and revealing truth. I hold fast to the hope that one day it may lead you back to me.

Until that day, let your dreams lift you high, like wings on a breeze. And should you ever be ready I will be here waiting, arms open, loving you . . . forevermore.

Love, Dad

Raven's hands shook as she set the letter aside. The words swirled around her like a storm. The weight of her father's absence pressed on her, squeezing until it hurt to breathe.

"Rae?" Cole's gentle voice broke through.

His relentless blue eyes reeled her back.

"I—" Her voice cracked, choked by buried memories forging to the surface.

The letter slid from her lap. She gasped, her breath coming in sharp, broken stutters. And then—she wasn't holding herself up. Cole wrapped his arms around her as she fell against him, gripping fistfuls of his shirt like it was the only thing keeping her from shattering.

Tears streamed down her face, hot and relentless, each one a testament to the years spent wondering what she'd done wrong. Believing that she was the reason he'd left without a trace, like Mom had said. Raven had convinced herself that avoiding feeling it, and anything else for that matter, protected her.

Cole's hand rubbed slow circles on her back as he whispered. "It's okay. Let it out."

Raven clutched at him.

Memories surged—her father's laughter, the scent of peppermint from his favorite tea, the soothing hum of his voice as he read poems to her, the ink-stains on his fingers, his black-rimmed glasses that slipped to the end of his nose. All those morsels she had locked away, believing they would never fit together again.

"I didn't know . . . " Words fell out between sobs. "I thought he didn't care."

Cole squeezed her tighter. His body radiated warmth, melting the chill inside her. For the first time in years, she felt truly held, for as long as she needed.

"I asked God to give me something. Every night I prayed. I begged. I did everything I was supposed to. And what did I get?

Nothing." Her voice muffled against his shoulder. "After a while, I stopped expecting God to show up."

Cole's chin settled atop her head.

"I get it. I stopped expecting a lot of things too. But maybe the showing up part starts now." He pulled back just enough to look at her. "Maybe He took the scenic route to get back to you."

A soft laugh bubbled up from Raven's throat. Strange, like sunshine in a snowfall, but she clung to it.

She met his eyes, tears glistening down her face. "Scenic route?"

The corners of Cole's mouth lifted into a crooked smile.

He brushed a tear from her cheek. "Sometimes the best intel is off the main path."

Raven studied his face. How could he still have this effect on her? His eyes held hers, unravelling her defenses. She found a steadiness there, a safe harbor in the storm.

Silence stretched between them. But reality crept in. She leaned back and he eased his arms to his sides.

"Thank you." She tucked her hair behind her ear.

What was she doing?

She wanted to stay in his arms, where his assurance wrapped around her. Convincing enough to make her believe she belonged there. But she couldn't make that mistake again. Not with Cole. Not with anybody.

Just *friends*.

For a long while, he sat with her. Letting her spill everything—what she'd remembered about her father, what Gram's house looked like now, and everything that had happened the last five months since they'd talked. He offered support. He held back his real opinion of her mother, but she knew how he felt. Just as she finished the last cookie, the door burst open with a force that made her jump.

Cole leaped to his feet, shoulders tight, eyes sharp.

"Raven!" Zoe's voice sliced through the air, filled with frantic energy. She stumbled into the apartment, curls in a wild frenzy.

Cole's solid presence offset Zoe's whirlwind entrance. Raven scrambled to her feet, wiping crumbs from her mouth.

"I tried calling you back a thousand times." Zoe dropped her Louis Vuitton purse and rushed to Raven's side. "I had my phone on silent at work and then hit crazy traffic because some loon stood in the middle of Main Street protesting plastic straws. Can you believe that?" Her words spilled out rapid-fire and she threw her hands up.

Raven held back a laugh and shot a quick glance at Cole, whose lips twitched fighting back a smile.

Zoe's eyes darted between Raven and Cole. "What's going on? Are you okay?"

"Yeah. Just . . . a lot happened," Raven said.

Zoe's eyes shifted to Cole. "Has she been crying because of you? Because I've already had a day and that would not work out for everyone right now." Her finger pointed so close to him she nearly shoved it down his throat.

Cole raised his hands in surrender.

"Zo, stop. I asked him to come over." She paused. "I got Gram's will today."

"Oh." Zoe dropped her finger and faced Raven. "What did it say?"

Raven took a breath, her eyes drifting to Cole. He gave her an encouraging nod.

"Gram left me her house. I didn't read the details yet."

"Seriously? That's huge."

Raven walked back to the couch and plopped down. She grabbed the envelope with her father's letter in it. "She also left me this. A letter from . . . my father."

Zoe's eyes widened as she hurried to the couch and dropped next to her. "Your father? But I thought—"

"I know." Raven brushed a stray hair from her face.

Zoe placed a hand against her chest. "Oh, Rae." She wrapped an arm around Raven's neck, pulling her close.

Raven leaned into Zoe's embrace, looking over her shoulder at Cole. He had a look on his face she couldn't quite read. As she pulled apart from Zoe, he grabbed his keys off the table.

"Hey, I'm going to head out." His voice low, almost a whisper.

"You don't have to go."

"It's okay. Spend some time with Zoe. Call me later."

She nodded. Part of her wanted to ask him to stay. But logic pinned her tongue.

Zoe grabbed Raven's arm and widened her eyes as he walked toward the door. Zoe nudged her head toward him. Raven's heart thumped a quick beat, wrestling with what to say to him.

"Cole!" His name burst from her lips before she could second-guess herself. She sprung from the couch toward the door. He paused mid-stride, his hand already on the doorknob. He turned back to face her.

"Um, thanks for the cookies." Lame. So, lame.

He gave a nod, that easy grin returning. "Anytime."

As the door clicked shut, Zoe whirled to face her. "So, you're telling me Mr. Tall-Dark-and-Brooding didn't cause those tears, but actually helped mop them up?"

Raven let out a breathy laugh, some of the heaviness lifting away. "Yeah. Kind of."

"Okay." Zoe nodded. "Points for him. Now tell me about this letter."

They both sank into the couch. After Raven shared highlights, she let Zoe read both letters from Gram and her father. Zoe listened, holding Raven's hand, squeezing it at emotional intervals.

"You were like seven years old when he left, right? Why would he think you didn't want to see him?"

"Where does it say that?" Raven grabbed the letter again.

"Right there." Zoe pointed. "Where it says I understand you don't want to see me."

Raven must have brushed over it the first time. Only one answer came to mind.

Mom.

She shook her head at Zoe, keeping her lips pressed together.

"Ugh! I knew it. That woman is a cancer," Zoe said.

Raven looked down at the letter, drawn to keep reading. At the end, she recognized something familiar. His word choice . . . she had seen it somewhere else. Somewhere recently.

Raven shot off the couch, pacing the living room as her mind churned. The subtle nuances in the letter scratched at the edges of her memory. Lack of sleep warped her brain most days, but this felt important.

"Forevermore." The word tumbled out in a whisper. "Where did I see—"

"Rae, don't even think about her." Zoe's voice cut in. "Now you have proof he wanted to see you. All this time you thought he wanted nothing to do with you. That's some closure, right?"

Raven barely heard her. She walked toward the kitchen, pressing her fingers to her temples. "That word . . . I know I've seen it."

"Rae?" Zoe's voice edged with concern.

Think.

The word pulsed in her mind like a beacon. She spun toward the bookshelf, fingers shaking as they skimmed across the spines. "It can't be—"

"Girl, what are you thinking about?"

Her eyes locked onto Zoe. "That's it!"

The puzzle piece slid into place with a near-audible click. There. *Whispering Pines* by J.C. Nevermore.

She yanked it from the shelf, flipping open the worn cover. Her breath caught as she landed on the dedication. Her fingers trembled while tracing the words. She turned the book around to show Zoe.

"I don't understand. What—"

"The dedication. Look at the way it's signed." Raven pointed to the inscription.

Zoe squinted. "I don't get it."

Raven grabbed her father's letter and held it up next to the book. "Look."

Zoe grabbed the letter. "You've got to be kidding me. Who's the author? Do you think it's him?"

"J.C. Nevermore." Raven whispered his name, as if tied to her very soul. "Wait, J.C.?"

Her father's name, Jeffrey Cunningham . . . J.C. . . . . Her hands shook and the book became heavy in her grip.

Zoe snatched the book from Raven's hands, flipping through its pages like they held answers. "It can't *really* be him, can it? I mean, he was a writer and all but—"

"I don't know. But something in my gut tells me it's crazy enough to be true." Raven yanked the rest of the Shadows of Hawthorn series from her bookshelf.

She opened the cover of the second book, brushing her fingers over the same dedication. She's probably seen it a hundred times. But now, the words seemed to take on a different weight, as if he'd been leaving clues all along . . .

Waiting for her to find them.

The morning sun slanted through the living room blinds, striping the worn recliner in pale gold. Cole shifted, rolling his right shoulder to work out the lingering stiffness. A dull burn radiated down his arm, the familiar pins-and-needles sensation creeping through his fingers.

He flexed his hand, then checked his phone, swiping away an email notification.

Curled at his feet, Radar licked his paw.

Jaw tight, Cole set the phone down on the side table—too fast. The quick motion sent a jolt through his arm, a sharp zing of nerve pain shooting to his elbow. He sucked in a slow breath. Maybe he shouldn't have thrown that extra thirty pounds on the bar this morning.

His mind drifted to yesterday. Raven in his arms. She hovered in his mind, whether or not he'd seen her. Too bad he hadn't brought something better than dumb jokes and cookies.

His phone buzzed on the side table. He snatched it—but only another generic update from HQ about pending administrative processes. Nothing promising. He tossed the phone aside and grabbed the remote. Radar barked at the back door, and Cole let him out. Moments later, the dog charged back in, pouncing on his favorite squeaky duck. Cole grabbed a bottled water from the kitchen.

A loud thud followed.

Cole stepped around the corner and stopped short. "What did you do?"

His pulse hammered in his ears. Vision tunneled until all he saw were Preach's things scattered in front of him—worn gloves, a faded photo of the two of them, grinning like they hadn't a care in the world. . . and his journal.

Cole's hands shook as he crouched. One by one, he placed everything back in the box. He hesitated over Preach's journal before putting it back. The worn leather creased, soft in his hand.

Memories came in waves, stronger than he was ready for as he slid on the box lid. His hand lingered as if to steady himself. He stood and pushed the box into the corner against the wall, snagging a glimpse of the label as he forced himself to look away.

M. Ramirez 75 RR, 3rd Bn

The squeak from Radar's toy snapped like a gunshot.

Too loud. Too close.

The floor disappeared—only dirt, heat, and the raw scent of blood and burning.

Living room walls blurred.

The photo of Preach on the floor distorted, his face flickering between past and present.

A shrill ringing filled Cole's ears.

Everything muted except the sound of shouts under enemy fire. Preach groaning as he bled. The acrid smell of burnt flesh . . .

Cole squeezed his eyes shut, clenching his fists while his heart hammered against his ribcage. The room spun, and he forced himself to take control, bracing a hand against the wall. Air came in shallow gasps, thick and stifling.

Focus. Breathe.

He forced his mind to ground itself. Cole's chest tightened, breath coming in short bursts. The walls felt too close, the air thin.

Not here. Not now.

He gritted his teeth, locking his knees to stay upright. His heart slammed against his ribs, the pressure in his chest building like it might crack him open. He couldn't breathe, couldn't move—until the words forced their way out.

"Recognizing that I volunteered as a Ranger . . ."

His voice was low, barely above a whisper, but he pushed more out.

" . . . fully knowing the hazards of my chosen profession."

Breathe in. Hold. Breathe out.

The tremor in his hands started to settle.

"I will always endeavor to uphold the prestige, honor, and high esprit de corps of my Ranger Regiment."

His heartbeat slowed, the weight on his chest easing, the room shifting back into focus.

By the time he reached the final line of the creed, his breathing had steadied. He swallowed hard, pressing a hand to the back of his neck.

Radar's bark broke through the haze, sharp and familiar. Cole latched onto the sound like a lifeline, his hand finding Radar's soft fur as the dog licked his face.

Not gone. Not fixed. But for now, it was enough.

The ringing eased.

His breathing slowed.

Cole pushed himself to his feet, gripping the back of the couch for support. He took a few deep breaths. He snatched his earbuds and phone and bolted out the back door. The screen door slammed behind him. He jammed the earbuds in, letting heavy metal pound out every thought.

He ran, the only thing he knew how to do when his mind betrayed him.

Run.

Outpace the memories. Leave them bleeding in the dust behind him.

His feet slammed against the road, his heart thumping, sweat streaming down his face. Tension coiled in his right shoulder, knifed down his back and seared through his legs. The music in his ears drowned nothing out. No matter how fast he went, memories assaulted him.

Run.

Each step brought flashes—Preach, blood, compressions. His chest tightened, the pounding deepening.

He stopped, hands braced on his knees. Gasping for breath, feeling free air move in and out of his lungs.

When his head cleared, realization struck.

Second episode since he'd been home.

Therapy three times a week hadn't helped. But it checked the box. Even Hank agreed. But here he was—one cracked-open box enough to drag him backward.

It was fine. Manageable. Just a rough patch. Once the Medical Board decision went through, once he was back where he belonged, it wouldn't be an issue.

He straightened with a groan, rolling his shoulder as he glanced back toward the house. The ranch-style home sat at the top of the hill. Its pale blue siding and white trim stood out against the backdrop of the apple trees. A wraparound porch stretched across the front, the old wooden swing. Still not quite home.

He swiped the sweat from his brow and started a slow jog back. The small creek trickled through the orchard, its banks lined with smooth stones worn down by years of spring floods. He jumped the narrow gap with ease and landed near the weathered wooden bench where he'd spent countless afternoons fishing as a kid.

He took a seat. He rested his arms on his knees as he caught his breath. The air carried damp earth and ripe apples, the same scent that had clung to his clothes after long days in the orchard. Some things never changed. The sun pressed against his neck, but the autumn air bit, sharp and cold.

"You've got a twisted sense of humor, don't you?" He shouted up.

God's muteness mocked him. He shook his head. "You should've taken me."

A breeze rustled through the orchard, dead leaves falling around him. He heard footsteps crunching on the leaves and jumped up.

Pop trotted down the hill towards him, two fishing poles in hand.

"Saw your truck. I thought maybe you'd want to throw a line in."

"What are you doing home? Not staying at the lake tonight, too?" He walked toward Pop and grabbed the tackle box.

"Your mother wanted to make it home for the antique show with Aunt Jean. Negotiating old silverware is not my idea of fun."

Pop handed him a pole, and they baited their hooks. Cole's first cast landed under a branch. He gave it a quick yank and swished it in the current. The familiar motions steadied his pulse. The worm danced across the water, sending ripples outward. Pop settled beside him, casting his own line with a practiced flick. The lure plunked into the water. More circles rippled over the creek's surface.

"Whatcha doing out here?"

Cole shrugged. "Needed some air."

Pop glanced sideways at him, brows raised. He adjusted his faded camo hat. As they settled into the rhythm of the creek, Pop's quiet presence grounded Cole. Even as a man of few words, Pop being there, close and constant, hit him. He thought of Raven, that letter from her father—a stranger, really—arriving now, years too late.

He stared back at the water. "Thanks Pop."

Pop glanced over, gave a quick nod, then recast his line.

Cole stared at the water, reminded of the many times he and Raven ran through it. Especially the last time. The hurt in her eyes when he told her about going to the Army. Looking back now, he wished he had been gentler, taken more time to explain. He'd turned into another person in her life who had left.

Cole ran a hand over his face, exhaling slowly. That box needed out of his living room. Out of his hands. Preach deserved better than dust and a dark corner. And his parents deserved more than a package in the mail. They deserved someone who could look them in the eyes and say, "He mattered." He owed them that much.

No more putting it off, no more excuses. New Jersey couldn't wait any longer.

CHAPTER 6

RAVEN HAD READ HER father's letter so many times, she could recite it by heart. But knowing the words wasn't enough. She needed something, anything, that could lead her to him. But where did she start?

The envelope had no return address. The letter looked newer than it should have, probably because Gram kept it safe all these years. Her fingers hovered over the keyboard. One good lead. That was all she needed.

But she should've been working. She needed to work. The blinking cursor on *Chapter Three: Touch and Go (Literally, Know When to Touch and When to Go Away)* offered no help. She needed a better subtitle. But Jo stood firm on this one, insisting the humor is necessary.

Three hours at her desk, and Raven had managed half a paragraph. At this rate, she'd need divine intervention, or a suitable excuse. The first draft was supposed to be finished by the end of the month. How was she going to write five chapters in barely four weeks? And she was the one who had set the timeline. Not that Jo ever stuck to anything they'd discussed. Raven exhaled, tapping her fingers against her desk.

Maybe a quick break would help.

She got up from her desk and wandered into the kitchen, popping open the fridge. A single yogurt cup, a carton of egg whites, and a Chinese takeout container stared back at her. Nothing exciting. The pantry wasn't much better—protein bars, crackers, and a questionable granola mix she'd bought during a health-conscious phase and never touched again.

Sour cream and onion chips it was.

She grabbed the bag from the counter and poured a handful into a bowl, because she wasn't completely unhinged. Snagging a can of diet coke, she headed back to her desk and plopped down with a sigh.

She clicked out of her manuscript and pulled up her browser. Just for a minute.

Articles, obscure fan forums, a handful of dead-end links, and the only social media account she could find for J.C. Nevermore, with a single Poe-esque raven logo and zero personal details.

Her fingers hovered over the keyboard. One more search. Just in case she'd missed something. Her phone buzzed next to her. A text from Jo.

Jo-Pet Whisperer: You must come to the farm. Authenticity is key in good writing. Next weekend looks good. You need hands-on experience.

Was she serious?

Raven: Super busy next weekend. Maybe next time.

She exhaled, setting her phone aside, knowing full well that wasn't the last of Jo's attempts. Raven rubbed a smudge of oil from her fingertips onto her sweatpants.

She slid the mouse to open a new browser tab. If her father truly meant what he'd said in the letter, why hadn't he reached out again? No calls, no other letters, nothing.

Her phone buzzed again.

Jo-Pet Whisperer: Be here next Saturday before sunrise. Pack boots.

Raven: I appreciate the offer, and it sounds fun, but I can't.

Jo-Pet Whisperer: You eat meat? I'll be smoking ribs.

Raven stood from her desk, stretching her legs. Pack boots? She had no intention of going to the farm. It was over two hours away and the last thing she wanted to do was clean stalls. But the dogs might be fun . . . and the ribs . . .

Ugh, boundaries, Raven, boundaries.

After a quick lap around her 850 square foot apartment, she returned to her desk chair. Doubt loomed, making her wonder if her father would want to see her. He'd written that letter sixteen years ago. She'd looked him up a few times over the years. Jeffrey Cunningham returned hundreds of results, from New Jersey all the way to Canada. She'd spent hours wading through articles, and even obituaries. At a desperate point, she'd paid for a DNA kit and sent it to an online database. She'd received a few alerts, but nothing solid.

What if he'd moved on? Maybe he has another family. That thought burned.

She looked up at the ceiling at nothing in particular. "I know You're up there. But if I'm being honest, God, it feels like You've been busy . . . or maybe I stopped checking in."

Her fingers tightened around the edges of the letter. "I mean, how do I make sense of this? The dad I thought abandoned me didn't. Mom lied. And You. . . ." Her voice cracked. "You just watched it all happen. Why?"

Silence. Of course.

She swigged her diet coke. Her fingers trembled as she typed "J.C. Nevermore family" into the search bar. A quick hesitation, but she hit enter. Within seconds, links filled the screen—book reviews, speculative blog posts, and news articles, all purple from already having been clicked. But no indications of a family.

Her phone buzzed again. Please, no more farm talk.

Zoe: Any luck yet? J.C.'s a weird hermit.

Raven: Not much. Lots of fan stuff.

Zoe: Found an IG that might be your dad. Was he into weapons?

Raven: Not from what I can remember. I think he was in the military after high school, not sure of details.

Zoe: This guy has a Red F250 as a profile pic. The license plate says knives.

Raven let out a quick laugh and set her phone down. She clicked on one of the fan forums. The users buzzed about J.C. Nevermore's latest book, *The Unseen Thread,* a mystery centered on family secrets. Oddly enough. She scrolled other recent posts.

Her phone buzzed again. Then again.

> Zoe: NVM. That guy looks like he is a hundred.

She chuckled, shaking her head. Another message from Jo she left unread.

Her eyes drifted back to the website. One thread caught her attention: *Speculation about Nevermore's Next Appearance.* She clicked on it, chewing her bottom lip. Fans debated the reclusive author's whereabouts. Most posts were guesses, but one linked to his new book on the publisher's website.

"That's different." She clicked the link.

The page loaded with a high-resolution image of the book's dark, moody cover. Her mouse hovered over it for a second before she clicked. The author's bio appeared below, along with a small banner she almost missed at the bottom of the page:

Upcoming Event: J.C. Nevermore Book Signing at McFinn's Bookstore, New York City

Raven blinked, leaning closer to the screen.

Clicking the banner brought up the event details—a date, time, and location. Her heart raced.

She texted Zoe.

> I think I found something.

What is it?

A book signing.

The three dots bounced.

Hold up. Like an actual book signing? Not a livestream scam?

Yeah. In New York City

SHUT UP! When?

Five days from now at McFinn's Bookstore. It might not be him. What if it's some publicity stunt?

And what if it's not? What if it's the real deal? We have to go.

Raven stared at her phone, thumbs hovering. This was the most tangible lead she'd found, but the idea of going terrified her.

Zoe: UGH. Wait. I leave for Boston on Wednesday for the trade show. CURSE MY RESPONSIBILITY. But you must go. Fate demands it.

Raven couldn't drive to New York City by herself hoping her father, whom she hasn't seen in twenty-two years, was at a book signing. A bonkers idea.

Raven exhaled and set her phone down. Zoe's encouragement only half-silenced the doubts swirling in her mind.

She needed to go, didn't she?

Even if it turned out to be nothing, she'd regret not taking the chance. She leaned back in her chair, twisting her ring. Her focus shifted to J.C. Nevermore novels still stacked on her desk. The dog-eared pages marked her favorite passages as a kid, a world she hadn't visited in years. She skimmed each dedication again, then looked back at the letter.

Dad loves you forevermore.

The dedication could be coincidence, couldn't it? Just a stylistic quirk of a writer she'd admired? Maybe he had copied it from the books. That seemed more logical than the reckless conclusion floating in her mind. She sat straight up, the swivel chair creaking beneath her. A nagging thought plagued her.

What did Mom do to keep him away?

Raven couldn't let it go. After years of half-truths and dead ends, she needed answers. She grabbed her coat and keys and rushed out the door.

Sliding into the driver's seat of her car, she tossed her bag into the passenger seat and stared at her reflection in the rearview mirror.

"Get answers and get outta there."

She navigated her way to Maplewood Lane for the second time in two days, this time to Gram's house. Her grip tightened on the wheel, knuckles white. A sharp exhale fogged the windshield as she blinked hard, her pulse warring between fight or flight. The road blurred ahead—too many thoughts, too many what-ifs—but she kept driving, hands steady.

Mom opened the door as Raven pulled in, then crossed her arms, a mug in one hand. Raven barely had the car in park before Mom called out. "You gonna sit out there all day or what?"

Too late to turn back now.

Mom looked more weathered than the last time Raven saw her, at the funeral. Not like Raven hadn't left voicemails and texts, trying to be there for her. "Get-togethers" had never been her thing. Especially not with Raven.

The lines on Mom's face carved deep into her paper-thin skin. Dirty blond hair, now streaked with silver, hung in uneven strands at her shoulders.

Raven climbed out, shoving her keys into her jacket pocket. "Hi, Mom."

Mom waved the mug in the air. "Look who finally decided to visit. I was starting to think I'd need to send out a search party." The familiar slur in her words confirmed it. Not coffee in the mug.

Raven forced a tight smile. "I've been busy."

Mom huffed. "Too busy for your own mother? That's rich." She turned back inside. "Well, don't just stand there. You're letting the heat out."

This was a mistake.

Still, Raven followed her inside, inhaling the lavender air freshener that almost, but not quite, masked the stale cigarette smoke. The house looked the same—Gram's crocheted afghan still draped over the couch, the same photos on the mantel—but it felt emptier somehow. Hollow.

Mom slumped into a chair at the kitchen table and flipped through a stack of mail. Raven hesitated, then straightened her shoulders. No arguments. No letting her steamroll. Just get to the point.

"You want some?" Mom lifted her mug.

"No, thanks." Raven leaned against the wall between the kitchen and living room.

"So, to what do I owe the pleasure? You didn't come over here just to check in. Handling me as if I need your charity." Mom stumbled as she opened the fridge. "Miss Independent. Doesn't need anyone."

Just keep it together.

"Always doing things on your own. Not afraid to shut people out. You get that from your father no doubt."

Mom poured more wine into her mug. The sharp clink of the wine bottle against it sent a jolt through Raven, dragging her back to her childhood. Heat rose up her neck. That sound had been a warning back then, the first note in a symphony of chaos. It meant the night was only going to get worse.

Raven swallowed hard, forcing her hands into her jacket pockets. Just be out with it. Lingering wasn't an option.

"I need to ask you something . . . about my father."

Mom set the mug on the kitchen table, then straightened a stack of mail. "The electric company doesn't let up. How do they expect me to pay 352 dollars when I'm on social security?"

"Gram told me something about him . . . That he wanted to see me."

Mom busied herself with the mail and let out a bitter laugh. "Your grandmother always had a vivid imagination. She liked her stories, you know that."

"She wasn't making it up."

Mom's eyes flicked to hers, something hard flashing in them. "You know, I don't appreciate being interrogated in my home. Especially when all I've ever done is try to protect you."

"*Protect* me?"

"You just don't get it, do you? Your father didn't want you. You think he would've stuck around? Chasing dreams all the way to New York City. No roots, no responsibility. A complete loser. He couldn't make enough rent for a one-bedroom loft." Mom stumbled when pulling out the kitchen chair.

"Do you know he tried—" Mom cut herself off with a silent burp.

Raven's pulse kicked up. "Tried what?"

"You know, Tim wants to knock down that stupid wall in the living room." She pointed, her voice sliding into something syrupy. "Open floor plans are all the rage. Said it'll make the house more attractive to buyers."

Raven clenched her jaw. She could already picture it—Gram's cozy house gutted to fit Tim's half-baked renovation ideas.

"Of course, none of that can happen if I don't figure out how to pay this outrageous electric bill. Tim says we should start renting out your old room. He has some friend that would want it. City money. But I don't know. The last thing I need is some stranger judging me."

The house wasn't hers. But Raven nodded, waiting for the moment to pass.

Mom's eyes slid back to her. "What are you doing here? Thought you had all the answers now."

Raven's grip tightened around the keys in her pocket. She was done asking. If Mom wouldn't give her answers, she'd find them herself. "I just . . . Nevermind. I have to get going."

She turned to the door.

Mom let out a short, bitter laugh. "Well, I'm good. I think I have enough candles in case they shut off the electric. Or I can stay at Tim's."

As Raven walked past her, Mom stuck out her cheek expecting a kiss.

Raven leaned down slow, giving a quick peck on her cheek. "Do you need some money for the electric?"

Mom batted her hands as if surprised. "Oh no, don't you worry about me. I mean, if you're offering I'm not going to refuse. But you don't have to do that. I know writers don't make any money."

"It's okay. I'll send something once I get home."

"Well, aren't you the generous one? I'll pay you back after Tim gets his check from that Squirrel Hill business." Mom followed Raven to the door and eyed her up and down as she walked outside. "Still dressing like you just rolled out of bed, I see. No wonder you're still single."

Raven's nails pressed into her palms. "Bye, Mom."

She sucked in a deep breath, got in her car, and slammed the door. Mom knew how to worm her way under Raven's skin. And what was the point? Her words couldn't be trusted anyway.

Raven clutched the steering wheel, trying to shake off the frustration curling through her chest. She should have known better. And yet, a small part of her still wished things could be different. That just once, Mom would look at her without bitterness clouding her gaze. But that hope wore thin over the years.

This had been pointless.

And yet, her mother had slipped up. New York City. And something about her father trying . . . to do what?

If Mom refused to give her answers, she'd find them herself.

Cole tossed his duffle bag onto the bed, the worn canvas carrying the weight of journeys far heavier than this one. But none as personal. He hadn't fully unpacked since coming home—because home was temporary. The trip to Jersey gnawed at him, but it was necessary. One day, in and out. Maybe stop at camp on the way back. He had weights in the truck, and he'd get a run in on the trails. That mountain air could heal anyone.

A quick visit, a duty fulfilled. A Ranger finished what he started. Cole owed Preach that much.

The smell of Mom's stew filled the house, thick and rich, setting off a sharp hunger. Guess Mom's cooking was a perk of being home. He tossed the duffle on the floor and headed to the kitchen. He swiped a quick spoonful from the Crock-Pot.

"Hey! That's not ready yet." Mom smacked his hand with the dish towel.

"Tastes ready to me." He muttered through a mouthful, then hissed in pain as the broth torched the roof of his mouth.

Mom smirked. "Serves you right. Now out of my kitchen."

Cole swiped his water bottle from the counter and walked into the living room, where Pop reclined in his chair, eyes locked on the Steeler game, a Pepsi in one hand, remote in the other.

"How they looking, Pop?" Cole dropped onto the couch across from him.

"Terrible. Defense needs to wake up." Pop tipped back his drink. "You'd think they had money on the other team."

Cole reached for a handful of cashews from the tray on the table. The two of them settled into a familiar rhythm—watch, react, critique the coaching like they could do better.

During the commercial break, Pop set down his drink and gave him a knowing look. "Wake up late this morning?"

Cole knew where this was going.

Before he could answer, Mom's voice rang from the kitchen. "Since when is the gym more important than church?"

And there it was.

Cole rubbed a hand over his jaw. Mom appeared in the doorway, arms crossed, towel draped over one shoulder.

"It's called staying in shape, Ma." He stretched his arm, rolling his shoulder. "Movement's a good thing."

"You're not invincible. Training every day puts too much strain on you."

Cole clenched his jaw.

Pop swigged his soda. "So, how long you sticking around?"

Cole hesitated, then took the opening. "Was thinking about stopping by the camp for a night or two."

Mom brightened, but barely. "That'll be good for you."

Cole nodded. "Also, gotta make a quick stop in Jersey." He took a sip of water. "Nothing big."

"What for?"

"Something I gotta take care of."

Pop didn't react, but Mom's gaze sharpened. "You talk to his folks yet?"

He shifted in his seat, grabbing a handful of cashews. "Not yet."

"You're just gonna show up?" Pop looked at him.

"It's fine."

Mom scoffed. "Cole—"

"Can we not do this right now?" Cole popped a cashew in his mouth, focusing on the game. "Ref's blind. That's PI if I've ever seen it."

Behind them, Mom's voice cut in. "You keeping up with therapy?"

"Viv, let it go for now," Pop said.

Mom's lips pressed into a thin line, but she turned back toward the kitchen, banging pots louder than necessary.

At halftime, the Steelers edged the Ravens by ten points. They could pull it together, if they read the blitz. Cole grabbed his jacket and stepped onto the back porch, Radar at his heels. He sank onto the wooden step, rubbing the dog's ears as the cold air settled the weight pressing on his chest.

This trip to Jersey wasn't just a stop, it was a debt. A final duty to Preach.

But did his parents need details?

His mind churned. What was he supposed to say to the Ramirezes? They deserved better. That box was just another reminder of what everyone knew but wouldn't say, at least not outright.

Cole hadn't done his job.

The back door creaked open behind him.

"Hey, go easy on her." Pop lowered onto the step beside him with a groan. "She didn't leave your side, you know. At the hospital. The old marine in her came out when they tried telling her about visiting hours."

He hadn't remembered much about the hospital. Tried to forget most of it.

Pop stretched out his legs, staring out at the yard. "No mother should ever hear that her son might not make it." He let out a heavy breath. "She's only trying to help. Wants to make sure you're not being too hard on yourself."

Hearing that made something knot in his chest.

For all her nagging, prying, and pushing—she did it because she still had a son to worry about.

Pop stood, groaning as his knees cracked. "Come on. Let's eat."

Cole followed Pop back inside and sidled up next to Mom as she ladled stew into a bowl.

"Sorry, Ma." He pecked her cheek.

She sighed, but a faint smile tugged at her lips.

"I know you are." She handed him a bowl, then reached for the rolls. "Just . . . be careful at camp. That storm last month knocked some trees down. Watch for loose branches."

Cole smirked and grabbed a roll. "Yes, ma'am."

They gathered around the table.

The conversation shifted to safer territory, Pop's latest attempts at fly fishing and the antique lamp Mom found at the flea market. After dinner, Cole lounged in the living room with Pop, catching the rest of the game. Steelers pulled it off.

His phone buzzed in his pocket.

Raven: Hi. Can you meet up? Maybe get some dinner?

He stared at the screen, thumb hovering.
Three dots bounced.

Raven: Or some pie. Apple pie is the feature this month, I think.

A smirk tugged at his mouth. Like she had to convince him.

Cole: Sure. Right now?

Raven: Yes, perfect. See you in 10. Main Street Diner.

Cole slipped his phone into his pocket. He wasn't hungry, but he could make room for pie.

He snatched his jacket off the hook by the door.

Mom arched a brow.

"Be back later."

Radar perked up, tail wagging as if he'd been invited.

"Not this time, buddy." Cole scratched the dog's head, then stepped outside.

The cold air bit as he hopped into his truck. The Main Street Diner wasn't far, ten minutes, tops. Should he tell Raven about Jersey? She'd have questions. If she knew the full story . . . she'd never look at him the same.

Once he pulled up to the Main Street Diner, he parked across the street. The place smelled like French fries and bacon. Tempting. He spotted Raven sitting in a corner booth with her head down as she thumbed through her phone.

Cole pulled off his jacket and slid into the booth across from her. "How's it going?"

The moment Raven looked up, her smile caught him off guard. Maybe he'd seen that smile thousands of times before, but tonight, it hit different.

"Hey. Thanks for meeting me. I needed out." She set her phone down.

"Of course. What's on your mind?"

"Okay, I know this might sound crazy, but I think my father might be the author J.C. Nevermore."

Cole tilted his head. "Never heard of him."

"He wrote those old mystery books I used to read, remember? He's pretty reclusive. You'd think for a famous author, there'd be more out there, but it's like he's a ghost."

Cole nodded. "What's your plan?"

"I keep hitting walls trying to find any information linking them together." She stirred her coffee. "I'm about to hire some cliché PI who skulks around in a trench coat and eats donuts in parked cars."

"Don't do that. You'd get scammed, and we're way too old for Hardy Boys antics. Just keep digging, you'll find something."

"That's the problem. I feel like I'm chasing my tail. The more I uncover, the more tangled it all gets."

"What do you know for sure? Something solid." He leaned forward, resting his forearms on the table.

She blew out a breath, brushing a strand of hair from her face. "Okay, um . . . my father's letter, the way he signed it, 'forevermore,' it matches the dedications in J.C. Nevermore's books. That can't be a coincidence." She paused. "Oh, Nina got me a virtual meeting with an editor friend of hers next week. She works with authors at the same publisher as J.C. Nevermore. It's a huge imprint, but maybe she knows him or someone who works with him."

"Really? That's great."

Her eyes dropped to her phone, her finger tracing the edge. "I did find something last night, though. J.C. Nevermore is supposedly going to be at a book signing. Four days from now at McFinn's Bookstore in New York City."

Cole's brows shot up. "Are you going to check it out?"

"I don't know. Zoe said I should, but I don't really want to go alone. What if it's not him? Or what if it *is* him? I don't know what I would say."

He nodded. "I get it."

Her fingers tapped against her coffee mug. "I got nothing but grief from my mother yesterday. I should've known it was a waste to go over there."

"Did you tell her about it? I thought—"

"No, not the letter. I asked about him, but of course it was a bad time." She let out a bitter laugh. "I walked in expecting a conversation and got a monologue about her electric bill and Tim's grand plans to rip apart Gram's house."

"I thought your gram left you the house. They can't just rip it apart."

"She did. But I couldn't get into it, not when Mom was . . . it doesn't matter. The less she knows, the better. At least until I can figure this all out."

He wanted to say something, tell her she didn't owe that woman a second of her time. But he stayed quiet.

She leaned back, staring at the scratched-up Formica table. "I don't know why I even bothered. Maybe I thought, for once, she'd give me a straight answer."

"She didn't say anything?"

"Oh, she said plenty." Raven smirked. "How my dad was a loser, how I'm just like him. Classic material. But as far as anything useful? No."

Cole caught the server's attention and ordered a coffee.

"She did say something about New York."

"What about it?"

"It was probably nothing. Just her usual drunken rambling. Something about him chasing pipe dreams or whatever."

Maybe. But he saw a flicker of hope in her eyes, no matter how much she tried to downplay it.

"Rae, that's something."

She scoffed, taking a sip of coffee. "It's a place—and not just any place—the biggest, loudest, most overcrowded city in the country. A place where people disappear into chaos every single day. And knowing my mother, it could mean anything. For all I know, she pulled it out of thin air."

Cole leaned forward. "You don't believe her?"

"I believe she had no idea what she was saying. I don't want to get my hopes up over something she blurted out between wine refills."

Cole hadn't pushed, but something about the way she said it. Like she'd already decided it couldn't be true. Something she wasn't ready to face.

Still, he nodded. "Fair enough."

She let out a breath, rolling her shoulders. "I don't know. This whole thing might be worth looking into. Just . . . not right now."

"Look. Don't let fear hold you back. Sounds like you have a solid lead with that book signing."

"Maybe I should wait to hear what the editor says and go from there."

Cole's trip to New Jersey needed to be quick, and not something he wanted to unpack. No distractions, no complications. But then Raven looked at him with that flicker of hope too fragile to crush. The kind of hope she rarely let in. And something about that settled in his chest, heavy and immovable.

"I'm heading to New Jersey tomorrow. Why don't you come with me? We'll be close enough to swing by that book signing. I'll help you chase down whatever you need."

Her eyes widened. "Seriously? You'd do that?"

He leaned back, shrugging like it was no big deal. "Think of it as a road trip. We can stop by my family's camp along the way. You always said you found peace at camp. Maybe it'll help you focus, with writing or whatever."

"That sounds amazing. But I don't want to mess up your plans. Why are you going to New Jersey?"

He rubbed the back of his neck. "I need to return something. It won't mess up anything. You need answers and you shouldn't go alone."

For a moment, she studied him. Then, a small smile crept onto her face.

"Okay. I'm in."

Cole nodded, but inside, something twisted. This was supposed to be a simple trip. One day, in and out. Then fishing and training. He didn't need company. Didn't want it.

But now Raven was coming along. And he needed to help her find answers.

CHAPTER 7

RAVEN TWISTED THE OPAL ring on her finger, the cool metal biting into her skin. She glanced at the clock above the kitchen sink for the hundredth time. 6:26 a.m. Cole was supposed to be here any minute, and her nerves were bouncing between mild anxiety and full-blown panic attack.

This wasn't a spring break road trip. It wasn't some nostalgic getaway to camp. She was going to New York for answers, to find the truth about her father. And she wasn't about to let Cole—his charm or frustrating ability to unravel her—get in the way.

On speaker phone, Zoe let out a groggy sigh. "Relax. It's a road trip, not a marriage proposal. Now, I'm going back to sleep."

"But what about the camp? I mean, it's beautiful there. Separate rooms and all, but it'll just be us. Remind me, why did I agree to this?"

Zoe snorted. "You're right. A few nights in the Poconos sounds awful."

Raven gripped the edge of the counter. "This is—"

"A bad idea?" Zoe cut in. "Don't tell me you're chickening out."

"No, but . . ." She paced the tile between the counter and the fridge. "It's Cole. So, it's different."

"Different how?"

She paused, twisting the ring tighter. "It's just . . . I haven't spent this much time with him in years. What if it's weird?"

Zoe's laughter huffed through a yawn. "You're overthinking this. It's only a few days and you've known each other forever. Plus, you've been to that cabin with his fam. It's not exactly the Hilton. Don't you have to pee outside?"

She stopped and leaned against the counter. "What if this whole thing is a waste of time?"

"Then you'll both have gloriously dull memories to add to your collection. But either way, you need this. You never take a vacation and the chance to relax in the mountains and possibly get answers about your estranged-turned-long-lost father is a perfect reason to get away."

Raven bit her lip, peering through the blinds. A flash of head-lights gave her heart a jolt.

"He's here. I gotta go."

"Deep breaths. Text me later, preferably during normal human hours."

Raven slid her phone into her back pocket. She straightened her spine, trying to summon courage from thin air. She caught her reflection in the microwave door—low ponytail, loose but soft sweater. Decent. Should she put on more lip gloss?

The truck pulled up and parked. A moment later, Cole stepped out. He was all broad shoulders and casual confidence, jeans fitting a little too well. Did he get more handsome every day? He was like a Chia pet, except growing sharp jaw lines to add to his smolder.

Nope. Not marveling at how ridiculously good he looks before sunrise. Treat him like a solar eclipse—brief glances only or risk permanent damage.

She opened the door before he could knock. "Hey."

His grin made something flutter in her chest. "You ready?"

"Define ready."

He laughed. He stepped inside and grabbed her duffel bag by the door. "This is it?"

"I travel light."

"Minimalist approach. I like it." He winked and headed back toward the truck.

Raven followed, her feet heavy as she walked down the porch steps. "You sure about this?"

"Never been more sure of anything." He tossed her bag into the back. "Besides, I heard there's a place along the way famous for their pancakes. Be a shame to miss out."

She arched a brow. "Pancakes. That's your major selling point?"

His expression turned mock-serious. "You mean there's more to life than pancakes?"

"Some would argue."

"Well, they'd be wrong." His grin widened.

Against her better judgment, she smiled back.

Remember, permanent damage.

As Cole pulled onto the road, the silence between them settled. Raven ran her fingers over the smooth leather seat, willing herself to focus on anything but the faint scent of his cologne mixed with the vanilla from the tree hanging on the mirror. They fell into conversation as they drove, reminiscing about old road trips. Especially after his basic training graduation in South Carolina, when he belted "Livin' on a Prayer" by Bon Jovi so loud on the drive home he had lost his voice.

When they stopped for gas, Raven ran inside while Cole pumped fuel. After a quick bathroom break, she grabbed a large coffee. She was adding hazelnut creamer when she heard a familiar voice mid-stir.

"Well, if it isn't Raven Cunningham."

She turned to see Amber Willis, former high-school queen bee, standing near the counter, magazine in hand.

Raven forced a smile. "Amber, hi."

Amber looked like she belonged on a reality show, perfectly polished from her platinum blonde ponytail to her gleaming white sneakers. She wore cerulean scrubs that clung to her surgically enhanced curves.

Amber's lips pursed as she gave Raven a once-over. "Didn't expect to see you still in Elkwood. I'm just passing through for coffee. I work for Dr. Larkin now, you know, the plastic surgeon." She tossed her hair. "So, are you still stacking books for a living?"

Raven gritted her teeth and nodded.

Amber's eyes flicked past her. "Was that Cole out there? I'd recognize those arms anywhere. He certainly filled out."

Raven tightened the lid on her cup.

Amber's smile turned pretentious, her signature move. "I always thought Cole would end up with someone a little more . . . ambitious. Unless he still has you in the friend zone."

Raven's cheeks burned. Friend zone? Really? Amber had always resented their friendship, especially after he'd turned Amber down for the Sadie Hawkins dance in seventh grade.

Maybe Raven should bring *that* up.

Raven's fingers curled around the strap of her bag. "At least he doesn't pretend to be my friend just to suck the joy out of my soul like some kind of dementor."

Amber blinked.

Oh. That was not how normal people talked.

Before she could backtrack, Cole's voice cut in. "There you are."

Relief rushed through her as he rounded the corner, a plastic bag in hand.

Amber straightened, her smile turning coy. "We were just catching up."

Cole's expression didn't change. "Is that right?" He stepped closer, slipping his free hand into Raven's. "We should hit the road. Right, hun?"

Raven froze. *Hun?*

What game was he playing?

"Uh, yeah." She grabbed her coffee and let him steer her toward the door.

Amber's smile faltered, her gaze bouncing between them. "Take care."

Cole led Raven outside, his hand grazing the small of her back. When they reached the truck, he opened the door, his smirk lingering.

Raven turned to him, brow raised. "Hun?"

He shrugged. "Didn't seem like a conversation you wanted to finish."

"That was some quick thinking."

He slid into the driver's seat, flashing a cocky grin. "I have my moments."

Raven sipped her coffee, the tension in her shoulders loosening. She should be focused on the trip, on finding her father, but Amber's words still dug under her skin.

Unless he still has you in the friend zone.

"Good to hear I'm not sucking life out of your soul."

Raven's head whipped toward him, mortification heating her face. Why—why did she even speak?

"You still do that when you're nervous?" Cole gestured toward her hands.

"Do what?"

"Twist that ring. You used to do it before every science exam in high school."

Raven stilled her fingers, suddenly self-conscious. "I didn't realize I was doing it."

His smirk softened. "It's kinda cute, actually."

Her cheeks warmed. She turned to the window, hoping he wouldn't notice.

Rain streaked down the windshield as Cole flipped through radio stations. A Rascal Flatts song filled the cab, and memories stirred—late-night drives, summer bonfires, the ease of old familiarity. She peeked into the shopping bag. Doritos, beef jerky, waters, and protein bars. All the essentials. Cole reached for the beef jerky, his arm brushing hers.

"Beef jerky at 6 a.m.?" Raven said.

"Breakfast of champions. It'll hold me over until pancakes. C'mon, you know you want some."

Raven grabbed a piece of salty jerky. Amber's barbed words lingered like a stubborn itch.

Friend zone.

As if it was so ridiculous that she could be with Cole. Times like these she wished she had Zoe's knack for biting comebacks.

Those two words fostered a decade of unspoken what-ifs lingering between them.

Until that day in the hospital. The moment Raven had convinced herself she saw love in his eyes. Bandaged and weak, he'd asked her to stay, his grip firm despite his fading strength. And she had, right next to his bed.

Then in one foolish whim, she whispered the truth her heart had carried for years. "I love you, Cole."

She thought she saw him mouth the words back. Or maybe she only wanted to. But when she brought it up before he went to rehab, he waved it off like it was nothing.

"You know I love you, Rae." He said it in that way a big brother would before he punched you in the arm.

She tried to forget. Tried to believe she'd misread everything. But she couldn't shake the way he'd looked at her that night, like she was the only thing holding his world together. Like he meant it. And yet, the moment he was strong enough to be released, he shut her out. Ghosted her. As if none of it mattered.

Raven shook her head, forcing her gaze to the window. She had to push it out of her mind. What good would it do to dwell on moments like that? Whatever she thought she'd seen, it didn't matter now. Cole Walker had mastered the art of holding people at arm's length, and she wasn't about to be fooled again.

She'd checked her phone, scrolling the J.C. Nevermore social media fan forum for any clues. It buzzed in her hand.

A text from Zoe.

> Zoe: I'm now awake and have to know, did you fall in love yet?

> Raven: OMG, stop.

> Zoe: You didn't answer my question.

> Raven: I'm ghosting you now.

She glanced over at Cole, studying his face. There was maturity there now, a rugged steely calm that hadn't been there before. She wondered about what he'd gone through in the Army, how it had changed him. He never shared details. Not even about Preach since the funeral. Not that she'd gotten much out of him at all. He'd avoided conversations about Preach . . . about anything. Eventually she'd stopped calling.

She bit her lip, her voice barely louder than the rain. "Can I ask you something?"

Cole gave her a quick side glance. "Sure."

"When you were overseas . . . did you ever get scared?"

"Nah."

"Really?" She tilted her head.

He rolled his shoulders, eyes fixed ahead. "Fear's part of it. You learn how to work through it. Do what you're trained to do."

She stared at her hands. "Is that what you did? Just . . . pushed through it?"

He hesitated, something shifting in his expression. "Most days. Some days were harder."

The silence that followed throbbed with things unsaid. She could push, but she shouldn't. She wanted to know what had happened to him on that mission with Preach. But if she pushed, he'd probably turn around.

The truck hit a patch of slick road. Her heart jolted. Cole's grip tightened on the wheel. His jaw locked again, that same closed-off look settling back in.

Her phone buzzed in her lap.

> Mom: Did you send the $ yet? I didn't see it in the account.

> Raven: I sent it to your Venmo last night. It should be there.

The rain picked up, smearing the view ahead into streaks of gray. She turned her screen face-down in her lap, then glanced at Cole again. Even in the dim cab, he looked solid. Steady. Like someone who didn't rattle easy.

Another buzz.

Mom: Okay. I see it now.

A weather alert lit up next: *Severe storm warning in your area. Use caution.*

Great.

She flipped her phone over again, not ready to let anything steal this opportunity from her. Maybe it wouldn't last. Maybe it was all pretend. But for the next stretch of road, she let herself believe in the possibility that she could find answers.

And maybe figure out what Cole was still hiding.

Three hours into the drive and the rain still hadn't let up. A storm tracked east right behind them, and Cole tightened his grip on the wheel, pushing to stay ahead of it. He glanced at the speedometer—just under sixty-five—but the truck skimmed across the slick highway like it was skating on glass.

He flexed his right hand, trying to will the tremor in his arm to ease. It wasn't bad yet, but he knew the signs. The burn always started low, sparking like a frayed wire. Yesterday's workout had pushed the limits, and now he was paying the price. But he didn't have the luxury of rest. He only had so much time to get back to pre-injury state.

He ignored the burn crawling up his arm and focused on the road. He'd driven through worse. But that didn't stop the unease from curling in his gut. The storm behind them wasn't the only thing weighing heavy. The box in the backseat, Preach's box, pressed in hard. Heavy with things he hadn't said. Truths Raven still didn't know.

A flash of lightning lit the clouds above, and the rain intensified, streaking across the windshield faster than the wipers could clear.

"Should we pull over?" Raven clutched the door handle.

"We're alright. Just gotta take it slow."

The highway curved ahead. He adjusted the wheel, instincts sharp. A faint reflector glowed on the edge of the lane. He adjusted the wheel to the left, testing the traction.

The rear tires hit a patch of standing water. The truck jolted sideways, the back end kicking out.

Cole's pulse spiked.

Adrenaline surged.

He feathered the brakes, worked the wheel.

The truck fishtailed.

Raven gasped, bracing herself.

"Hold on." He counter-steered, but they slid onto the shoulder.

The truck slammed into a shallow ditch, the thud jarring them to a halt.

His arm shot out in front of her, holding her in place. "You okay?"

"Yeah, I think so." She shifted.

The truck tilted to the right.

"Stay put." He threw the hazards on and killed the engine.

His training kicked in. Check the damage. Secure the vehicle. Keep them moving forward.

He stepped into the mud, boots sinking. Rain pelted his face as he crouched near the front tires.

No sparks. No leaks.

But the slope of the ditch angled straight into a narrow culvert. They couldn't stay here long.

He popped the tonneau cover, grabbed two flares, and lit them before placing them on the shoulder.

Back at the driver door, he leaned in. "Seatbelt stays on. I'm checking the tires."

Raven nodded. She looked pale but composed.

He swept mud from the treads. The tires were intact. Four-wheel could work—if he could get traction. He slung the tailgate down. A few tools rattled in the storage box. If the mat wasn't enough, there might be some downed branches he could use.

He shoveled quickly, ignoring the burn slicing through his shoulder. He laid the mat beneath the rear wheels and climbed back inside, soaked through.

He flipped the truck into low gear. "Brace yourself. This might get bumpy."

Raven clung to the door handle as he eased off the brake and tapped the gas. The wheels spun, caught, then launched forward. The truck clawed up the slope.

"Come on!" He pressed harder.

Mud sprayed. The engine roared.

With a final jolt, they were free.

He exhaled, releasing his grip on the wheel. "We're out."

Raven let out a shaky breath beside him.

"Remind me to dodge hydroplane zones next time." He jumped out, grabbed the mat and flares, and tossed them in the bed before slamming it shut.

He wiped rain from his face with an old blanket and draped it over the seat before getting in.

"You're soaked." Raven gave him a crooked smile. "You sure you didn't plan this to show off?"

He chuckled as he twisted the cap off a water bottle and swigged. "Please, I'd rather run a marathon in full gear than hydroplane into a ditch with you watching."

A smile tugged at her lips. "Well, consider me impressed."

The rain softened to a drizzle. For a moment, they both breathed easier. Cole leaned back in his seat, the adrenaline ebbing away. He pulled back onto the highway.

"Maybe we could stop at the next exit." Raven scrolled her phone. "Looks like there's a diner about two miles ahead."

"Pancakes?"

"Absolutely. My treat." She confirmed with a small laugh.

He shifted into drive, guiding them back to the road. The chill soaked through his wet clothes. He needed to change.

The rain lightened to a drizzle by the time they pulled off the exit. He should have been relieved. They were safe, the truck was fine, and pancakes were minutes away. But a strange tension coiled in his chest, stubborn and unrelenting.

He glanced at Raven. "You sure you're okay?"

She looked up, eyes wide. "Yeah, why?"

"Just checking." His jaw tightened. What if it had gone worse? What if she'd been hurt?

She tilted her head. "Are *you* okay? You've got that look."

"What look?"

"The one that says you're overthinking ten things you won't say out loud."

He offered a smile. "Just thinking about pancakes."

She laughed. Didn't press him.

As he merged off the exit, something in him shifted.

Whatever this was between them, it was more than road trips and rescue plans.

He had to push that thought to the back of his mind. Because, whether or not he could admit it aloud, one thing had become clear.

He needed to get her to that cabin.

Safe.

Before anything else went wrong.

CHAPTER 8

THE RAIN HAD LET up, but the sky hung heavy and gray as they pulled off Interstate 99. Raven's stomach still flipped from the near crash. But Cole had gotten them out of the ditch. Of course he had. That was what he did—fix things.

He shifted the truck into park and leaned back with a satisfied sigh. "There it is. Salvation in the form of breakfast food."

Raven gave a half-hearted chuckle, glancing out the window. The Sunrise Café looked like a set piece from an old movie—retro red booths blurred behind fogged-up glass. Her boots splashed in a puddle as she stepped out. Cold October air sliced through her sweater. She pulled on her wool coat and buttoned it quickly.

"Give me one sec." Cole stood at the back door, towel in hand, wiping mud from his arms.

He tugged a white T-shirt from his duffel and peeled off the soaked one. Raven pretended to admire the pumpkin and haystack display outside the entrance. But her eyes betrayed her, trailing—okay, ogling—his chiseled abs as he pulled on the dry shirt.

Good grief.

A tattoo curled across his left bicep. Scars marked his right arm.

"See something interesting?" Cole slipped a black Steelers hoodie over his T-shirt.

"Just admiring nature's bounty." She nodded to the pumpkin display, tucking a loose strand of hair behind her ear.

"Oh right, the pumpkin bounty." He zipped his bag and shut the truck door.

She gave him a playful shove as they walked toward the entrance. He held the door, motioning her inside.

Warmth wrapped around her instantly. The scent of fresh coffee and cinnamon rolls tugged a growl from her stomach. Cole pointed to a window booth, and she slid into the seat across from him.

The Sunrise Café was like a page torn from time, its interior cozy and welcoming. Wooden beams lined the ceiling. Oak-paneled walls gave it a rustic charm Gram would've adored. Mismatched paintings of red barns and sunflower fields added character. A chalkboard above the counter listed daily specials in colorful script: blueberry pancakes, country-fried steak, homemade apple pie.

Raven pulled out her phone and leaned back, snapping a photo of the waitress delivering omelets and steaming sausage gravy to the sweet older couple next to them.

"Do you know them?" Cole said.

She laughed. "No, I wanted a pic. I love the farmhousey vibe to this place. Don't you?"

His brows came together, but he smiled. "You mean uneven floor planks and the sound of a cash register?"

She pretended not to hear him, already pulling up her notes app. "This place is *begging* to be the setting for something."

The waitress arrived to take their orders. After she left, Raven resumed typing, thumbs flying.

Cole leaned in, lowering his voice. "Are you logging details in case that guy in the corner ends up on a true crime podcast?"

Raven kept typing, not looking up. "Taking notes."

"Well, if this place is the setting, he's definitely your villain."

She smirked, reading aloud as she typed: "Rustic diner with mismatched chairs and worn floors. Elderly couple splits a newspaper, arguing over the crossword. Waitress with hair in a messy bun is all business, but you know she's a softie. A lone military man slouches in the corner booth, muddy jeans. His black coffee sits untouched, his expression distant, unreadable."

He laughed, leaning back in his chair. "You forgot devastatingly handsome."

Her fingers hovered over the screen as she added: *Diner hums with life, yet everyone seems lost in their own world. A place where stories overlap but don't always touch.*

When she looked up, he was watching her. "What? You're not going to make fun of me?"

He shook his head. "Nope. Just getting a kick out of watching your brain work."

She flushed but tried to hide it behind a sip of coffee. The warmth steadied her. Maybe the adrenaline hadn't fully left her system, or maybe it was the absurdity of sitting here with Cole Walker on a spontaneous road trip. A trip that may possibly lead to her father.

Across from her, he smirked. "What's on your mind?"

"I'm trying to figure out what I'm doing here."

"At the Sunrise Café?"

"You know what I mean. This whole trip."

He sipped his coffee. "You're here because you want answers. Are you second-guessing it now?"

She fiddled with the edge of her napkin. "There's no part of you that thinks this is nuts? I mean, I have no proof he's J.C. Nevermore other than a ridiculous whim. And the last I heard, from the most unreliable of sources, my father lived somewhere in

New York. A city with, I don't know, eight million people? I could be chasing shadows."

"Then we'll get creative." He leaned forward, resting his elbows on the table. "Look, you've got nothing to lose and maybe everything to gain."

She wasn't sure. The not-knowing had been safer. Familiar. Answers meant change, and change meant risk.

"The craziest part is this feeling that I *am* on the right track. But I don't know what the track is. Does that make any sense?"

His eyes softened as he nodded. "Sometimes you have to follow your gut. Even when it feels like you're groping around in the dark with nothing but a matchstick for light."

She studied him. "How do you always sound like you've got everything figured out?"

He laughed. "Spoiler alert. I'm winging it, just like you."

She chuckled and sipped her coffee, feeling a small weight lift from her shoulders.

Their food arrived. Cole's stack of pancakes towered like a dare. Hers was more modest—eggs, toast, two pancakes—but smelled like comfort. They ate in a relaxed silence.

Afterward, Raven slipped to the restroom. When she returned, Cole was at the door, waiting.

"You paid?" she said.

"I owed you. For the cookie in fourth grade." He rubbed his arm with a wince.

"You okay?" She pointed to his arm.

"Fine. Let's hit the road."

They stepped out into the crisp air. The rain had finally stopped. She slid into the passenger seat of the truck as Cole fired up the engine. Once they merged onto the highway, a low grinding noise echoed beneath them.

"Do you hear that?" Raven said.

"Yeah, something doesn't sound right. Maybe it's mud in the undercarriage." He flicked on the turn signal and changed lanes.

The noise grew louder as they picked up speed. But as he passed an eighteen-wheeler, the grinding turned into a clattering rattle.

Cole glanced at her. "Can you look up a mechanic near here. Sounds like the bearing might be loose."

She searched. "Kenny's Auto Service is a few miles off the next exit. Good reviews."

"Kenny's it is."

Raven tapped the screen, pulling up the directions.

They maneuvered down the off-ramp, following roads lined with trees shedding their vibrant autumn coats. A few turns later, Kenny's Auto Service appeared. They pulled into a gravel lot in front of a worn-down shop that looked straight out of a Route 66 postcard. Cole talked with a gray-haired mechanic. The mechanic gestured toward the truck before leading Cole to a service bay.

The place had a forgotten, dusty feel to it. Raven wandered through the office door, petting a sleepy hound dog curled up on a flannel bed. Inside, a space heater hummed next to the counter. Despite the shop's worn appearance, it was tidy and organized. Tools hung from pegboards and the counter around the ancient computer looked clean. Raven sat on a cracked leather seat in the waiting area, petting the hound dog when he sauntered toward her.

Moments later, Cole returned, wiping his hands on his jeans.

"Looks like we're stuck for a couple of hours." He dropped onto the seat beside her, giving the dog a quick scratch. "The wheel bearing is shot and needs replaced."

She groaned. "Guess our road trip gets an intermission. At least we have until Friday for the book signing. But I know you were hoping to get some solid fishing in before then."

He shot her a grin.

She leaned her head back on the seat and stared at the ceiling tiles. "So, what's the plan, wingman?"

"We can wait here. Or we can take a walk. Kenny said it's about a mile into town."

"A walk might be nice."

Cole stood up and held out his hand. He helped her up, crooking his elbow. She hooked her elbow through his, laughing. Part of her knew he was just being himself. *A friend.* But another part wanted to pretend the sincerity behind his eyes might be something real. Meant just for her.

As they walked alongside the two-lane road, the swirl of color invoked everything she loved about autumn. The chilled air smelled like woodsmoke and wet leaves, ideal for a cozy-up-with-a-book kind of day. The sun broke through the gray clouds. Raven let go of Cole and took a few pictures.

"I'm sorry about this." Cole pushed a tree branch out of her way.

She gasped, feigning offense. "You mean this wasn't part of your plan? Hydroplane into a ditch, break the truck, and whisk me into a one-horse town?"

He huffed a laugh, shaking his head.

"Besides, this reminds me of when we walked to that bus station in Virginia."

Ugh, why mention that? Do not say another word.

Cole paused and stopped to face her. "Me too."

Her chest tightened. Senior year spring break. The beach. The way he'd chased her to the edge of the waves, looking at her like . . .

Change the subject, fast.

"Remember the guy in the puffy coat who offered us a ride? Pretty sure he wanted to human traffic us."

"You thought everyone was sketchy, getting all worked up for no reason." Cole tossed a rock along the road.

"Right. But what about that time you left me and Emily to fend for ourselves at the boardwalk in Ocean City?"

"Those guys were hippies, completely harmless."

"You don't know that. One of them had a chain with handcuffs hanging from his pants."

Cole laughed while shaking his head.

"I guess I worry too much, huh?" Raven laughed along with him.

"I wouldn't let anything happen to you."

She believed him. And everything in her wanted to relish in the safety of his presence. His shoulders were like two mountain peaks carved from stone. The pride and confidence in his stance screamed of a military man, a protector, and was anything but subtle. Her eyes darted between him and the ground as she struggled to push past doubts filtering through familiar comfort.

Solar eclipse. Permanent damage.

She didn't know where this road led, not with her father, and definitely not with Cole. But for now, she wasn't going to shut him out. Not completely. Maybe they could be friends again. Maybe that was enough . . . or maybe it was the beginning of something she wasn't ready to name.

Either way, she didn't pull away when he smiled at her. And that was something.

Roaming an empty backroad in rural Pennsylvania wasn't how Cole pictured this trip going. He shoved his hands in his pockets, boots crunching loose gravel. One thing at a time—fix the truck. Then . . . everything else.

Raven walked beside him, seemingly enchanted by the detour. She let her hair down, and the wind caught it, framing her face like something out of a painting. Her eyes darted to every oddity they passed: a faded "Welcome to" sign whose name had peeled, a leaning mailbox barely holding on, and a half-collapsed barn with a murder of crows perched on the roof like sentries. She snapped pictures.

He slowed his stride to match hers. The grind of the busted wheel bearing echoed in his mind, mocking him. He shouldn't have let this happen.

"You're awfully quiet," she said.

He forced a grin. "Just thinking about how much better this trip's gonna be once we're at the cabin."

She laughed, and the sound hit him harder than he expected. He couldn't let her see how much this was bothering him, any of it. Not the truck. Not the delay. Definitely not the thought of seeing Preach's parents, and the look on their face when he told them the truth.

"You're doing that thing again." Raven tilted her head.

"What thing?"

"Where you get all stoic and distant."

He raised a brow. "Maybe I'm pondering life's mysteries."

She arched her brows. "Sure, Walker."

He couldn't tell her the truth.

The wind picked up, carrying the faint smell of damp earth and gasoline, a combination that always put Cole on edge. It reminded him too much of the motor pool back at base. Too many bad memories rode in on that scent.

Raven stretched her arms overhead. "Well, if life's mysteries are anywhere, I'm sure they'll reveal themselves on this scenic tour of Pennsylvania's most forgotten road."

Before he could respond, his phone buzzed in his jacket. Unknown number.

"Hello?"

"Cole? It's Kenny." An air compressor hissed in the background.

"What's the verdict?"

Kenny sucked in a breath that seemed to stretch. Not a great sign. "Well . . . it's the right front wheel bearing. Thing's shot. We can't patch this one up. Needs replaced."

"Alright. No problem, do what you gotta do to get it running. You think it'll be ready today?"

"We need to order the part, and it's probably going to take a day to come in, maybe two."

Cole pinched the bridge of his nose. A day or two? He'd planned to spend that time in the woods. Training. Processing. Fishing. Not stuck in a town with no name.

"Fine. Order it." He shoved the phone back into his pocket.

Raven's brow lifted. "What happened?"

"They need to order the part. But it's not going to be here for another day or two." He started walking again, back toward the shop.

She fell into step beside him. "Maybe it's a sign."

"Yeah. A sign I should slow down in a rainstorm."

She chuckled, nudging his arm. "Come on, every misadventure makes a better story later."

"Right."

"Oh please." She gestured broadly. "I'm sure we'll stumble into something riveting. A haunted ice cream truck? A fight club where they bet with potatoes, maybe?"

He huffed a short laugh and slowed his pace as they neared the repair shop. He greeted Kenny with a handshake and thanked him. Kenny offered to have his son-in-law drop them at a bed-and-breakfast in town run by an old friend. Cole grabbed their bags out of the truck and placed a blanket over Preach's box behind the seat.

When he stepped into the office, Raven stood at the counter talking with Kenny about the photo of a 1967 Corvette and what looked like a much younger version of himself. She had a way of unlocking people, softening them with genuine interest. That kind of warmth was rare.

"Hey-oh." A short, bearded man walked over. He and Kenny exchanged a hearty handshake and clapped each other on the back.

"Rex, thanks for coming out. This here is Cole and Raven. Take em' over to the Heartland." Kenny faced Cole. "Ask for Martha. She'll get ya set up with a nice room."

Rex tipped his baseball cap. "Nice to meet yinz. You can hop in the front."

They climbed into the truck—an old F250 with a leather bench seat that had seen better decades. Raven hesitated before Cole offered his hand to help her up. She slid in beside Rex, who unintentionally swallowed half the middle seat.

Tight fit.

Cole sat snug against Raven, arm braced behind her as the engine rumbled to life. Raven pressed the right sight of her body against his to keep from bumping Rex.

As the diesel fired the truck into gear, Raven jumped. She slid slightly toward Rex until Cole's arm pulled her gently back.

"You okay?" Cole said.

"Me? Oh, yeah. No problem. All good here." She stared straight ahead.

Rex chatted the whole way—cars, tattoos, small-town life. Raven nodded politely, brow creased in that quiet, curious way she had when she was filing someone away for a future story.

Her phone buzzed. She swiped the screen fast and glanced at him.

"Spam." She tucked it away.

They passed barns and flat fields, similar to home. A pothole sent the truck bouncing so hard Cole's head nearly hit the roof. Raven yelped and grabbed his knee.

"Sorry 'bout that," Rex said. "Road maintenance 'round here just means putting up a couple orange cones and calling it good."

"No kidding." Cole tried to ignore how long Raven's hand lingered.

They pulled up to a white Victorian house with striped awnings and a sign that read *Heartland Bed & Breakfast*. Quaint. Wrought-iron railings. A wraparound porch like home. But it wasn't the cabin with its mountain air and biting smallies.

It wasn't part of the plan.

Cole helped Raven down and thanked Rex. While she admired the porch, he pulled out his phone—nothing nearby for car rentals. Not within fifty miles. Great.

"This is cute. Don't you think?" Raven tapped his arm.

"Sure." He still scrolled. No Plan B. Just . . . this.

Everything about the trip had veered off course. Preach's parents were still waiting. The box still sat behind the seat of a busted truck. And Raven smiled like this wasn't a disaster.

Maybe it wasn't. Not for her.

Cole let out a slow breath and pocketed his phone.

This trip was out of his control. But maybe that wasn't the worst thing.

CHAPTER 9

RAVEN TRIED TO STAY positive, but it was hard to ignore the obvious—this trip had already started unraveling. Still, a strange sense of comfort came with the chaos. She never expected things to go smoothly because they rarely did. At least this time, she wasn't alone. Even though Cole looked like he'd rather be anywhere but Brookhaven, Pennsylvania.

He probably regretted bringing her. He could've been reaching Jersey by now.

"I checked rental car places near us," Cole said, shifting their bags over his shoulder. "Closest one's fifty miles out. I can get us a ride if you want."

"I thought we'd stay here. I mean, I don't want you leaving your truck in some random town."

"I'm not worried about the truck." He met her eyes. "I'm worried about getting you to that signing. I don't care if we have to jump on a horse-drawn carriage."

"It's four days away. We have plenty of time. But, a horse-drawn carriage? I'm holding you to that." His sincerity surprised her. Somehow, that look in his eyes made everything feel . . . less derailed. Like this wasn't a roadblock, just a pothole.

The scent of freshly baked bread drifted onto the porch as they stepped inside the bed and breakfast. Cole held the door. A cat lay on the polished oak surface. Behind the counter stood a plump, rosy-cheeked woman with blonde and silver-streaked hair tied back in a neat bun.

"Welcome to Heartland Bed & Breakfast. How can I help you folks today?"

Cole explained the situation. "Kenny sent us. We're hoping to get two rooms for the night."

"That Kenny, he's such a doll. You're in luck. We just had a cancellation. But I'm afraid we only have one room available."

Raven froze. Did she just say *one* room?

"Thank you. But we'll need two. Any other options nearby?" Cole said.

She admired how quickly he took charge. Always fixing things.

The woman shook her head. "Most places fill up this time of year. Folks come from all over for the harvest festival."

"Are you sure there's nothing else?" He glanced at Raven as if seeking backup. "Look, I'll take a cot in a basement or even a tent is fine."

Cole's determination was both respectable and borderline dramatic. They'd had plenty of sleepovers as kids, including one in a trampoline during a meteor shower. Though back then, cooties were the biggest threat. Now? Different stakes entirely. Still, she appreciated the effort. It meant he respected her boundaries, even if part of her wasn't sure where those boundaries edged.

Martha's eyebrows arched so high they nearly touched her hairline. "The basement? Good heavens, no. And a tent? This isn't a campground, sweetheart." She reached for a brass bell on the counter and gave it one sharp ring. "Earl! Come here a minute!"

A wiry man with sagging suspenders poked his head through the kitchen door. "What is it now?"

"These folks need space. And this one wants to sleep in a tent." She pointed to Cole.

"A tent? In October?" Earl let out a deep chuckle that sounded like gravel being churned by an old tractor.

"You think you can get the attic ready?"

He sighed but nodded. Then he disappeared again, muttering something about city folk.

Raven pressed her lips together to hide a smirk.

Cole turned to Martha as she slid the key card across the counter.

"Room three. Top of the stairs, second door on your left if you want to drop your bags and get situated." She winked. "But Earl might take a little while spiffing up the attic. Man moves slower than molasses in January, but he gets the job done."

"Thank you. We appreciate it." Cole accepted the key with a tight smile, and they made their way up the creaky wooden staircase.

The Heartland's charm—ancient floral wallpaper, antique furniture, the faint smell of lavender sachets, framed cross-stitch samplers—all reminded her of Gram. But it also screamed shared bathroom territory and her inner germaphobe rattled a bit. At the top of the stairs, Cole paused and glanced back at her before sliding the key in.

As the door swung open with a faint creak, Raven froze mid-step, her breath catching in her throat. This had to be a mistake. Surely, Martha had handed her the wrong key, or maybe the universe was pulling some sort of cosmic prank.

This wasn't just a room. This was *the honeymoon suite.*

"Oh boy," she muttered under her breath, stepping inside.

Soft golden light spilled from an antique glass lamp, bathing everything in warm, honeyed hues. Front and center stood a quilted canopy bed, its high wooden posts carved with intricate floral patterns. The layers of plush burgundy fabric on the bedspread screamed "romance" louder than any bad Valentine's Day commercial.

And then there were the heart-shaped pillows.

"Oh no." Her stomach flipped as she took an involuntary step back. Were those . . . rose petals? She squinted. No, just a floral pattern on the rug, thank goodness. But still.

What was Cole thinking right now? Probably something ridiculous, like how he should start calling her "The Mrs." for laughs. She pinched the bridge of her nose.

Get a grip. It's just a room. At least you're not sharing it with him.

If she made it through the night without dying of embarrassment, it would be a miracle. Cole brushed past her and set down their bags near the foot of the bed. He didn't seem phased, either oblivious or pretending not to notice. Every detail swept her into a weird ball of nerves. This moment was the most single she'd felt in a long time.

"Well, this is . . . cozy." He rubbed the back of his neck.

Raven laughed. "That's one way to put it."

Thankfully the bathroom was tucked right inside the room. While Cole took a quick shower, Raven slipped off her coat and scanned the space. She sank onto the edge of the bed. Her hand ran across the quilted comforter. She sighed as she looked around. Despite the awkwardness, she had to admit it beat another sleepless night at home. A sudden urge to write about the detailed decor tugged at her. Even the awkwardness of the whole thing.

She pulled her phone out of her purse, thumb hovering over the notes app, and started typing:

Swept into a honeymoon suite with all the romance of a Hallmark movie and none of the fiancé to match. Carved bedposts scream 'serious commitment,' but also look sturdy enough to fend off an intruder or perhaps prop up a blanket fort for someone sleeping solo. Heart-shaped pillows? Overkill.

She snickered to herself as she typed. The absurdity of the situation was less like a roadblock and more like . . . well, maybe an anecdote she'd laugh about later. Much later.

A quick text from Zoe buzzed in her hand.

What's going on with the truck?

It's getting fixed, but we have to stay overnight.

In the middle of nowhere?

Yep. Classic small-town vibes. Might not be too bad.

You two fall in love yet?

STOP asking me that.

That's not a no . . .

It IS a no. And I swear, if you don't stop, I'll block you. He almost saw your last text about that. Thanks for nearly killing me.

Oh, come on. That means you're bad at hiding feelings. Or maybe he's curious?

You're impossible. I mean it. Blocked.

Love you

Goodbye. Forever.

Raven stuffed her phone in her bag, shaking her head. Zoe would have a field day if she knew about the honeymoon suite. Nope. Raven couldn't handle that conversation yet. Or ever.

The bathroom door creaked open. Cole tugged down his T-shirt as he stepped out, his hair still damp.

Seriously? Who looks that good fresh out of the shower? Like some kind of rugged, all-American heartthrob, the kind who chopped wood shirtless and had a loyal dog named Duke. And the worst part? He wasn't even trying.

"What?" Cole towel-dried his hair with an easy grin.

"Oh, nothing. Just documenting our detour for future generations."

"Right, future generations will definitely want to hear about how I got banished to the attic."

They shared a laugh. Wait, did he think she meant *their* future generations? Again, why did she even speak.

"Wonder what this festival is all about." She wandered to the window and pushed the lace curtain aside.

Colorful banners and hay bales lined the streets below, and for a moment, she imagined herself there—blending into the cheerful crowd, sipping cider, walking arm-in-arm with someone who stayed. Someone who wouldn't retreat at the first sign of her flaws, or fade into excuses when things got messy.

She shook the thought off.

Behind her, Cole had flopped onto one of the bedside chairs, entirely too large for the delicate furniture. The chair shuddered under his weight, but he didn't seem concerned.

"Think they've got a pie-eating contest at this thing?"

She raised an eyebrow. "You're hungry again?"

"Pancakes were just the pregame."

"You've got weird priorities."

Was he saying he wanted to go? She could go for a snack, too. Festival food was her love language. Plus, it was after two o'clock already.

He leaned forward, a mock serious tone creeping into his voice as he balanced his elbows on his knees. "When the day comes that you're staring down a table with twenty pumpkin pies lined up and a timer set for five minutes, you'll realize this isn't just about food. It's about legacy."

"Oh my gosh, you're ridiculous." She laughed.

"Do you want to check it out? Unless you want to hang in here with the honeymoon pillows."

She stiffened. Her heart skipped at his simple charm. Her first instinct was to deflect, joke, stall.

Instead, she looked back at him. And made a choice.

"Let's go. I'm not letting you win that pie contest unchallenged."

The town looked like a cornucopia had exploded onto everything. The cobblestone streets and red brick buildings looked old, probably early 1800s. A cannon statue sat in the middle of the town square, where people dressed in farm gear gathered.

What was this place again?

Cole glanced at his phone. Brookhaven. That sounded familiar. Just a few miles north of Penn State College.

"Look at that!" Raven pointed to a bakery where two women in bonneted dresses urged kids to crank an old butter churner. "I wonder if they use it."

She flipped through the brochure Martha had handed her. "Oh, my goodness. Pumpkin races? That's so great."

"Let me guess. First one to roll their squash across the finish line wins?" he teased.

She grinned. "Fastest pumpkin takes the crown, Mr. Sarcasm."

He laughed under his breath and tucked his phone back into his hoodie pocket. He wanted the truck fixed and out of this town. But then he glanced at her, eyes wide with wonder, cheeks pink from the cold. Maybe this wasn't the worst detour after all.

"Any pie contests?"

"Not until the weekend." She scanned the flyer. "But there's a puppet show."

He raised an eyebrow. "Hard pass."

"Okay, okay. No puppets." She motioned to the tents around them. "But come on, they've got candy apples, cake pops, and kettle corn."

She grabbed his sleeve and tugged him toward the vendor rows before he could object. The air swirled with cinnamon and fried sugar. If autumn had a scent, this town wore it like cologne. He skimmed over candles and jewelry but slowed near the handmade leather gear and the military surplus booth. Real, solid things. Familiar things. But no way was he rolling a pumpkin down the street.

Meanwhile, Raven knelt to talk to a little girl with a butterfly painted on her cheek. "I love your dress," she said.

The girl smiled shyly, thumb still in her mouth.

Raven always saw people, even when they didn't want to be seen.

"You're smiling." She rejoined him with a triumphant smirk. "You're having fun. Admit it."

He shrugged, shoving his hands in his pockets. "It's . . . tolerable."

"Tolerable." She nudged him with her shoulder as they continued down the row of food vendors. "You know you want one of those deep-fried Oreos." She twirled toward the food truck, scarf flying out like a ribbon, and he swore the entire street warmed by ten degrees.

Brookhaven, yes, he knew he'd heard it before. His army buddy Tick never shut up about this place and some urban legend tied to it about a radio frequency. Why hadn't he thought of Tick earlier? If anyone could find intel on Raven's father, it was him.

Cole texted Tick.

> Cole: Hey man, you still in Brookhaven? Got a case for you.

As they strolled past the band, Raven swayed to the beat.

"You gonna start dancing in the street?" Cole said.

"Maybe. Care to join me?" She shot back, twirling again so her scarf flared out behind her.

He shook his head with a smirk.

"Oh, I forgot. You were the king of wallflowers."

They rounded a corner near a cluster of carnival games.

Before he could argue, a sudden crack split the air. His arm shot out in front of her.

Pop-pop-pop.

His lungs seized. Sound bled into memory.

The music blurred into chaos. Children's laughter shifted into screams. Dust filled his mouth. Heat flared across his back.

Another pop. Another flash.

His mind spiraled. Voices blended into a roar.

His breathing shallowed.

Chest tightened as if trapped under a thousand-pound block.

He couldn't breathe. Couldn't move. The world folded in on itself, crushing his chest with invisible hands.

He squeezed his head with both hands, trying to pry it out of the vise grip. He staggered then hunched over. Ringing faded in and out.

"Cole, what's going on?"

Breathe.

Pulse quickened. Breaths shorter. Faster.

Focus.

He squeezed his eyes shut, unable to lock in.

"Cole, look at me." Raven yanked his arm, pulling him face to face with her. "Describe one thing you see."

He squinted. "Brown hair," he forced out.

"Good. What else?"

His jaw tightened and his muscles coiled.

"You're safe. Remind your body you're safe." Her chestnut eyes held his, pulling him from the brink. "Right here, with me. I've got you."

"I can't get . . ."

She stepped closer. "Four things. Tell me four things you see."

He opened his eyes and latched onto her voice. "White . . . white tent."

"Good. Three more."

"Balloons. . . Your boots . . . grass." His breath snagged, but the pounding eased.

"You're doing great. Keep going. Two more things you see."

"That oak tree. A bench." His vision focused and his lungs opened.

"One more thing you see."

His breathing slowed. "You." He kept his eyes on her.

She smiled, cupping her hands over his. "Good. Now, four things you can touch."

His pulse slowed, and the ringing stopped. "The ground."

He ran his left hand over his chest, the other still holding hers. "My hoodie. Your . . . coat." He brushed the edge of her sleeve. ". . . Your hand." He wrapped both hands around hers.

Her touch seeped into the hollow places, reaching the pain not avoiding it. Her presence said what her words didn't: he wasn't alone.

He exhaled slowly, shoulders lowering.

"That's great." Her thumb grazed his knuckles. "I think you're back."

Cole blinked, festival sounds trickling back in through the fog. He swallowed hard as if trying to push down a lump lodged deep in his throat. He didn't speak—wouldn't trust himself if he could.

He searched her face, the curves of her cheek, the strand of hair drifting in the wind. Her expression untouched by fear or pity—but something else. Worry? No, something deeper. An understanding that didn't require explanation or pretense. Those deep brown eyes weren't just looking at him—they were cutting through every defense like they knew where he hid.

"How do you feel now?"

He wanted to say grateful, exposed, afraid. All of it.

"I'm okay."

She didn't let go. Neither did he. She stood closer than she'd ever been. Except . . . one other time. The faint scent of her perfume crept through the chaos still settling, something floral and earthy.

Another pop rang from the shooting gallery. His body jerked, too fast to stop. She felt it too.

"You don't have to pretend," she said gently.

"I said I'm good." He stepped back quick.

"Cole."

He met her eyes, and the truth surged to the surface—about Preach, the mission, the blood, the box in the truck. But the words stayed trapped behind the wall he'd spent years building.

And she saw it. Not with judgment, but with that same unrelenting insight she'd always had.

"I just . . ." He stopped. "Thank you."

She nodded, brushing her hair behind her ear. "Does this happen often?"

"No." Too sharp. "Not really."

She didn't push. Just watched. And somehow that was worse.

He hated that she could *still* see right through him. But he also didn't want to look away. The look she gave him wasn't disappointment. Worse—it was discernment. Like she already knew he was a coward.

And it burned him that she might be right.

CHAPTER 10

RAVEN FOLLOWED COLE INTO The Copper Kettle, a cozy red-brick café tucked a block away from the festival noise. White string lights twinkled along the windows. Shelves lined with mason jars, small copper mugs, and green plants gave the space a warm, lived-in charm. The scent of coffee beans and cooling cookies coaxed her nerves to quiet.

They ordered and sat at a small bistro table tucked against the wall. Raven wrapped her hands around her spiced caramel coffee. Across from her, Cole hadn't said a word—just stared into his drink. She couldn't stop thinking about the pain etched on his face. For a brief moment he'd started to let go. If only he'd let her in.

Why hadn't he told her?

She took a slow sip, then put down her mug. "So, do you want to talk about it?"

"About what?" He stared at the table, squeezing his right hand as if it had fallen asleep.

"C'mon Cole, you know what." Why didn't he trust her?

"I get migraines." He shrugged, his tone as flat as a pancake. "No big deal."

She raised her eyebrows, taking another slow sip. She stared at him. He wouldn't meet her eyes. Classic Cole dodge. She knew that move too well—keep everything bottled, stay in control. But this time, she didn't call him out. He didn't need her poking at him when clearly something wasn't right. Instead, she leaned back in her chair, letting the silence stretch long enough to swallow the café noises around them.

His jaw tightened. His hand curled around his mug as if it were about to grow legs and run away if he didn't grip it in place.

She took a deep breath. "A beer bottle."

His head jerked. "What?"

Raven traced the rim of her cup. She hadn't planned on saying it, not like that. But now it hung between them, sharp and unshakable.

"I was twelve. My mom hit me with one." She tapped her temple, lifting a lock of hair to show the scar near her hairline.

His brow furrowed. "Rae—"

"She was drunk. Big surprise right? I yelled back at her, for once. She grabbed the bottle, aimed for the wall, but it hit me instead. I woke up on the kitchen floor with blood dripping down my face and glass in my hair."

Cole's mouth opened, then shut. His eyes darkened as he looked away, jaw tight.

"She didn't mean to, not really. She wasn't aiming for me. Got mad at me about something, I don't remember what it was. I'd said the wrong thing, and she lost it. She was screaming, throwing things." Raven's voice wavered, and she took a deep breath to steady it. "I don't know what I was thinking, standing up to her like that."

He looked back at her and his brows pulled together.

"I blamed myself for years," Raven said. "Told myself if I'd just kept quiet, it wouldn't have happened."

"That's not on you." His words laced with fierce protectiveness.

"After that night, the panic attacks started. Not the small kind, if there is such a thing. These were full-on. My chest would tighten like a vise, making it impossible to breathe. My heart would race so fast, I thought it might explode, and my hands wouldn't stop trembling no matter what I did. I'd feel this heat rising, like my whole body was on fire, and my mind was spiraling out of control, convinced I was dying. It eventually got better, but I worry about it coming back sometimes." Raven adjusted in her seat.

"I never told anyone. Not even Gram." She'd never told Cole either, but he'd witnessed the fallout of an episode or two. He'd never asked questions, just sat with her.

"And Ethan, or he-who-shall-not-be-named as Zoe calls him, thought I was crazy when I had an episode in front of him. I was sobbing, screaming, barely making sense, and . . . I scared him. Maybe that's what finally pushed him away." She glanced at her bare ring finger. "That, and the paralegal at his firm he'd been spending too much time with."

"I didn't know. I'm sorry."

"Don't be, it's okay now. I learned that stuffing it down doesn't work. It just waits until it can hit you harder."

She looked up, forcing herself not to flinch under his stare. "You're not the only one who's carried something heavy. Whatever you're fighting, don't carry it alone."

His eyes held hers. Something cracked there. For a heartbeat, she thought he'd say it—the truth he kept buried.

But then his phone buzzed.

He grabbed it, exhaling as he read the message. "Finally."

She tilted her head. "Everything okay?"

"Yeah." His thumb hovered over the screen as he typed out a quick reply. "I sent a buddy of mine a message earlier."

He set his phone on the table and leaned forward. "I heard what you said. It kills me that anyone could do that to you. And the Ethan thing, that wasn't your fault."

His eyes held hers, full of something—anger on her behalf, maybe. The space between them felt smaller than it had been a second ago. The hum of the room faded into the sound of her heartbeat pounding in her ears.

For a moment, she thought he might reach for her hand, and part of her wanted him to. But instead, took a gulp of his coffee and stood.

"C'mon. We gotta go meet a buddy of mine."

"Who?"

"Tick. He lives near here."

"Tick?" She tried to remember.

He flashed a smile. "It's a nickname. He's the kind of guy that gets under your skin, know what I mean?"

She raised an eyebrow. "Like an actual tick? That's . . . charming."

"Trust me, you'll get it when you meet him." Cole pocketed his phone. "He's meeting us at the dive bar down the street."

"Right now?"

"Yeah, let's go. Tick's the guy you want around when you're chasing breadcrumbs. He did cyber recon. Found people before they knew we were looking. Hacking and tracking kind of stuff. If anyone can help find your father . . . it's him."

She studied him for a moment, her curiosity twitching. It was clear Tick was someone he trusted, so she had little reason to doubt it.

"Okay." She knew better than to have expectations.

The sun lowered, streaking the sky in orange and red, matching the foliage. After a short walk, they reached the bar—a mix of local grit and small-town charm. Raven hadn't caught the name of the place. The dim orange lighting reflected off wood-paneled walls. The low hum of conversation mingled with the clink of pool balls from a corner table. Cole scanned the room, then led her to a booth in the back.

A man slouched in the booth, one boot resting on the opposite seat, the other tapping an erratic rhythm on the floor. His disheveled hair stuck out in wild tufts, as though he'd walked through a wind tunnel—or an explosion. He wore a tattered coat over a shirt that might have been white once and cargo pants with stuffed pockets.

"Is that . . . Tick?"

Cole smirked. "In the flesh."

"Doc, you made it!" He leaped to his feet, nearly tripping over his own boots. He clapped Cole on the back after they fist-bumped. "Who is this radiant creature? Randall Tucker, at your service." He swept into an overly dramatic bow facing Raven, then straightened and gave her a wink. "But you can call me Tick. Everyone does."

Raven tried not to laugh. "Raven. Nice to meet you."

"He's always like this. Don't pay mind to it," Cole said.

Tick placed a hand over his heart, his expression wounded. "It's not every day you bring a goddess of mystery and beauty into my lair of intellectual genius. This is a moment to be treasured!"

Cole shot Tick a look. "We're searching for her father."

Tick plopped into the booth. Cole guided Raven in the booth opposite him and sat next to her. Cole seemed unfazed by Tick's antics. In the same way a parent tolerates an unruly toddler.

"Now, tell me, are we looking at, a classic gone-off-the-grid scenario? Or perhaps he's been swept up in some grand international conspiracy? No, wait—hold on." Tick's manic energy vibrated as he tapped an invisible keyboard on the table. "Is he a rogue FBI agent? Nah, too predictable. CIA on the run from a

Russian mafia boss? Maybe he intercepted some highly sensitive documents detailing their secret vodka pipeline?"

Raven laughed despite herself.

"Stay with me!" Tick waved his hands like he was orchestrating a symphony of chaos. "He's probably hiding somewhere exotic. I'm talking untraceable Pacific atoll, or an underground labyrinth beneath Paris, booby traps and all! Or maybe—wait for it—he's leading a double life as the head of a shadowy think tank dedicated to predicting apocalyptic events using quantum algorithms no one else knows how to spell." He paused, eyes gleaming. "Boom."

Tick sounded as if he was spinning the theory into a Netflix series pitch.

"Tick." Cole reigned him in.

"Fine. What's the mission?" Tick crossed his arms.

"We're looking for breadcrumbs. Can you help?"

"Breadcrumbs? Lay it on me. And don't worry." He pulled a small device from his pocket that beeped with blinking lights. "This place isn't bugged. I already checked."

Once the antics settled, Cole explained the situation.

Tick's grin faded. "A mystery author? C'mon. Give me a *real* challenge."

"Can you do it or not?"

"Of course I can. If there's a trail, I'll find it." He picked up a sugar packet and twirled it between his fingers, his eyes gleaming with a kind of manic mischief that was both unsettling and mesmerizing.

Raven hadn't known what to expect from him. But this? This jittery man-child with theories about Russian pipelines and apocalyptic think tanks? Her skepticism hitched up a notch. He wasn't ordinary, that much was clear, but she couldn't tell if that worked in her favor or was another cosmic joke at her expense.

"You're sure you can find something?" she said.

Tick met her eyes, his grin returning in full force. "Let me make this clear: If there's a breadcrumb to follow, I'll find the whole loaf."

Cole crossed his arms. "You still doing contract work?"

Tick gave a half-shrug. "Now and then. Enough to keep my clearance warm."

Cole smirked. "Just don't crash anyone's system."

Tick gasped, clutching his chest. "You wound me! I'm a professional. Now, I must go."

As Tick disappeared out the door, Raven sat back.

Cole turned to her. "He's a lot. But he's the best at what he does."

Raven stared at the door. Her instincts screamed to pull back. Tick was unpredictable. Cole had dodged her again. And she'd spilled more of her brokenness on him.

Trust was a risk. And she'd taken two steps forward with both feet dangling off the edge of a cliff. She wanted to believe, or hope, that maybe this wouldn't fall apart.

But the part of her trained by disappointment—the part that had been hit and left and forgotten—whispered that hope was the first mistake.

The festival lights glowed at dusk. Cole walked alongside Raven through the festival, back toward the bed-and-breakfast. Bars had never been her thing. Plus, his room in the attic should've been ready. Maybe he belonged in a dusty attic room to let the memories lose some of their grip.

A beer bottle over the head.

Her mother had done some unspeakable things over the years, but that topped it. The image pressed inward like barbed wire around his ribs. Picturing her lying there, bloody and scared—he knew there was more to the story back then. The memory jogged forward, her saying something about falling off the back porch.

He shoved his hands deep into his hoodie pockets as they walked. He shouldn't have lost control. Not in front of her. She'd helped him during his episode with a calm, steady presence. But he hated that she'd had to . . . or that he'd shown her that side of him.

As they strolled past the festival, people gathered in front of a small stage where a country band strummed. The lead singer wore a cowboy hat too big for his head and jeans so tight they probably squeaked when he moved. He belted out a rendition of "Take Me Home, Country Road."

"That guy's one high kick away from a public indecency charge," Cole said.

Raven laughed, tugging her jacket. The cool breeze carried the scent of fried dough and kettle corn.

Her eyes darted toward the food trucks parked near the edge of the festival. "Oh no."

"What?"

"Donuts. They're my kryptonite. We can't stop, or you'll have to roll me back to the B&B."

"Noted." He strolled closer toward the food trucks, exaggerating his steps.

"Stop, I've already been eating enough junk." Raven reached out to grab his arm—missed, and nearly tripped on a hay bale instead.

"Whoa, watch your step there." He steadied her with a hand on her elbow, a half-smile tugging at his lips.

She shook her head, her laughter bubbling between them. But as it faded, Cole circled back to what she'd said earlier at the café, about the panic attacks. He needed to know more. How she kept going. How she faced the fear and found her footing again. Because when it hits him, it knocks him flat, and no one is there to drag him back.

He cleared his throat. "What you said earlier . . . about your mom." He paused, searching for the right words.

Raven glanced up at him those warm brown eyes reeling him closer. "It was a long time ago."

"I'm not used to talking about this stuff," he said, voice low. "As the medic, it was my job to spot when someone was unraveling. To catch it before they cracked. But Preach . . . he was the one who read me."

She looked at him.

He swallowed. "I didn't have to say anything. He just knew. I've been trying to white-knuckle it on my own. But maybe that's not working."

He looked at her then. "When you said I don't have to deal with it alone . . . I don't know how to believe that. But I want to try."

"Then start with me. I'm listening."

He took a deep breath. "These episodes, they got worse after Iron Torch. Preach and I . . . the mission went bad. By the time I got to him . . ." Cole's voice caught. "It was too late."

The band's music faded behind them as they headed back toward the bed-and-breakfast. Gravel crunched under their feet.

"I thought I could handle it. But it's like everything I buried comes back at once. I get stuck in loops. Sounds. Smells. I'm right back there. I can't breathe, can't think. I'm just . . . gone."

The wind stirred, carrying the distant hum of the band. He felt her eyes on him as they walked. Feelings were like gear—too much of it, and it'd slow you down. He kept the load light, even with those he trusted. But Raven's earlier confession had scraped away his usual defenses. He didn't dare look at her. He wasn't sure what he'd see in her expression, and didn't want pity. But he owed her something.

"For what you've seen, I can't imagine how you handle all of it." She stepped closer. "You ever feel like you're two people? Like there's the person you are now, trying to be normal, whatever that looks like, and then there's this other version of you? The one who keeps replaying everything you've been through, over and over like some broken record."

How did she know?

"That's . . . yeah, that's exactly it."

The words had knocked the air out of him. His mind raced, flashes of the last five months playing out—Preach's death, the sleepless nights, failure burning him from the inside out. He'd barely admitted it to himself, let alone said it out loud. He hated that she knew from experience. Maybe she saw him more clearly than he saw himself.

"I think that's how it starts. The doubling, I mean. You split yourself so you can survive. One version gets hurt, deals with all the chaos. The other one checks out, pretends everything's fine because otherwise . . ." She sighed. "You don't make it."

He stopped walking and turned to her. "How'd you change it?"

Raven stopped and looked at him. "Well, I didn't. Not really. Not until I surrendered it to God. I still struggle with why it had to be so hard . . . and believing He can work all of it for good."

That wasn't what he'd expected.

"For years, I thought I had to fix myself. That if I tried harder, took the meds, did the therapy, avoided conflict, then I'd get better." Her eyes drifted to the ground. "But I got to a low point, where I didn't know if I should even be here."

The air left his lungs. He'd heard the same from too many of his brothers—some who'd made it, too many who didn't. Raven ever thinking she didn't belong in this world sent ice through his veins.

"No. Don't say that. Don't believe that."

Her eyes dropped. Her shoulders curled inward.

"You couldn't—" He stopped himself, dragged a hand over his face. "Your mother stole your childhood. Your dad left you with questions no one should have to ask. But none of that is on you."

She stared at the ground. "I didn't want to die . . . I just didn't know how to live anymore."

Cole stepped closer and reached out. His finger tilted her chin up. "You're not broken. You've got this light . . . and I don't even think you know it."

Tears gathered in her eyes with a look, as if something cracked inside her.

"This world needs you." He reached for her hand, his grip firm, needing her to hear him. "*I* need you."

Cole didn't want to disappear. He didn't want to go back to the attic. He wanted this.

Her.

"Come with me." He pulled her back toward the festival.

She wiped her eyes. "If this ends with me holding a fried Twinkie . . ."

He laughed. "No Twinkies. Just trust me."

CHAPTER 11

Raven couldn't remember the last time the weight she carried every day had lightened, if just for a little while. Maybe it was the string lights dangling between tents, the dancing, or the funnel cake weaving through the air. But Cole's hand clutching hers probably had something to do with it. For once, she didn't want to overthink it. She didn't want to pull back. She wanted to be in this moment—with him. Fully as friends, like they used to be.

"C'mon, up there, by the stage." His grin was reckless, boyish, familiar.

Her heart stumbled.

They raced from the tent-lined street to a nearby baseball field where the band played on a large wooden stage surrounded by outdoor heaters. Cole wove them around clusters of people dodging families and teens and folding chairs. Raven laughed as she tried to keep up with his long strides, her boots crunching over stray popcorn kernels and hay.

The music grew louder with every step, a mix of jaunty fiddle and thumping bass. A sea of people bobbed and turned under the glowing heaters above. Couples spun and swayed to the rhythm, their boots kicking up dust and straw from the makeshift dancing area. The crowd cheered as the fiddler struck a wild refrain, urging everyone into a faster tempo.

She tugged on his hand. "Where are we going?"

His grin tilted, that same way as when he'd sneaked her into the movies when they were kids. "Change of plans." He pulled her into the outer edges of the crowd. He helped remove her jacket and scarf and placed them on a nearby folding chair. "We've got to make the most of our time while we can, right? Thought you loved to dance."

"I do, but—"

He pulled her in with that classic Cole confidence, so sure of himself it made her breath hitch.

"You don't dance." A smirk played on her lips, but he looked serious.

He loosened his grip only to let their fingers twine in a way that sent goosebumps racing up her arm. "Maybe tonight I do."

Who was this *man* in front of her? He must have thrown the bow-legged wallflower version of himself into a closet.

As the music picked up, he twirled her under his arm, then caught her back to his chest, hands firm on her waist. His strong hands and those electric blues pulled her into a two-step. He spun her out from him, the motion so sudden that laughter escaped before she could stop it. Every part of her lit up like the fairground around them. They moved together—spinning, laughing, twirling through songs like the world had pressed pause.

The band struck up a fast-paced tune, and the crowd moved in synchronized stomps and spins. Around them, boots slapped against the dirt and straw, the rhythm infectious. Cole moved in time with the beat, his boots slamming down as if he'd been born to do it. She'd never seen him dance like this. At prom he stepped on her foot so hard she had to run for a first aid kit, blood dripping onto the gym floor. But here he was, stomping and spinning like a pro.

"Where did this come from?"

He winked and caught her against him, closer this time, his hand sliding to the small of her back. "I've got a few secret talents."

Her heart skipped. She'd known him most of her life, but this man version of him leading her across a straw dance floor was someone . . . different.

This wasn't supposed to happen. She wasn't supposed to feel anything.

But the way he looked at her now . . . like she was more. Like *they* were more. It shattered her resolve with every breath. Maybe he wasn't the same man who'd left. Maybe she wasn't the same, either. And maybe it was too late to pretend she hadn't already fallen for him all over again.

They danced song after song, twisting around in a frenzy of stomping and laughter. He'd twisted her around as if they were the next contestants on *Dancing with The Stars*, prompting a few people to cheer during a dramatic dip.

The music changed mid-spin, slowing into a sultry rhythm. The band transitioned into a folk version of "You Make It Easy" by Jason Aldean. Couples around them shifted to gentle sways. He pulled her close. His arm draped around her waist, fastening her to him as if she might float away. His other hand remained wrapped around hers, but instead of guiding her through another spin or playful maneuver like he had earlier, he lifted it and pressed it against his chest.

She leaned into his warmth, letting her head fall lightly against his shoulder. Let herself breathe him in. Let herself believe—for just a heartbeat—that this could be more than nostalgia.

He drew back to meet her eyes. "Is this okay?"

She nodded. Yes. It was everything she'd tried not to want.

Their hands stayed locked. His fingers laced with hers. As her hand pressed against his chest, she felt tension in every muscle beneath it. His chest rose and fell beneath her palm, the thrum of his heartbeat strong under her touch. Her hand trembled as she slid it up to his shoulder. The sharp, clean scent of his cologne hit her, frying every coherent thought she had left as they swayed.

Her heart leaned into it, reckless. She glanced at him as he looked to the side, but he turned. When his lips dipped toward hers, her breath caught. Time stilled. She hadn't dared look up. Those eyes would latch onto her, and she'd never let go. No way could she take that risk.

But she didn't have to look up. The tiniest tug at her waist told her what was coming. Her heart hammered in her chest, louder than the music. He tilted his head, just enough for his stubble to brush against her face. His lips paused close to her cheek, his breath warm and completely unfair.

"You're thinking too much." His voice was so low and quiet it almost didn't reach her over the song.

"I'm not—" Her voice cracked. She swallowed hard and tried again. "I'm not thinking about anything."

Liar. Every part of her was thinking, feeling, hoping.

He pulled back just enough to give her a doubtful grin. "Right. That's why you're looking anywhere but me."

She let out a weird high-pitched laugh, and way too loud. His lips brushed close to her ear, sending a shiver skittering down her spine.

"You're a terrible liar." His voice rumbled through her.

"I'm trying not to step on your feet." She shot back, daring to meet his eyes. Regret punched her in the gut the second she did. Those deep pools of blue locked onto hers like they were about to unravel every layer of armor she'd built against them.

Just friends. That's the line. Don't be stupid enough to cross it again.

Panic fluttered in her chest like a trapped bird, but she couldn't make herself look away this time. The way he looked at her—like she was the only person who mattered on the straw dance floor. Or the entire world.

Then he smiled. Not his usual teasing smirk, but something dangerous.

And he leaned in.

Panic screamed at her to move, to say something, to do anything besides stand there like a deer in headlights. But she couldn't. She didn't want to. His hand tightened just slightly on her waist, grounding her, stealing away every ounce of resolve left.

The space between them disappeared like it had never been there in the first place. His lips hovered over hers, so close the whisper of his breath mingled with her own. Everything pressed on her heart—his chest against hers, his fingers intertwined with hers, the hint of nervous energy in the way his grip tightened.

"Rae . . ." The way he said it against her lips caught somewhere between a plea and a promise. She closed her eyes, waiting.

And then—applause.

A burst of clapping, whoops of laughter and cheers shattered the moment like glass hitting stone. Raven opened her eyes, the world snapping back into focus.

The song ended.

Couples untangled from each other on the dance floor, some laughing, others shouting playful boasts about their moves. The band announced a quick intermission before their next set.

Cole didn't move. His lips still hovered inches from hers. Then, he let go—first of her waist then her hand. He stepped back, clearing his throat. With a sharp inhale, as though realizing all at once where they were. Or maybe who he was with.

Had she been wrong, again?

She had let herself believe—just for a second—that maybe this time would be different. That maybe he'd finally meet her halfway.

Her throat tightened. Maybe she'd misread everything—every look, every touch, every whispered word.

Stupid.

Cole rubbed the back of his neck. The move was too familiar—it usually meant he was about to make a joke or dodge something real. She couldn't tell which one it was this time.

"We should probably head back." He handed over her jacket and scarf. Their fingers brushed, barely.

"Right. Of course." The weight of the almost-kiss still lingered.

He glanced at her, his expression unreadable, like he was battling some inner war. She started to walk but he hesitated.

"Rae?"

She turned around, her chest tightening.

"Never mind."

There it was. Same Cole. Same story.

She'd let herself believe—again—that maybe this time would be different. That maybe he'd fight for something more.

But he didn't. He never did.

She'd always want more than he could give. That was the truth she kept trying not to look at head-on. So, she wouldn't. Not anymore. No more maybes.

From now on, she'd guard her heart like it was on lockdown. Because if she didn't, he'd break it all over again, without meaning to.

Friends was all they'd ever be.

The walls she'd lowered snapped back into place, sharp and fast.

The air had turned colder since they'd left the festival. They'd walked back in near silence, only trading a few clipped words, each one landing like a missed step. Cole held the door open for Raven as they stepped into the bed-and-breakfast.

"Thanks." She brushed past him.

He clenched his jaw. She looked beautiful, and that was the problem. She always did, and he never knew what to do about it.

Coward.

What had he been thinking back there? Almost kissing her, then pulling back like some confused teenager.

Inside, Martha wiped a small coffee table. "Back already? Festival goes until ten."

"It's been a long day." Raven unwrapped her scarf. She avoided Cole, her tone polite. Detached.

Martha walked to the check-in counter. "Here's your key to the attic. That radiator's been acting up again. If it quits, give it a good kick. Not too hard, though, or you'll take it clean off."

He grabbed the actual brass key from her with a short laugh. "Noted."

"There's a finesse to it." Martha winked. "Goodnight, you two."

"Goodnight." Raven had already headed for the stairs.

Cole followed a step behind. He tried not to look at her. But every tiny movement pulled at him. When they reached the second-floor landing, she paused at her door. Her hand rested on the knob, and for a second, she hesitated.

"I had a nice time tonight. Thanks for . . . everything."

The wobble in her voice hit him. Was she mad or nervous?

"Yeah, me too."

Idiot. That's all you've got?

"Goodnight Cole."

She looked at him—just for a beat—like she was waiting. And then she was gone. Door shut. Moment over.

He stood there, staring at nothing.

What's wrong with him? He'd faced gunfire and blood and chaos. But Raven undoes him with a look. And he still let her down.

He turned toward the attic stairway, boots heavy.

"Cole?"

His pulse kicked at the sound of her voice.

"You forgot this." She stepped into the hallway, clutching his bag with both hands.

He took it from her, their hands brushing. "Thanks."

Neither moved.

She smiled just a little. "I figured you might need it."

He opened his mouth, but nothing came. No joke. No charm. Just silence.

"Well . . . goodnight."

"Goodnight," he said, quieter this time.

She disappeared again, and he turned toward the attic.

When he pushed the door open, his breath puffed in front of him like smoke. The room was what he'd expected—cold, drafty, and full of silence he didn't know what to do with. He kicked the radiator. It groaned but sputtered to life. He ducked under the slanted ceiling as he tossed his bag onto the floor next to an end table. Not bad. He'd slept in much worse.

He dropped onto a chaise, the old thing creaking under him. He rubbed his hands together and blew on them. Dust clung to the lone circular window in the corner. A faded painting of what he guessed was the town of Brookhaven hung crooked next to it. The whole space smelled like cedar and mothballs.

He leaned back, phone in hand. Minutes ticked by in silence. He opened a puzzle app. Swiped tiles around the screen. Pointless. His mind was still back on the dance floor.

Back with her in his arms.

The phone buzzed in his hand. A message lit up the screen.

> Tick: Meet me in the Heartland lobby at 0600. Got some info for you.

> Cole: Got it. See you then.

No greeting, no explanation, just a time and a promise of answers. It was exactly what Cole needed—something concrete to focus on, and a way to be useful. He glanced at the phone.

Should he tell Raven about meeting Tick?

He thumbed to the chat with her. Then set the phone on the nightstand.

No. Not tonight.

She already thought he couldn't show up when it mattered. He wouldn't give her one more reason.

He dragged a hand over his face.

He was an idiot. She was right there, open and vulnerable, and he'd shut the door.

Again.

That flicker of hope in her eyes, and he hadn't even tried. What was he afraid of?

Losing her?

He'd left her standing there, hoping for something he couldn't give.

He didn't want her to regret this trip. She needed answers. Deserved them. But screwing up their friendship wasn't an option.

She deserved someone reliable, not like that fool Ethan. As good as she was at reading people, his slick charms had blinded her. Somehow, he'd wormed his way into her life.

Friends. That was all he could offer. Anything more, and he'd screw it up. Tomorrow he'd meet with Tick. Get the information. Give her something solid. That was what she needed. Not feelings. Not maybes. Just answers.

That was what he'd do. That was something he could control.

CHAPTER 12

Raven woke the next morning with one relentless thought. What just happened?

The song, the almost-kiss, the need in Cole's voice—had she imagined it? It felt like something that would happen to Zoe, not to her.

But it had happened, and she remembered every second. That look in his eyes . . . but he cut faster than a dull subplot axed in first round edits.

She closed her eyes. No over-analyzing. She was done with that.

New day. Time to focus. She sat up and grabbed her phone, brushing hair from her face. Zoe was definitely still asleep.

Time to get back to why I came here in the first place. Find answers about my father.

After all, she'd stopped reading into signals from Cole in high school. She knew better than to fall for those baby blues. But he has this irritating way. After her impromptu confession, and his swift retreat into ghost mode, she'd buried the thought so deep it might as well have had a headstone. But he was like one of those revolving doors in a fancy hotel—impossible to know when to step in without getting stuck. And yet, here she was, stuck again.

Why did he have to stroll back into Elkwood? And then, because God clearly had a sense of humor, twirl her around in that stupidly perfect fall aesthetic, smelling so good she couldn't let go.

She groaned into her pillow, kicking her legs under the blanket in frustration.

Her phone buzzed with a message from Jo.

> Just had a breakthrough. If your dog bites the mailman, don't reward him with treats. Reward the mailman for surviving.

Raven blinked. Was that even legal?

> You need to come to the farm. I think one of the llamas is grieving and projecting onto the barn cat. That makes for a good story.

Raven groaned and collapsed back on the pillow. Her phone buzzed again.

> Don't ignore me. That's how emotionally avoidant dog owners end up with chihuahuas that run their house like mob bosses. I need your ghostwriting genius.

Raven stared at the screen and exhaled. She'd answer Jo later. Right now she had bigger mysteries to solve than why a llama was being rude to a cat.

She opened her laptop and started a new file.

J.C. Nevermore: Collaborators/Leads.

She remembered he'd co-written a few other books. If her father had worked with anyone, even once, maybe they knew something.

She made a list. A quick Google search turned up Monty Usher, a reclusive poet and professor who'd co-edited a gothic collection with J.C. Nevermore. Raven added it with a note to reach out later. Another author, A.G. Pym, popped up. He and J.C. Nevermore wrote *The Hollow Hour*. Raven clicked on the blurb:

Time remembers what we try to forget.

When 27-year-old Iris Caldwell inherits her late uncle's crumbling estate on the cliffs of Brier's Hollow, she expects peeling wallpaper and drafty windows—not clocks that tick backward, hallways that shift at night, and a grandfather clock that chimes at the wrong hour . . . for someone who isn't there.

But the strangest discovery isn't in the walls—it's in the attic. Hidden beneath a floorboard lies a weathered journal from 1873, written by a man named Elias Ward, who once lived in the same house. His entries mirror Iris's descent into obsession. His warnings come too late. As the line between past and present blurs, Iris must unravel the house's secrets before it unravels her.

In a place where time bends and memory lies, the truth is never where you left it.

She made a mental note to add the book to her TBR list.

After going to the author's websites, she saved the contact information available and their current publishers. She could reach out to them, right?

Sure, she could. After all, she was an author too, sort of. That was what she'd do, reach out to them.

She got up and splashed cold water on her face in the bathroom, trying to shake off the strange weight in her chest—equal parts excitement and dread. She needed food, coffee, and space to think.

Downstairs, the dining area looked cozy and charming in a way that made her forget, for a moment, the weight of everything. Warm light from lantern fixtures on the walls shed soft gold streaks across the circular tables. The lace tablecloths that adorned each table looked like they belonged in Gram's kitchen. Small vases in the center of the tables held sprigs of autumn wildflowers: goldenrod, asters, and baby's breath. The scent of cinnamon and nutmeg made Raven's stomach growl.

The small buffet contained a mismatch of ceramic plates and platters, an impressive spread for such a tiny space. There were croissants, delicate scones with cranberries, glass jars brimming with homemade jam, *and* little donuts.

She poured a cup of coffee, grabbed three powdered donuts, and slid into a corner seat by the window. She was halfway through checking Jo's last unhinged email from yesterday when someone slid into the chair across from her.

Tick.

Dressed in a Mortal Kombat hoodie and smelling like motor oil, he grinned like he hadn't materialized out of nowhere.

"Morning, sunshine." He stole a donut from her plate. "Do you mind? I'm starving."

She stared. "No, please."

He devoured it and glanced around. "This place feels like a retired clockmaker's dream. I'd bet they dust the lamps with cinnamon."

Raven sipped her coffee. "Are you here to see me, or . . ."

"No. I thought you were here to see *me*."

Raven squinted her eyes and shook her head.

"Really? Not here to see me?" Tick leaned back, drumming his fingers. "Strange. I just gave Cole some very interesting information. He didn't tell you?"

Her breath hitched. "About my father?"

He grinned. "I found something."

"Are you serious?"

"But there's a hiccup." He reached across the table for another donut, and she slapped his hand away.

"You'll get more donuts after you tell me what you know."

"Ooh, playing hardball." Tick leaned back in his chair, arms crossed over his chest. "All right, here's the deal. Your father, Jeffrey Cunningham, is definitely J.C. Nevermore."

"Are you sure? How do you know it's him?"

"I tracked down copyright filings for J.C. Nevermore's books. The earliest ones listed a name as the copyright holder: Jeffrey Cunningham. After that, he published under the pseudonym J.C. Nevermore, probably to keep a low profile. Makes sense with his backlog. I cross-referenced a few other databases, the kind civilians don't know about. Some records got murky, but it was enough to connect the dots."

"I can't believe it." She blinked back tears.

Thank you, God.

"Don't get all gushy. It's not airtight. Something happened—maybe he dropped off the grid— but it ain't random. Trail's too clean to be chance. Jeffrey Cunningham *is* J.C. Nevermore. I don't have every step locked down yet. There's still—"

"Hey, there you are." Cole appeared at the table.

"Cole, he found him! He found my father, who actually is J.C. Nevermore. I can't believe it. I mean, I'm blown away."

Cole nodded, eyes on Tick. "Yeah. He told me."

Raven jumped up from the table and gave Tick a hug. He patted her back as if no one had ever done that before.

She sat back down, buzzing with adrenaline. "So, what's the hiccup?"

His posture straightened. He shrugged, eyeing Cole. "Still working out the trail. Some gaps. But I'll keep digging."

Cole's presence seemed to flip a switch in Tick.

Tick cleared his throat and checked the oversized watch strapped to his wrist. "I'll update you in . . . the next twenty-three hours."

"Didn't you need to update your Roomba?" Cole said.

Tick froze for a beat, then snapped his fingers. "Oh! Right. Yep. Good call, Doc, very observant." He stood. "Also need to grab goat wax."

Raven blinked. "Goat wax?"

"Yes. It's imperative." He sprung from the table and grabbed Raven's hand, kissing it as if she were royalty. "It's been a pleasure to serve you."

Tick bolted for the door, nearly tripping over a chair in his haste.

Raven let out a breath, laughing at the absurdity—but also the truth.

Her father *was* J.C. Nevermore.

And for the first time in years, she wasn't just wondering. She might actually see her father again.

Cole yanked on his jacket, rolling his shoulders to loosen the stiffness. His phone buzzed, but he let it ring. He'd call Hank later.

Jeffrey Cunningham . . . not her biological father.

That truth settled heavy in his gut. He didn't have all the intel from Tick yet—and until he did, he wasn't going to be the one to wipe that hope out of Raven's eyes. Not over breakfast. Not when she'd finally looked like she believed in something again.

Delay the damage. Keep her stable. He'd distract her if he had to. Anything to keep her whole until the truth was solid.

He still had work to do, on his body and on his future. But that fight felt easier. He shoved his phone into his pocket and stepped out the attic room door.

In the lobby, Raven lit up the moment she saw him.

She held a pamphlet in her hand, beaming. "Feel better? Because I've got ideas."

He raised a brow. "What kind of ideas?"

"Fun ones. Martha said we can't leave town without seeing the World's Largest Tea Kettle." She paused. "And before you ask—yes, that's a real thing. Apparently, it's only a ten-minute walk from here."

"A giant teapot."

"Don't knock it. We're doing this. Then, festival games. No shooting ones, though. I saw something about a tug-of-war." She gave him a pointed look. "You're not afraid of a little competition, are you?"

"Please. You better get your money ready because when I win, you're buying me a funnel cake." He smirked, slipping his phone from his pocket as it buzzed. Kenny.

"Hey Kenny. Any luck?"

"Part's coming in this afternoon. If all goes well, I'll have it fixed tonight."

He glanced at Raven, who was practically bouncing with energy. "Copy that. Looks like we'll hit the road tomorrow. Thanks, man."

"What did he say?"

"Truck won't be ready until tonight. You okay with staying here another day?"

"Of course, because now I *definitely* need to see the World's Largest Tea Kettle." She started toward the door.

"You're set on the tea kettle thing, huh?"

"Absolutely." She grabbed the door handle. "Come on. Live a little."

The crisp morning air bit as they stepped out of the B&B. Raven walked ahead, pointing out a map with their route to the teapot. Her ponytail bounced like the world had nothing in it to hurt her. He quickened his stride to match hers.

She was so full of hope, it twisted his gut.

How could he tell her without breaking her?

The landmark was as ridiculous as expected—a bulbous red-and-white structure fenced in like royalty. It stood at least ten feet high, and looked like a relic from the 1950s. Chipped spout and a faded plaque detailing its historic significance.

Raven circled it with a grin. "This is absurd. I love it. Come get a pic with me."

He pushed off the fence, walking over to her.

She held up her phone. "Come on, Walker. Look like you're having fun."

He bent down to fit into the frame beside her.

She snapped the picture. "One more—do something silly."

"Silly?"

"Yes." She nudged him with her elbow. "Lean into it."

With a laugh, he leaned toward the teapot, pretending to sip from the spout. Her laughter rang out bright and full as she caught it on camera.

"You're so distinguished."

She was supposed to be the one laughing. He was supposed to be the one keeping it light. But that look she gave him—like he belonged in the moment—it chipped away at his walls.

Back at the festival, the main square had vendors already set up, and it was barely noon. Booths lined the streets, offering everything from caramel apples to pumpkin carving. Raven dragged him to the center of the same field as last night. Two teams gathered at the end of a rope. An enormous hay bale marked the midpoint. Seemed fitting. The longer he kept the truth from her, the more it felt like he was stuck in his own tug-of-war.

"We're doing that," she said.

"Nope. Where are the food trucks?"

"Come on." She nudged him with her shoulder. "You'll be great at it. Look at you. You're built for tug-of-war."

"Fine. But after you owe me a funnel cake."

"Deal."

The rope burned in his hands, but he held tight, boots digging into the dirt. In front of him, Raven let out a war cry so fierce it drew cheers. The bale shifted, inching toward them. When it tipped, the crowd roared.

She turned to him, breathless and glowing. "You're not bad at this."

He managed a smile. "I think you carried us."

She snapped a few photos of their team and the rope, then turned. Her camera captured him before he could look away. She pulled her phone down slowly when he caught her eyes. Something flickered in them. He wanted to lift her in his arms and never let go.

She paused. Her eyes held his just a little too long.

And that was the danger.

He wasn't supposed to want this. But he did.

She stepped back, putting the phone in her jacket pocket.

He glanced around the park. A group of people gathered near a booth with a big wooden sign that read: *Pumpkin Bowling: Strike for a Prize!*

He nodded toward it. "What do you say? You up for some pumpkin bowling?"

She laughed and hooked her arm through his. "You're on. But I'm terrible at bowling."

As they walked toward the booth, he let himself relax.

Not because he was supposed to. Not because it kept her smiling. But because part of him wanted this to last. That was the problem. He'd made a plan—delay the damage. Keep her smiling. Keep his distance. But the weight of what he hadn't told her pressed in and coiled tight.

Sooner or later, the truth would land. And when it did, he wasn't sure if he'd be the one cleaning up the wreckage . . . or the one who had caused it.

CHAPTER 13

Raven had made a quiet vow that morning after the news about her father—no more bracing for disappointment. At least, not today. Even though Tick had to dig for more truth, what he'd found had already given her hope of seeing her father again. And for once, the edges of her life didn't feel jagged and broken.

So, she leaned in. Enjoyed the fall festival, the chill in the air, and the company of someone who she'd known long before life got complicated. For one day, she was going to let herself hope—just a little.

The festival buzzed around them, and Raven soaked in the warmth of it despite the thirty-degree wind chill. She glanced at Cole, who laughed as a pumpkin he'd bowled veered wildly off course and slammed into the side of a hay bale. Something about the way he could shift from gruff and serious to boyish and competitive made her crazy.

When they were kids, she'd been free to be herself around him. And right now, with cider in her hand and pumpkin guts on his sleeve, it felt like maybe she still could be. As long as she kept her heart on a short leash.

Her phone buzzed in her pocket. She pulled it out to see a text from Zoe.

Sorry I didn't see your last text until now. Packing, ugh. I told you this trip would be good for you. You owe me big time.

Yes. You were right.

You love it when I'm right. Now, what's the deal with military boy? Did he say anything about the almost kiss? Or do I have to take a detour on my way to Boston and shove you two together?

STOP. I don't want to unlock that safe again.

Sure. That's why you're texting me in all caps after he took you dancing, dipping you like Johnny Castle. Just admit it. He's INTO you.

Can we please not do this right now?

If that was true, why the freeze? She couldn't say that. Better to leave it lie.

Three dots bounced.

Fine. I'm just saying. I won't be surprised if he tells your dad that nobody puts Raven in a corner.

You haven't been this excited for anything in months. And I'm not just talking about the dad news. Call it what you want. You know I'm right.

Love you. Bye.

She laughed under her breath, tucking the phone away. Zoe always had a way of pushing just hard enough to make her squirm. Raven glanced at Cole, who was gesturing to the pumpkin as if it were to blame for his failed throw.

"Maybe it's not the pumpkin." She crossed her arms. "Maybe you're not as good at this as you think."

He shot her a look. "Big talk from someone who hasn't stepped up yet."

They spent the rest of the afternoon like kids again—competing in games, stuffing themselves with caramel apples and cinnamon rolls, and bickering over who got the better scarecrow keychain.

As the sun dipped lower, they ducked into a small café to warm up. He seemed lighter, more open. They'd laughed just like they always had. Cole's thick surface had nothing but heart underneath. Frustrating as it was, she also loved that part about him.

Her phone buzzed.

Mom: Call me. I know Gladys is hiding something about this house. Tim's looking into the paperwork.

Raven stared at the message, stomach knotting.

How could she know? Her thumb hovered over the call button. But instead, she shoved the phone into her purse. Not now. Not here. She pushed her tea aside and headed to the bathroom.

By the time they started back toward the B&B, soft orange hues from the light posts bathed the streets. The festival music sounded tempting, but tonight was karaoke. Raven couldn't carry a tune, let alone stand on a stage in front of hundreds of people. Her phone buzzed again. She pulled it out to see Gladys calling.

"One second." She motioned to Cole before answering. "Hello?"

"Honey, I hate to bother you, but we have a problem."

Raven cleared her throat. "What kind of problem?"

"Your mother's slippery boyfriend showed up at the courthouse. He knew exactly what to ask for. He's filed some kind of motion."

"I don't understand. How could he do that if Gram took care of this months ago? Not to mention he's not licensed."

"Please, don't get me started on what he *can* and *can't* do. They're trying to buy time. And unfortunately, with probate, they might be able to."

"What? How?" Raven dropped onto a nearby bench.

"They're claiming your grandmother wasn't of sound mind when she made the will. It's bogus, but it'll buy them time to stir up trouble. If they succeed, the house gets tied up for months, maybe longer."

Figures. Mom always knew how to get what she wanted. "They want the house. Mom mentioned something about flipping it."

"Doesn't surprise me. Your mother always wants control and then makes a mess of everything. You're going to have to make a decision, and fast."

"A decision? What can *I* do?"

"The lawyer said if you take possession by moving in, it could help move this forward. The house is yours in the will and I've filed everything. But if you start living there, it's harder for them to claim it. Show them it was meant for you."

A knot formed in her stomach.

"It's what your gram wanted, sweetheart," Gladys said.

"Okay. I'll figure it out." Raven tossed her phone back into her purse. She had no intention of moving in. Definitely not while Mom lived there. But how could she put her own mother out? She reached into her purse for the Tums.

Cole stepped closer. "What's going on?"

"My mom. She's trying to get the house. She doesn't know I already have the will, but Tim's got his fingers in everything, trying to sideswipe ownership."

Cole's brows came together. "Can they do that?"

"They're trying. Claiming Gram wasn't of sound mind. Gladys says it'll probably get tied up for months. Maybe longer." She let out a shaky breath. "They want to flip the house. Like it's some old couch from a yard sale."

He said nothing. Just sat next to her.

"I haven't decided if I want it. I just—I wanted time to think. I didn't ask for this." Her voice cracked, and she looked away.

He shifted beside her, quiet but present.

"Gladys says I should move in. Take possession, to make it harder to contest. But Mom lives there. I'd be kicking her out." She gave a bitter laugh. "It's poetic, really. I finally have something that's mine, and I'm supposed to use it to throw out my own mother."

"You wouldn't be throwing her out," Cole said. "You'd be drawing a boundary she's ignored your whole life."

Raven looked up at him, startled by the clarity in his voice.

"I know it feels wrong," he said. "But you're not choosing to hurt her. You're choosing to *stop* being hurt by her."

That hit deeper than Raven had expected. She blinked, trying to push back the sudden sting in her eyes.

"I told myself I'd enjoy today." She sighed. "Be happy for once. But it's like the second I do, something shows up to remind me why I don't trust good things."

Cole went quiet again.

Raven stared across the street at the festival lights reflecting on the houses. "I don't want to feel like I'm always fighting, or never getting ahead, or waiting for the shoe to drop. I don't want to just survive with a stack of ghostwritten books no one knows I wrote." She turned to him. "I want a home. A family. People who stay . . . who choose me."

Not sure where that came from.

His eyes softened, and for a heartbeat, he didn't move.

"Rae. You're someone worth—" He cleared his throat. "You deserve all of those things more than anyone I've ever known."

His words slipped past her defenses.

He leaned forward, locking eyes with her. "You've carried so much for so long. And you still show up for people."

Her breath caught.

"And if you don't see that yet, I'll keep showing you. As long as it takes."

The words cut straight through her. She swallowed hard and dropped her eyes, too exposed to look at him.

She let out a small cough. "That got weirdly emotional. I blame the sugar." She pushed her hair behind her ear.

He smiled but didn't look away.

"Do you ever think about the future?" Her words tumbled out.

He exhaled slowly, breath visible in the cool air. "Honestly? I used to think my future was staying in the Army. That made sense. But now . . . I don't know. Something quieter, maybe. One place to call home, you know."

"Yeah."

She hadn't expected that answer, so steady and grounded. Steady had never been her reality. Not with a mother who only showed up when she needed something, or with a father who had abandoned her, no matter what the reason. Even as a kid, she'd learned not to count on anything lasting—people, places, even love. Gram tried her best, but Mom feathered her way in and out, leaving chaos in her wake. Maybe that's why Raven gravitated toward stories. In books, the endings brought certainty. Promises meant something. And the people who were meant to stay . . . did.

But Cole was different. Like the one plot point that never changed, no matter how the story rewrote itself. And that terrified her just as much as it pulled her in.

She stared ahead, watching the last traces of sunlight melt into the horizon.

"When Gram got sick, it happened fast. One minute, she was herself, and the next . . . cancer was everywhere. I thought we had more time. I wanted to slow everything down, hold on to her for a little longer, but time stole that from me."

She paused, her throat tightening. "Then again, I guess that's been true my whole life. I'm always running out of time with the people I love."

He glanced at her.

She let out a slow breath. "But now, with my father, I feel like I've been given a second chance. Like I might be able to get back some of what I lost."

He nodded. Something unspoken passed between them. Feeling this safe with him was not supposed to happen. Sure, they were friends. And she knew falling for him led to disappointment. But the way he looked at her made it impossible to resist.

As they started walking again, her chest felt tight in the best and worst way—like she'd handed him her heart without meaning to. And the scariest part?

She wasn't sure she wanted to take it back.

The walk back to the B&B stretched, quiet and slow.

I want a home. A family. People who stay . . . who choose me.

The words hadn't left Cole's head since Raven had said them. They'd taken up residence, pressing hard. He wanted that for her, more than anything.

The image of her in that hospital room flashed through his mind—her voice trembling as she whispered she loved him. And he said nothing. Not because he didn't feel it. Because he knew, deep down, he wasn't the guy who could give those things to her. Not back then, and not now with the weight of the discharge hanging over him. She deserved better.

He needed to tell her the truth. All of it.

What he had felt that day. And even right now. But not just that . . . the information on that USB drive burned a hole in his pocket.

The truth about her father.

He wanted to believe she'd be okay if he told her, but there were too many shadows in the story. Too many cracks. If it was wrong, he'd take the one thing she had left to hope for. And then? Nothing would feel true anymore. He couldn't do that to her, not yet.

And him? He didn't know if he had a place to land in the life he used to know. Everything felt temporary. Fragile.

Still, he walked beside her. Dug his hands deep in his pockets to keep from pulling her close. Because even if he didn't deserve her, that didn't stop him from wanting her by his side.

The porch light of the B&B glowed as they approached. When they walked in, Martha's voice floated from the hallway.

"Dinner's in an hour, dears. You've got time to wash up."

"Thanks, Martha." Raven turned to him. "I'm going to head upstairs and freshen up."

"I'll hang down here. Make a few calls."

He watched her disappear up the stairs. He sighed and pulled out his phone. The phone rang twice before Tick picked up.

"Doc! I—"

"Tell me you've got something solid."

"Public records, property databases, and old contacts who owe me, but I'm not breaking any laws. Mostly. There's one forum where these retired guys swap information on—"

"Tick." Cole pinched the bridge of his nose.

"Okay, okay. I've got two addresses." Tick's voice dropped lower. "One in New York and one in New Jersey."

Cole's grip on the phone tightened. "Which one checks out?"

"Well, that's the million-dollar question. The New York one's . . . odd. It's tied to some historical building. Now it's a law school. Pretty high-profile, which feels wrong."

"And the Jersey address?"

"That one's a bit cleaner. The background's fuzzy but fits the timeline. Still checking it out, but doesn't look like it's Jeffrey Cunningham."

Cole's grip tightened on the phone. "What about the paternity test? Anything to disprove it?"

"Not yet. But it's sketchier than gas station sushi. The lab doesn't exist anymore, paperwork's got more holes than a fishing net, and the lawyer who filed it? Didn't even take the bar. I'd call it a red flag if it wasn't basically a neon sign."

Tension released in his chest. "So, it's not locked down."

"Nope. Uh, you okay? You looked like you were going to break my neck at breakfast."

"Yeah. I didn't want to kill her hopes before getting all the information."

"Don't wait too long to spill the beans. You ever hear about my cousin Dave and the ferret?"

"What?"

"My cousin Dave. Bought a ferret, right? Waited too long to train it. Thing took over his house. Stole his keys, his wallet, chewed through his internet cables. Guy couldn't leave his own place without getting ambushed. You wait too long to handle something, it handles you."

"Did you just compare this to your cousin losing a turf war with a ferret?"

"Exactly. Don't let this be your ferret, man."

"I'll keep that in mind. Please work fast."

Cole ended the call. He knew Tick was right. But telling Raven now felt like kicking up dust before the ambush—too risky, too soon.

Cole wandered into the dining room. Tonight, the menu said pot roast, mashed potatoes and brown gravy, green beans, and pumpkin pie. He took a seat, passing time with a puzzle game. He checked his wallet for cash. Earl and Martha deserved a nice tip. His fingers brushed a folded note—Raven's handwriting from twenty years ago. He'd almost forgotten about it. Her words still grabbed hold of him more than he wanted to admit. He slipped it back into the fold.

"Hey."

He looked up. And there she was. Black jeans. Red shirt. That smile.

Yeah. He was in trouble.

She sat across from him, brushing her hair over her shoulder. "Smells amazing in here."

He cleared his throat. "Comfort food week. Martha's going all in."

"Any word on the truck?"

"Not yet. I'll call Kenny after we eat."

"Imagine if we were stuck here forever. I could get used to this place, but *not* in the honeymoon suite." She flashed him a smile.

He couldn't take his eyes off her. He was falling hard, fast.

Who was he kidding? He'd fallen the second she showed up in his second-grade class wearing those yellow shoes.

Dinner tasted good. He'd made small talk here and there, but kept his eyes on his plate. Safer that way. He moved onto pie.

Raven took a slow sip of her water. "What's going on? Are you okay?"

He nodded while chewing.

She looked down at the table. "You don't have to go cold on me, you know."

His brows came together. "What?"

"You've got this look. Like you're here but not really. I've seen it before."

He sat back in his chair. "I'm fine. Just hungry."

"Right." She sighed and put down her fork. "Look, if this is about last night at the festival, you don't have to say anything. It's fine."

"What do you mean?"

"You do this thing where you pull back when things get . . . close."

His grip on the fork tightened. "I'm not pulling back."

"Yes, you are, but I'm used to it. You always get weird and run for the hills."

He put his fork down. "That's not fair."

She arched one eyebrow, then looked away. "It's fine. Don't worry about it. I just want you to own it. It's just like what happened with Sofia. The second you met her parents, you bolted."

He winced as if she'd hit him with a rock. Where was this coming from? "That's not what happened."

"Oh, sure. My mistake. You retreated like a soldier under fire." Raven let out a sarcastic laugh.

"Hey!" He shot her a look. "I reassessed priorities."

"Uh-huh. You reassessed yourself right out of there and ghosted her until you ran into her at the grocery store."

"She was too clingy, I told you that."

"She asked you to meet her mom because she thought you were serious. God forbid someone care about you for more than three seconds."

There she went, twisting him like a pretzel. Berating him out of nowhere for running out on Sofia. Raven hadn't liked her anyway, not sure what that was about.

Yes, he wanted to kiss her the other night. Of course, he did. Heck, he wanted to kiss her right now.

"I'm just tired," he said.

"No, you're not. You're overthinking."

He pushed his plate aside. "I'm trying not to mess this up."

"By shutting me out?"

"I'm not—" He stopped, ran a hand through his hair. "You don't get it."

"Then make me get it, Cole. Because you're here but not here. And I thought we . . . I don't know."

A beat of silence. Frustration boiled under his skin.

"Look, I can take care of myself if you want to continue on the trip without me." Raven tossed her napkin onto her plate.

"That's not it at all." He looked at her. Really looked. The fire in her eyes, the way she leaned forward like she *needed* an answer.

"You want the truth?" His voice lowered. "Fine."

She stilled.

"I'm not just on leave, Rae. The Medical Evaluation Board deemed me "unfit." PTSD, nerve damage, leaky heart valve—take your pick. Ten years in, and just like that, it's over. I'm still on limited duty, so the doc signed off on extra leave time. They said I could use the time to rest, get my head straight."

Her eyes widened.

"I put in for an appeal with the Physical Evaluation Board. It's scheduled in a couple weeks. If it goes well, maybe I get another chance. If it doesn't . . . that's it. I'm out."

He'd trained for war. Chaos. Not for sharing feelings.

"I didn't tell you because I didn't want to be that guy. The one who dumps his baggage at the door, looking for pity. I wanted to handle it. Control it."

Raven said nothing. And somehow, that was worse.

He leaned back, the breath shaking out of him. He kept his eyes on the table, forcing himself to sit in the silence. The kind that echoed with everything he couldn't fix.

"Thank you for telling me."

He looked up.

Raven's expression wasn't pity or disappointment. It was something else. Those wide doe eyes looked at him like he was already enough. And that wrecked him.

"I know you think you're doing the noble thing by carrying all this alone," she said. "But you don't have to. Not with me."

He swallowed hard, the knot in his throat tightening.

She gave him a small, crooked smile. "Besides, you're kind of terrible at pretending you're fine."

A breath escaped him—half laugh, half relief.

"What happens next then, with the Army?"

"I keep training. Get through the evaluation. Hope for the best."

She nodded.

He cleared his throat. "Tick found something. A couple new addresses tied to your dad. One in New York, the other in Jersey."

"Really?"

He pulled out his phone and tapped the screen. "The New York one's weird—some law school building, too public. But the Jersey one fits the timeline. Problem is, it might not be the same guy."

"That's still something." Hope flickered in her voice again. "We could check it out, right?"

"Yeah. Whatever it takes."

He wanted to tell her about her father. But that look in her eyes—soft, sure—held him back.

And that gutted him.

CHAPTER 14

Raven couldn't stop replaying the moment Cole had dropped his guard last night. Let her in. Not all the way, maybe. But it was enough to tilt her off balance. The confession about his possible discharge still echoed in her mind. All the mental weight he'd been carrying heavy on her heart—his health, the episode she witnessed, his grief over Preach. Now he might be *done*. And knowing how much the Army meant to him, that was like saying his compass had snapped in two and he was still trying to walk a straight line.

But instead of running from it, or her, he'd told her. That meant something. Especially right after she'd let her frustration spill out. She'd figured he was being classic Cole, already halfway out the door. Then he went and proved her wrong by being honest—so painfully honest it frustrated her all over again. Because that was exactly the kind of man she'd always respected him for being.

When Earl dropped them off at Kenny's shop early that morning, Raven decided she wasn't going to overanalyze. These next two days she wasn't going to dig or hover or try to label whatever this was between them. She would show up. For him.

In Kenny's small, grease-stained bathroom, she took a breath, closed her eyes, and . . . prayed.

God, please show me what to do. I can't keep playing emotional tug-of-war—not with Cole, or my mom, or wondering if my father will remember me. I'll make a mess if I keep trying to figure it all out. Please, help me do the right thing. In Jesus' name.

She opened her eyes and stepped out. Cole waited by the truck.

The truck rumbled to life, smooth and without the clunk it had before. Still, Cole barely said a word as they drove. Maybe he'd regretted telling her. Silence settled between them. Not cold, but taut.

He gripped the steering wheel tight and pulled onto the highway.

Her brows came together. She leaned back in her seat, eyeing him.

"Are we going to the cabin now?" She glanced at him, not sure if a joke was appropriate by the look on his face.

His jaw flexed, his eyes locked on the road ahead. "No. New Jersey. I have to drop off something first."

"What part of New Jersey?"

"Elizabeth." His eyes stayed on the road.

The word hit like a stone sinking in water.

She sat back, the weight of it settling in. "Oh."

Silence filled the cab again, heavier this time. Raven looked down at her hands, twisting her ring. Of course, it made sense. Preach's family lived in Elizabeth.

"Do you want to talk about it?" she said.

"I'm good." His answer was tight, clipped. Meant to shut things down.

Knowing Cole, he carried the weight of what happened with Preach like it was stitched into his uniform. She wished he'd talk about it, but she didn't press. Whatever he needed to do, she'd support him.

The road stretched on. She grabbed her phone, more to occupy her hands than anything else. One missed call. Three texts. All from Mom. She sighed and opened the most recent one.

> Mom: Tell me when you call her. Don't flake on me.

Raven gave her a vague "I'll call you later" hoping to buy a few hours of peace before the next barrage. How exactly was she supposed to bring this up?

Hi Mom, funny story, you know Gram's house you've been nesting in like a raccoon in an attic? Yeah. So, small update. It's mine now, legally. Surprise!

She could already hear the screech. Her mother would go full courtroom-drama mode in under five seconds, quoting laws that didn't exist and dragging Tim in for backup. Tim, who had once tried to use a grill lighter to fix a clogged sink.

She set the phone on her lap and glanced over at Cole, who hadn't moved a muscle. His eyes still locked on the road, jaw tight, knuckles pale around the wheel. He had his own storm brewing. Her problems could wait.

Zoe had texted from the Boston book show, something about a new wholesaler offering discounted reprints. Raven fired off a quick reply.

"There's something you should know." Cole's voice jolted her.

"Okay."

He kept his eyes on the road. "It's about Preach."

She stayed quiet.

"That day in Syria, when the IED hit, Preach was still talking. We took on enemy fire from everywhere. By the time I got back to the Humvee . . . He was down."

The hum of cars passing cut the silence.

"I should've dragged him out first. I should've known."

"Cole, you got shot in the chest. And your arm, you barely—"

"Doesn't matter."

She reached over. Her hand settled on his arm. "Don't do this to yourself."

"It was my job. My mistake. I'm not looking for reassurance. I just . . . thought you should know."

Raven let her hand fall after a bit, staring at the blur of trees along the highway.

About three hours later, Cole eased the truck to a stop in front of a small brick house with a chain-link fence. He parked but didn't move. Neither did she. She stared ahead, feeling the same tight, breathless weight that locked him in place.

The house looked quiet, but lived-in. Flowerpots filled with mums lined the porch steps, one of them slightly crooked.

"Do you want me to knock on the door?" she said.

He shook his head. "I'll take care of it. I just need a minute."

A few minutes later, the front door opened. Mrs. Ramirez stepped outside with a watering can, crouching to adjust that crooked flowerpot. Her dark hair had slight streaks of gray and she wore a teal robe. When she straightened, she looked up. Her eyes locked on the truck. She didn't move, didn't smile. Just stood there.

Raven glanced at Cole, watching his shoulders tense like a coiled spring. He inhaled, but it didn't seem to soothe him. His chest rose and fell, slower now. Mrs. Ramirez wiped her hands on her jeans and walked to the edge of the steps.

Raven sensed how much he wanted to throw the truck in reverse and drive off. He had that same look as when they were ten years old, after Emily fell into the creek, and turned blue.

Raven drifted back to that day—the way he had pulled Emily out, yelling for help, his face a mix of terror and remorse. Emily had been hanging around as they were fishing and then wandered off. It happened so fast. Raven remembered running to get Mr. Walker, who was able to bring Emily back, thank God. She'd spent only one night in the hospital. Raven and Cole stayed up the whole night praying. He blamed himself. Even during her leukemia treatments years later, as if in some way it was related.

His hands had clenched so tight then, just like they were now. Maybe he'd never gotten over it. Maybe that was why he'd gone into the Army. To get away from it all.

Cole exhaled and stepped out of the truck, shoulders squared. He didn't look back at her. He walked to the edge of the sidewalk and stopped. Raven opened the window a crack, watching.

Mrs. Ramirez walked down the steps toward him, then brought a hand to her mouth. She shook her head as tears spilled down her cheeks. "Oh, mijo . . ."

Cole didn't say anything. Didn't move.

By the time Mrs. Ramirez reached him, her sobs were audible. She threw her arms around him and pulled him into a tight hug. He froze for a second before his arms came up, holding her as her cries shook both of them.

"Mijo, you came. It's good to see you."

"I wasn't sure you'd want to see me."

Mrs. Ramirez pulled back just enough to cup Cole's face in her hands, forcing him to look at her. "You're family. You're always welcome here, you hear me?" Her voice trembled but carried a quiet fierceness, almost daring him to argue.

He nodded. "Yes, ma'am."

A ball formed in Raven's throat, tears pricking the corners of her eyes. She caught the emotion in his eyes, the way his throat bobbed like he was swallowing it.

"You're too thin. Come inside. You need to eat." Mrs. Ramirez swiped at her cheeks as she gave him a once-over.

Cole managed a small, tight smile. He turned his head, glancing back at the truck. He motioned for her to get out and join them. She hopped out after turning off the engine.

"Mrs. Ramirez, this is Raven Cunningham."

Mrs. Ramirez turned toward Raven, her hand still resting on Cole's arm. She squinted, then her face broke into a smile. "Ah, so *this* is Raven."

What did that mean?

"I'm happy to meet you in person. I've heard many things about you dear." She winked and pulled her into a warm hug. "Good things."

They all walked toward the house, Mrs. Ramirez's hand grasped Cole's arm. The screen door creaked as they stepped inside. The scent of cumin and slow-cooked beans permeated, making Raven's stomach growl.

"Miguel, come out here!" She bustled toward the kitchen. "Have a seat, I'll be right back."

Raven sat next to Cole on a faded floral couch beneath a picture of Jesus with his heart glowing. A crocheted blanket was draped over one armrest, and it reminded her of Gram's house. Well, how it used to be. Across the room on a small buffet table rested a picture of Preach decorated with a wooden cross.

Preach wasn't just a friend to Cole, he was family. She remembered early in Cole's first deployment, when he forgot his helmet and hauled a water jug around his neck for a week. He hadn't even complained. Said he needed to be better, sharper, because as the medic, his brothers looked to him to keep them alive.

But she wondered why he blamed himself—why he always had. Even as a kid, he'd shouldered things that weren't his to carry.

And maybe what hit her most was how much that looked like . . . her.

She did it too, tried to keep control. Carrying everyone else's expectations so no one could accuse her of failing them. Keeping her distance so she wouldn't get hurt. Neither of them ever said it out loud, but they both moved through life bracing for the worst. Maybe that's why she couldn't walk away.

The sound of footsteps shuffled from the hallway before Mrs. Ramirez reappeared, her husband trailing behind her. Mr. Ramirez was a stocky man with silver streaks in his dark, curly hair. His eyes fell on Cole, narrowing just enough to thicken the air.

"Cole?" Mr. Ramirez stepped in front of them.

Cole stiffened his posture as he stood. "Yes, sir."

"Come here, son." Mr. Ramirez tugged Cole into a tight embrace. "I'm glad to see you."

Mrs. Ramirez stood to the right of Raven, clutching a tissue and watching the two men hug. The weight in Mr. Ramirez's eyes lifted as he gripped Cole's shoulder.

"Please, sit." He gestured to the couch. Cole sat back down next to Raven, as Mr. Ramirez sat on a leather recliner opposite them.

"And who is this with you?" Mr. Ramirez turned to Raven.

"Dear, this is Raven." Mrs. Ramirez joined him on the armrest of the chair.

Raven smiled. "It's nice to meet you both."

"So, you knew Cole in his younger days. I bet he was wild," Mr. Ramirez said.

"Yep, he sure was." She looked at Cole, but behind his short grin, he looked . . . distraught.

Mrs. Ramirez wiped her nose. "I can't tell you how happy we are to see you."

Cole nodded. His eyes darted between Mr. Ramirez and his own hands clasped together in his lap.

"I—uh . . . " Cole's voice sounded deeper than usual. He shifted, rubbing his palms against his jeans. "I just . . . needed to see you both. I have some of Preach's things."

Mrs. Ramirez twisted a tissue in her fingers. "Oh, but I thought they'd be mailed to us?"

"No." He straightened his posture. "I'm sorry I haven't gotten them to you sooner."

Mrs. Ramirez looked at her husband with a furrowed brow. "You came all this way to drop them off? Bless you! What a wonderful gift today."

"Well, there's something else."

His words hung there, suspended. His hands trembled a bit, but enough for Raven to notice.

"I need to tell you the truth about what happened to Pre—Michael."

Mrs. Ramirez inhaled as she clutched her husband's arm. Mr. Ramirez said nothing, his expression solemn.

Cole swallowed hard. But then his shoulders dropped, as if surrendering to something heavier than himself.

"It was my fault. He'd be alive if I'd have gotten to him first, if I'd have—" He took a breath. "Either way. I know it cannot possibly make up for it, but I'm here to tell you I'm sorry." He took a breath and tightened his lips. Raven wanted to hug him, touch his arm, anything to let him know he wasn't collapsing under this weight alone. But she stayed still.

The room seemed to contract. Mrs. Ramirez's face crumpled, her trembling hand clutching at her husband's shirtsleeve as though it were the only thing tethering her. Mr. Ramirez's brows drew together, his head lowering.

"And I . . . I don't expect you to forgive me. But you deserve the truth."

His hands curled into fists. "The Army told you he died in the ambush. But what they didn't say is . . . I made the wrong call." He swallowed hard. "Preach was still breathing. Told me to help Tex first. So, I did. By the time I got back, another blast hit. Shrapnel tore through him. We were under fire. I couldn't get him out fast enough." Cole looked at the floor. "I let him down when he needed me most."

The air thickened.

"I hold myself accountable. Every day. And I wanted you to hear it from me."

Mrs. Ramirez pulled her hand up to cover her mouth. Mr. Ramirez reached for her as if on instinct, wrapping his arm around her small frame. A lump formed in Raven's throat witnessing the raw grief in the room.

The weight of Cole's words settled. For a moment, the only sounds were Mrs. Ramirez's quiet sobs and the faint creak of the chair as her husband leaned into her. Mr. Ramirez went still. His jaw tightened, his chest rising with a slow, measured breath as he reached beneath his collar. When his hand emerged, a pair of dog tags dangled from the chain. His knuckles turned white around them.

"You think we blame you?" Mr. Ramirez's eyes fixed on the necklace.

Cole opened his mouth to respond but said nothing.

"Son. You know what I told Michael every time he deployed?" His eyes lifted then, locking onto Cole. "I told him to trust God and to rely on his team. And to trust that every single one of you was doing your best to bring each other home. No matter what you think you did, we know you tried everything you could. War is ugly and unpredictable, taking good men even when you do everything right."

Cole's lips parted, but nothing came out.

"You were his brother out there. And do you know what Michael told me the last time he was home? That if anything ever happened to him, and I told him not to talk like that, but if it did. He said you were the one he trusted if we needed anything."

Tears pricked Raven's eyes and she couldn't stop them from dripping down her cheek.

"Mijo, we know he's with our Heavenly Father," Mrs. Ramirez said. "He loved Jesus, and he wouldn't want us to carry bitterness in our hearts. Not towards anyone, especially you." In one grand motion, she stood from the chair and knelt in front of Cole, cupping his hands in hers. "You must let this go. He loved you like a brother and we feel the same."

Cole's head dropped. Mrs. Ramirez pulled him into a tight embrace. His shoulders shook with silent sobs he tried to hold back. It took everything Raven had to push that ball into her stomach. She put her hand on his back. Mr. Ramirez came over and the two of them knelt in front of Cole, holding each other. Mrs. Ramirez's quiet voice filled the air, a prayer in soft, broken English.

Raven watched it all quietly, her heart full and aching at the same time. She had never seen Cole like this, so raw and exposed. She sat beside him, still and quiet, as Mrs. Ramirez's prayer filled the room like smoke curling around them. It was gentle and cracked with emotion, but every word held weight.

Raven bowed her head.

She'd talked to God plenty, mostly about her own mess. But this wasn't one of those prayers. This wasn't about her. It was for Cole. And somehow, it settled deeper, like the Holy Spirit was sitting with her, nudging her heart.

God . . . I don't know what I'm doing here. But I think You're here. I think You've always been with Cole, even when he didn't know it. So please . . . be close to him now. Let him feel it. Let him breathe again. He carries so much. Too much. And he won't lay it down unless You help him. And if there's anything I can do, please show me. I'll do it.

The prayer felt small, but she meant every word. Maybe more than anything in a long time.

Selfish.

Cole had gotten to spend Preach's last moments with him, an honor his parents could never experience. And they'd consoled *him*? That thought burned.

But this afternoon, sitting around the Ramirez family's table, something had shifted. The grace they'd offered him cracked his walls. He didn't deserve it, never would. But their acceptance meant a lot. The sense of belonging they offered unsettled him. It was unfamiliar outside of camouflage.

The Ramirez dining room had a handful of mismatched chairs around a sturdy wooden table scarred with years of family meals. The early dinner had been simple—tamales, rice and beans, tortillas hot from the stove. Authentic and delicious. Laughter filled the room as Mr. Ramirez told old stories about Preach. Mrs. Ramirez insisted on piling more food onto his plate every time he looked up. And Raven . . .

He looked toward the kitchen where she stood beside Mrs. Ramirez, her sleeves rolled to her elbows as they scrubbed dishes together. Raven's laugh carried over the clink of plates. When she glanced at him over her shoulder, her smile hit him square in the chest.

She'd been there for him all day. Holding space when he couldn't breathe. And now, fitting into his life, like she belonged there. She looked at him as if he wasn't some broken-down soldier but just, himself. The friend she'd trusted for twenty years.

Maybe they *could* be more.

He shifted in his seat, running a hand over the back of his neck. That wasn't a thought he should have. Not now. Maybe never.

Mr. Ramirez stood by the back door, gesturing with his head for Cole to join him. "Come on. Let's get some air."

Cole pushed himself up from the chair. "Yes, sir."

The cool air met him as he stepped outside. Mr. Ramirez stood near the porch railing, eyes fixed on the backyard. Cole stopped next to him, resting his hands on the rail. He noticed the mismatched pavers leading to the back door—some slate, some brick, all uneven, as if someone had started the project and stopped halfway through.

"Michael talked about you a lot, you know. We couldn't get much out of him, except about his brothers."

"He was the best man I ever knew."

Mr. Ramirez turned to look at him. "You were good to him. You all were. I know you think you failed him, but you didn't."

The words hit harder than Cole wanted to admit.

"It doesn't seem that way, sir."

"Sometimes we carry things we're not meant to. But you have to let that go. It'll snatch your joy, and you'll never have peace." Mr. Ramirez reached into his back pocket and pulled out Preach's journal. "Michael would've wanted you to have this."

Cole shook his head. "I can't take this."

Mr. Ramirez clapped a hand on Cole's shoulder, squeezing once. "You can, and you will."

Cole swallowed hard as he took the journal.

"Now, what about that girl of yours?" Mr. Ramirez grinned. "You look at her like a man who's already bought a ring."

"No, no. It's not like that."

"Sure. Keep telling yourself that. I said the s-a-a-me thing." Mr. Ramirez let out a hearty chuckle as he went back inside, leaving Cole standing on the porch.

The journal sank in Cole's grip. Or maybe that was everything else pressing down.

Preach had almost taken a bullet in the shoulder to grab his journal on the tour before Iron Torch. Preach had muttered scriptures every night from it. Annoying as it was hearing him read at 2 a.m. in the middle of a desert, it had been one of the few comforts Cole clung to. They all had.

Sleep didn't come easy out there—never did on a mission in some God-forsaken country where breathing too loud was an invitation for an ambush.

Cole's phone buzzed. He pulled it out to see a text from Hank.

> Army moved up your eval. Two weeks.
> You'd know that if you answered.

> Check your email.

Two weeks?

How was he supposed to pull that off?

He'd already been training for a month, pushing himself hard, against the Army doc's better judgment. They'd made it clear that they didn't think he had it in him. That was why he came home. To train on his own, on his terms. Two months. That was the plan.

Enough time to build back strength, to force his body to remember what it used to do without thinking.

Now he had two weeks?

His grip tightened around his phone, but the strength still wasn't there, not really. It was coming back, sure, but his grip was weaker, reaction time slower. The tremors still crept in when he wasn't paying attention. And if they caught that during his eval? He was done.

What else could he do, train harder? He was already past the edge. Pushing more might break him before he got to that eval.

If he wasn't good enough by now . . . maybe he never would be.

The sound of the screen door creaking made him turn. Cole shoved the phone and the journal into his hoodie pocket. Raven stepped out, holding a dish towel in one hand, her hair half-falling out of its loose ponytail.

"Hey." Her voice was soft. But there was nothing soft about the way her eyes pinned him in place. "Everything okay?"

"Oh yeah. He wanted to talk, you know. Man to man."

Raven smirked as she shook her head. "Man to man, huh? Should I break out cigars?"

A small laugh busted out. "Yeah, yeah."

Raven started talking, but Cole's thoughts kept drifting—how she'd been there for him all day, the way Mr. Ramirez had called her Cole's girl, the arch of her brows over those knowing eyes . . .

"Cole?"

"What?"

"Did you hear me? I said Mrs. Ramirez wants to have some coffee and dessert. She made an apple pie with the crumble on top. I know you can't say no to that."

He followed her into the house. The warm, buttery scent of cinnamon and apples hit him before he crossed the threshold. Mrs.

Ramirez stood near the stove, humming to herself as she pulled the pot from the coffee maker. Raven took a seat.

"Sit, sit." Mrs. Ramirez pushed him next to Raven. The pie steamed in the center. Cole could almost hear Preach's voice in his head. *That right there is proof God loves us.* He'd talked about his mom's cooking all the time, especially her desserts.

"Raven was telling me about this book signing in New York tomorrow." Mrs. Ramirez served him a huge slice of pie. "You stay here, not in some stuffy hotel. Cole, you take the pullout couch in the den and Raven you stay in the spare room."

They looked at each other with wide eyes.

"Is that okay with you, Cole?" Raven said.

Cole nodded with a smile.

Mrs. Ramirez beamed, clapping her hands together. "Good! It's settled then. I'll grab some extra blankets for the pullout. And I'll get those broken blenders and mixers out of the spare room. Miguel swears he's going to fix them all someday. I told him, you're not an appliance whisperer, you're just a hoarder."

Mr. Ramirez shook his head with a mouthful of pie.

Later, the house was quiet with everyone asleep. Cole lay on the pullout couch, staring at the ceiling. His thoughts ran circles, as usual. The Medical Board notice. Preach. Raven. It all tangled so tight he wasn't sure which thread he was supposed to pull first. The Ramirezes owed him nothing, but they'd let him stay. No strings. No judgment. That kind of grace hit harder than anything he'd experienced. He sat up and grabbed his phone.

The email stared back at him in black and white. He read it again. And again.

Thirteen days from now. Not thirty.

Cole let the phone drop to his lap, staring into the dark.

The Army wasn't giving him time to train. This was a countdown to prove he still belonged.

CHAPTER 15

THE CLICK OF RAVEN's fingers on the keyboard filled the small guest room. She sat cross-legged on the bed, laptop balanced on a pillow. The glow of the screen lit her face, keeping sleep far from her mind.

For the first time since Gram had died, words poured out of her—unfiltered and raw. She didn't question them, just typed. Scattered notes, thoughts, moments. Everything she'd been carrying.

The Ramirez home: warm, lived-in, crosses over doorways, cinnamon and incense in the air. A house that prays and forgives.

Mismatched frames, sun-faded photos. Smiling faces. Some gone now, but still here in a way. Memories don't leave, they just soften. Like light through old glass.

Cole at dinner. Quiet. Polite. His shoulders not so tight. The way he looked at me, just once, when he thought I wasn't watching. I need to figure out how to stop my pulse from racing in moments like that. Don't know if it was real or if I only want it to be –Good line. Use this somewhere.

Raven shook her head and kept going.

Porch mums, bright and stubborn. Defying the cold, daring to bloom against the dying season. Like hope refusing to kneel.

Cole's 'yes, ma'am' to Mrs. Ramirez shows a man shaped by discipline, by duty, but there was gentleness beneath it, something unshaken.

After dessert, Mr. Ramirez called me Cole's 'girl.' A name, a claim, a question wrapped in a joke. Cole didn't correct him. Didn't laugh, didn't look away. Just let it settle in the air. A pause long enough to mean something . . . maybe.

That quiet, almost-smile of his. Not possession, not amusement. A secret. A thought half-spoken. A door left cracked open.

Love isn't always fireworks. Sometimes, it's an ember, slow burning, waiting for air to catch.

She paused, chewing the edge of her lip.

Piece by piece words pricked her like they wanted out. Not pretty, but free. Raven sat back, exhaling as the heater hummed. She set the laptop aside and swung her legs over the edge of the bed. She needed a break, and sugar. Would it be weird to snag a piece of pie? What time was it?

She checked her phone. 11:53 p.m.

The floorboards creaked as she tiptoed down the dark hallway. A simple plan: get to the fridge and cut a small piece. Quick and quiet. But as she passed the den, a faint glow caught her attention.

She stepped closer to the doorway. Cole perched on the pull-out couch, thumbing through a small leather-bound book. He looked distant and heavy, like whatever was in that book weighed a hundred pounds.

She gave a light knock on the doorframe. "Can't sleep either?"

He looked up. "You're up late."

"So are you."

He shut the book and set it on the end table. "Everything okay? I hope I didn't wake you."

"You didn't." She leaned against the doorframe. "I was writing. Well, scribbling down thoughts before they disappear."

"Your story?"

"Not quite. Just . . . notes. About the trip. About everything."

His eyes lingered on her. "Where were you going?"

"Oh, to the bathroom."

Cole dropped his brow. "The bathroom is right next to your room."

She rolled her eyes and huffed. Caught. "Fine. I was making a secret mission to the fridge for leftover pie. Happy?"

He laughed and shook his head.

"That's not weird, is it? I mean, Mrs. Ramirez won't think I'm some kind of creep stealing her pie, right? I need a sugar fix."

"No, but I didn't take you for a pie thief. Especially after berating me about the cookie in fourth grade."

"I prefer the term pie enthusiast." She folded her arms. "Like you've never snuck into a kitchen at midnight."

He slid to the edge of the couch and stood. "Want some company? I can keep watch like the old days."

She laughed, leading the way to the kitchen. He flicked on the sink light. She retrieved the pie, and he passed her a plate. As she tugged the foil off the top, it smelled almost as delicious as when it was first pulled from the oven.

The silence settled warm around them. She handed him a slice and sat across from him.

"Mrs. Ramirez should enter this in some kind of contest. Pie this good deserves national attention." She scooped a forkful into her mouth.

Cole smirked, taking a bite.

She couldn't stop herself from sneaking glances at him.

"You doing okay?" He'd caught her again.

She paused her fork midair. "Me?"

"Yeah. Staying here wasn't planned."

She shrugged, setting her fork down. "The Ramirezes are great. This was an unexpected gift, especially to see you making amends with them and everything."

"What about tomorrow? You nervous?"

She shrugged. "I'm not freaking out. Just . . . what if he doesn't remember me? What if I say something stupid? Like, 'Hi, I think you might have fathered me, let's have lunch.'"

He smiled.

"I don't know." She sighed. "I know better than to get my hopes up, but this is the first real shot I've had at seeing him. And then my brain does this thing where it whispers some crazy thought, like, what if he actually *wants* to see me?"

She nudged a piece of crust with her fork, her lips pressing together. "I'm considering pitching my book idea when I meet with the editor next week. So, who knows, I might be losing it."

He perked up. "You should. Your book idea is good."

Raven laughed, shaking her head. "I don't know. That's not why she took the meeting."

"Maybe, but you don't have to have all the answers yet. Just have to believe you have something worth saying."

She looked down at her fork, then up at him. His words lingered longer than the cinnamon in the air.

"Whatever happens at the signing, I'll be there," Cole said.

She stared at him. "Okay."

"I mean it, Rae. You won't be alone."

His words slipped under her skin, warming her entire body. "You've got a way of saying things that makes everything seem easier, you know that?"

He chuckled. "That's not what people usually say about me."

The moment settled around them, heavier than the kitchen table could hold. She took another bite of pie.

"You've got something . . ." He gestured at her cheek.

"Where?" Oh my gosh. Of course, she'd slop up the pie like an animal in front of him.

He leaned forward, his thumb brushing her cheek. "There."

Her pulse thrummed in her ears. She looked up right into those dangerous blue eyes and couldn't look away. She wanted to say something—anything—but all the words left her. He held her eyes, his thumb still lingering on her cheek like he'd forgotten to pull away.

His hand dropped as he cleared his throat. "All good."

"Thanks." She finished the last bite and stood. "Well, pie mission accomplished."

"Hey, Rae." He hesitated, and for a second, it looked important. Like he was right on the edge of saying something that mattered. "Big day tomorrow."

And that was it.

She nodded. "Yeah. Big day."

She grabbed the plates, pretending everything was normal. No big deal. Just pie. And a moment that scrambled her thoughts like a plot twist she didn't see coming.

The next morning, they gathered their things early. Raven's thoughts still tangled in the night before. That moment in the kitchen—his words, his touch—had knocked her off balance, again. She'd barely slept thinking about it.

Whatever happens at the signing, I'll be there.

She didn't know what to make of it or of the look in his eyes when he'd said it. But she wrapped herself in the hope that he meant it.

Mrs. Ramirez squeezed Raven in a warm embrace.

Mr. Ramirez shook Cole's hand and clapped his shoulder with a firm pat. "Take care of yourself, son."

Cole offered a tight nod. "Thank you, sir. For everything."

As they stepped outside into the cool morning air, Raven shoved the confusion aside. Today could be a turning point. The answers were finally within reach.

Cole put their bags in the truck and climbed into the driver's seat.

She glanced over as he started the engine. "Today's the day."

Excitement mixed with nervousness twisted inside her. She reached into her purse and pulled out the Tums. After popping two in her mouth, she took a sip of water.

He shifted the truck into drive. "You ready?"

"Yep. Let's go." She turned toward the window, the golden light breaking through the morning haze, and let herself believe that today everything could change.

Twenty minutes into the drive, her phone buzzed on her lap with a number she didn't recognize. She hesitated, then swiped to answer.

"Hi, Raven. This is Valerie Campbell's assistant."

Raven's heart kicked up a beat. The editor. "Oh, hi. Yes, I—"

"I'm sorry, but Valerie had to catch an earlier flight. She won't be able to meet until next month. She asked me to reschedule and sends her apologies."

"Next month?"

"Yes, we'll email you options. Thank you for understanding."

The line clicked off before Raven could say anything else. She put her phone face down in her lap. Maybe it was for the best. She hadn't decided if she could go through with telling the editor the truth about her suspicions, the letter, or even the pitch. But it still stung. Not because of what she might've said, but because of what she wouldn't get to hear.

Cole glanced at her. "Everything all right?"

"The editor can't meet next week. Just a tiny, insignificant shift in plans. A mere detour in the grand scheme of my unraveling life."

She tapped her fingers against the phone. "It's fine. Totally fine. Character development, right?"

Trees blurred past. The optimism Raven had felt earlier slid through her fingers like sand. A tight knot settled in her stomach, uneasy and insistent.

But the truth remained . . . J.C. Nevermore *was* her father. And they were on their way to see him.

Cole should've told her about her father last night.

Back at the table, with pie between them and something soft in her eyes—he'd had the chance. But he chickened out. Again.

Tick said he'd have something soon. Maybe it was wishful thinking, but Cole was still holding out hope. Hope that he wouldn't have to blow up her world just yet. But now they were ten minutes out, and his window was closing fast.

He told himself he was protecting her, but guilt sat low in his gut, heavy. The DNA test had enough holes to call it into question. Maybe it was fake. Maybe someone didn't want her to know the truth. And if they were on the right track, he didn't want to be the reason it all went off the rails.

Cole maneuvered the truck down the narrow streets of the Seaport district in New York City. The fog clung to the edges of the buildings. Good thing he checked spots available ahead of time. He found the lot on Pearl Street, handed the valet the keys, and waited.

He hopped out and rounded the truck and opened her door. She smoothed down the front of her coat as they walked to the bookstore. Horns blared. Brakes screeched. Shouting from a construction site echoed through the cold air. Another perk of the quiet back home in the country.

At McFinn's Bookstore, a sign hung on the window about the book signing, but no crowd. He wasn't sure how these things were supposed to go, but it seemed off.

He caught her eye as they reached the door. "Hey . . . just so you know, we're not here to storm the castle. We'll look around, get a feel. You don't have to talk to anyone if you're not ready."

She gave a shaky laugh. "Let's get inside before I lose my nerve."

Inside, the store stretched deep. Brick archways. Shelves lined with stories. But no table. No banners. No J.C. Nevermore.

"Where's the table setup? There should be something." Her pace quickened.

A clerk behind the counter looked up. "Can I help you?"

"We're here for the signing, J.C. Nevermore." Cole said.

The guy winced. "That was canceled yesterday. Sorry. We were told to pull the display."

Cole turned to Raven. "Did you get an email or some kind of notification?"

Raven shook her head, already pulling out her phone.

"Any word on what happened, or a reschedule?" Cole said.

"We don't usually know those details. You'd have to talk to the publisher about it." The clerk shrugged then turned his attention to a customer checking out.

Cole touched Raven's arm. She ran for the exit, and out the door. As she leaned against the building, she stared at the ground, not saying a word.

He should tell her about her father now. Just get it over with. But watching her hold back tears—he couldn't pile more on. That seemed cruel. Once he said the words, there was no undoing them. And he wasn't sure he could stand being the one to break her heart.

A tear slipped down her cheek. She wiped it fast. Still wouldn't look at him.

"Let's get coffee," he said. "Figure out what's next."

He steered them toward a small café across the street. Keeping her from spiraling felt like the only move he had. He pulled out his phone. Still no response from Tick. Cole texted him again.

The coffee shop was one of those corner spots that pummeled people with the smell of pumpkin spice no matter what season it was. Cole grabbed their coffees and they moved to a table. She stirred her drink, staring out the window.

They'd only exchanged three words since they left the bookstore. Cole had to say something.

"It's not over."

Her eyes flicked up. "Feels over."

"It's not. We can dig up more leads."

"You keep saying that." Her voice hardened with every syllable. "I should've known better to hope. This entire trip is ridiculous. I mean, did I actually expect a man I haven't seen in twenty-two years to just become part of my life again? And as a famous author, nonetheless. I should take the hint."

"And what's that?"

"Isn't it obvious? If he wanted me, he would have tried. I mean, my mother is ruthless, but she only had so much control. She hasn't been my legal guardian since I was fourteen." Her voice cracked. "I keep trying to make the pieces fit. But maybe there's no full picture. Just broken parts."

Cole leaned in. "You've come this far. One setback doesn't erase all that."

"You don't get it, Cole." She finally looked at him. "This isn't just another dead end. It's *the* dead end. The big, flashing sign that says, 'Go home and stop dreaming.'" She looked at him. Fury and grief tangled in her eyes. "You've gotta be sick of this. Me spiraling, needing to be put back together. But hey, at least you're not the one wandering through life like a crossword puzzle with half the clues missing."

He leaned in. "Lest you forget I have my own issues."

She stared at him, eyes shining. Fragile. He hated that look. Defeat after yet another undeserved blow.

He reached for her hand. "Don't give up because some guy bailed."

She didn't pull away. But she didn't squeeze back either.

"You're not some broken puzzle. You're a masterpiece people are too blind to appreciate."

Silence.

Not relief. Not comfort.

She pulled her hand away. "I'll be right back."

Maybe he'd overstepped.

She stood, hesitating for a fraction of a second about to say something. But she turned toward the bathroom.

After a few minutes, his phone vibrated.

Tick. Perfect timing.

His pulse kicked up as he answered. "Please tell me you got something?"

"Doc, I'm telling you, this isn't adding up. The guy's not her father—paternity test proves it—but there's something off about the records."

"I need you to find something on him. The book signing was canceled. Can you check out where he's going to be next? Maybe another signing. An address. Anything, man."

"I gave you what I know on that USB drive. Jeffrey Cunningham's as slippery as they come. Fraud charges, credit schemes, a whole rap sheet of bad decisions."

Cole tightened his grip on the phone. "What kind of fraud?"

"Anything he could get away with. Financial, real estate, insurance scams—you name it. And here's the kicker, a lot of it points back to Margaret Sullivan. So, I've been checking into her."

Raven's mom? He clenched his jaw. "What are you saying?"

"Let's just say she wasn't some innocent bystander. She's got arrests tied to his scams—one even listed her under a fake alias. I'm telling you, this whole mess smells like old socks in a gallon of turpentine."

Cole rubbed a hand over his face. "And you're sure he's not her father? What about the DNA match? How could that be false?"

"It wasn't, but—wait. You haven't told her, have you?"

Cole glanced toward the bathroom.

"Doc. You can't keep stalling. Remember the ferret."

"I know. I just . . . I can't drop this on her yet."

"You're running out of road."

"I'll take care of it." Cole ended the call.

"What?" Raven's voice cut like a blade.

Cole froze, turning to find her standing a few feet behind him, eyes wide.

"Raven—"

"What do you mean he's not my father?" Her voice trembled, fury and fear twisting through it.

He stood slowly. "Please sit. Let me explain."

She didn't move at first. Then, she lowered herself into the chair.

The look in her eyes could bury him. "Who were you talking to?"

"Tick."

Her eyes narrowed, glassy and sharp. "And what did you mean when you said he's not my father?"

He looked down and took a deep breath.

"Cole, tell me the truth." The volume of her voice caught the attention of a nearby couple.

"I was waiting until I had all the answers, until I knew for sure. Tick said there are still holes in the story. Jeffrey Cunningham is J.C. Nevermore but . . ." He hesitated.

"But what? Tell me."

"He's not your biological father."

She blinked once. Then again. As if trying to reset the scene in front of her.

Her eyes blazed with hurt. "He's not my father?"

Cole shook his head.

She looked down, then back up. "And you were just going to keep that to yourself?" Her voice rose. "You knew. You sat there, pretending, letting me hold on to hope, and you didn't say a word? Letting me go to that bookstore . . . I can't believe you."

"Listen—"

"No, *you* listen. You keep acting like you're protecting me, like you're the one who gets to decide what I can and can't handle. But all you're doing is trying to control everything, so you won't get hurt. Typical."

"It's not like that."

"Then what is it like?" Her voice dropped to a whisper. "You know what? This is what you do. You avoid things. You act like nothing's wrong, like it's another obstacle to muscle through, but the second something gets too real—too hard—you shut down."

Cole's jaw tightened. "That's not true. I didn't want—"

"Isn't it?" She let out a sharp laugh. "You never even told me about the Army, about your discharge, about how you've probably been pretending everything is fine to everyone instead of actually doing the work to fix it."

"You think I haven't done the work?"

"Have you?" She leaned forward, fire in her eyes. "Or did you push yourself past breaking, and hope no one noticed that you're barely holding yourself together?"

He held back from saying something he'd regret. "I didn't want to hurt you."

"Well, you did. And you always will, won't you? You always do this." She looked away. "You hold back until it's too late. And then someone else pays for it." She stood and started toward the door.

The chair scraped as he stood. "And what about you, huh? You've avoided things your entire life, Raven. Maybe that's why you let your mother call the shots, why you keep letting people walk all over you instead of standing up and demanding the truth."

She whirled around to face him. "That's not the same thing."

He let out a short, bitter laugh. "Isn't it?"

"At least I *tell* the truth."

His eyes locked onto hers, pulse drumming in his ears. He'd tried to protect her, and all he'd done was push her away. Again.

She shook her head. "I trusted you."

His chest caved. He wanted to say something. But he didn't.

She slung her purse over her shoulder and stormed away.

"Where are you going?"

"To figure this out on my own. Like I should've done in the first place." She shoved the doors open.

He caught up with her outside and grabbed her hand. "Stop. I'll take you wherever you need to go. Just . . ."

She turned to him. That look of disappointment and pain sliced him to shards.

"Rae—"

"I need a minute."

He let go, and she disappeared around the corner.

He didn't argue. He couldn't. Because deep down, he knew this was his fault. And she was right. He'd tried to protect her, to hold back the truth until it wouldn't hurt, and now?

Now he'd lost her for good.

CHAPTER 16

THE TRAIN STATION WAS cold and hollow, just like Raven. She clutched the strap of her bag as Cole followed her to the automatic doors, his boots scuffing against the concrete like he didn't want to be there anymore than she did.

He held out a USB drive. "Here. Everything Tick found. I should've given it to you sooner."

She stared at it. Then him. "And now you think this fixes everything?"

"No. But you deserve the truth. Even if I'm too late."

Her throat tightened. Her fingers curled around the drive, brushing his hand. She ignored the spark. Ignored the way something in her ached to stop, to not walk away. She shoved the drive into her bag.

This was over. It had to be.

He fidgeted, like he wanted to reach for her, but didn't. "If you need anything . . . I'm here."

He meant it. She knew that. And that was what made it hurt so much.

She met his eyes, and there it was—the thing neither of them could say.

But it didn't matter.

She had to let go. Whatever she wanted with him was never going to happen.

People brushed past them into the station, and a muffled voice echoed over the speaker behind them. A thick chemical smell and the faint whiff of soft pretzels lingered.

She turned toward the station. Walked inside. Didn't look back.

Cole didn't stop her. And maybe that was the worst part.

She made it through the doors and past the crowds, got her ticket and waited, trying not to replay the last hour. Once the train arrived, she found her seat. Window side. Alone.

The train rocked beneath her. Raven slumped by the window, buildings blurring past. She couldn't stop seeing Cole. That look in his eyes.

She blinked fast. Angry tears pricked her eyes, hot and unwelcome. Her shoulders tensed as a sob clawed its way out. She pressed a fist against her mouth, forcing in a breath.

She wasn't crying over him. She wasn't.

But she had believed. In him. In them.

Out of all the lies she'd been fed lately, the worst was his. Because he should've been the one person she could count on. And he wasn't.

The train rattled along, metal on metal, the vibration buzzing through the seat beneath her. Anger tightened, like a knot between her ribs.

She could still hear his voice in her head.

If you need anything, I'm here.

Like it mattered.

Her phone vibrated in her bag. Raven sniffed, pulling it out. Zoe.

She hesitated, then swiped to answer.

She pressed her forehead to the window. "Hey."

"Where are you?"

"On the train. Heading home."

"Okay. My mom said she'll pick you up. How are you?"

Raven let out a bitter laugh, swiping at another tear. "Oh, living the dream. It's not just the fact he didn't tell me, Zo. It's that I thought this time might be different."

"Oh, Rae."

"I should've known better. "

"Don't blame yourself. Take a breath. He cares about you, that's—"

"Then why lie? He knows what that cost me."

"Maybe he was waiting to make sure it was the truth. I can understand after everything you've been through. Maybe he thought he was protecting you. You've got to at least consider that."

Raven sat up straight. "Are you taking his side?"

"Of course not. I'm on yours. But don't throw this away. You've loved him forever."

Raven froze. That word.

Loved.

Maybe it was already over. Another tear slipped down her cheek.

"I don't know if I can trust him again. Or what I'm supposed to do now. This whole thing—my father, Cole, all of it—is one big mess. And I have no idea how to take the next step."

"Give yourself some grace. You don't have to know. Plus, maybe the truth is more complicated."

Raven nodded. But she didn't care if the truth was complicated. She needed to know.

"But, if you want me to completely ruin his life until he grovels properly, I'm more than happy to take the lead. I can spam his inbox with fake job offers for 'emotional support punching bag.' Or I could sign him up for a subscription service that delivers nothing but creepy porcelain dolls to his doorstep every month."

Raven dug into her bag for the USB. She pulled out her laptop and plugged in the drive.

"Or I could anonymously send him a series of cryptic letters in cutout magazine ransom-note font that says 'You better say sorry.' Really keep him on edge."

Raven smirked. "I appreciate the creativity."

"Oh, I'm just getting started."

Raven shook her head, flipping her laptop open. "I have to go, I'll call you later."

She ended the call and took a deep breath.

God, I don't know what you're trying to show me. But help me out here, please.

She plugged the drive into the port. The files popped up on the screen, organized and methodical. Not what she'd expected from Tick.

Her eyes skimmed the folder names, her pulse kicking up as she read them.

- *Paternity Test Results – J. Cunningham*

- *Fraud Investigation Notes*

- *Financial History – J. Cunningham*

A chill curled down her spine.

She clicked the paternity test first. A scanned document filled the screen, legal jargon crowding the margins. At the bottom, an unfamiliar signature. But then—a name she knew.

Margaret Sullivan – Parent/Guardian Providing Sample.

Why was her mother listed as the one submitting the test?

She leaned in, eyes narrowing at a handwritten note in the margin.

Filed at request of guardian. Chain of custody unclear.

Her stomach turned.

The words slammed into her brain, sparking doubt that wouldn't settle. Chain of custody unclear, which meant . . . what? That Mom had controlled how the test was processed? If that was the case, then no doubt she had manipulated it.

Raven's fingers hovered over the trackpad.

No. That was insane. Right?

How could Mom fake a paternity test?

Raven clicked the next file.

A table filled the screen—date, charges, locations. Intent to defraud in 2002. Fraudulent claims in 2003.

She scrolled further, until her father's name appeared.

Jeffrey Cunningham – Ongoing Financial Dispute, 2005

Fraud Investigation: Wiley & Putnam Publishing Legal Complaint – 2006

A publisher? Why would he defraud his own publisher?

She clicked open the document, skimming, searching—until a name popped up that she recognized.

Timothy Calloway. Mom's boyfriend? How was he involved back then?

Her heart pounded against her ribs. She exhaled, sitting back. She scrolled back up to the paternity test document, searching, and her breath hitched as she saw his title.

Filed by: Timothy Calloway, Esq.

Esq. As in "Esquire." As a licensed attorney.

Raven let out a sharp, bitter laugh. "You have got to be kidding me."

Tim had never passed the bar. And he'd been skirting legal work for years, cutting deals, filing paperwork under technicalities and loopholes. Raven recalled him bragging about it, usually over a beer. "You don't need a license if you know the right people," he'd say. "Courtrooms are for suckers. Settle in the backroom and walk away clean."

She twisted her ring, trying to make sense of it.

Her phone rang. She ignored it.

How was his name on an official document about her father? Mom hadn't met him until . . .

Her pulse hammered.

So, she had known him back then . . . was that why she left?

She clicked the next file. A list of transactions filled the screen. Money transfers, payments. She scrolled down to another document. Legal correspondence. Her father had tried to fight for custody. There were letters. Court filings. Attempts to gain visitation.

But the case had been dismissed.

Raven clenched her fists. Why? Why was it dismissed?

Her eyes scanned the last note at the bottom of the page.

Defendant deemed unstable due to ongoing fraud investigation.

A knot twisted in her gut. No doubt her mother had done this.

She had buried him. Smeared his name. Destroyed his chances in court by making him look like the unstable one.

Raven shut her laptop and pressed her fingers to her temples. This was a mess. A disaster.

Her phone rang again.

With an irritated groan, she grabbed it and swiped to answer. "What?"

A pause. Then, in the calmest, most amused voice imaginable. "Well, hello to you too, dear."

Raven pulled the phone away, squinting at the screen. Jo? Great.

"Sorry. It's been a long day. What's up?"

"Ah, well, I was brainstorming some fantastic ideas, and I had to call you immediately. I think we should introduce the book with a dramatic reenactment of my first-ever conversation with a cat."

Raven sighed.

"I think the best way to capture it for the readers would be to stage it with an actor. Perhaps someone with strong, expressive eyebrows. I'll let you handle the details, of course, but I was thinking in Chapter—"

"Jo."

"Yes?"

"I am not, under any circumstances, writing a dramatic reenactment of your first cat conversation."

A pause.

"Not even as a sidebar?"

Raven groaned. "Not as a footnote. Not as a dedication. Not even as a 250-word epigraph tucked before the acknowledgements.

It's not necessary for the book. And more importantly, it doesn't fit the story we agreed on."

She took a breath, keeping frustration in check. "I need you to respect the process we've outlined, because we've gone over it a hundred times already. I value your input, truly, but at some point, we must stick to what works. And this? It doesn't work."

Another pause.

She softened. "Trust me to do my job. That's why you brought me on this project in the first place."

Jo sighed. "I see."

"Now, I'm in the middle of something, so if this can wait—"

"You're putting your foot down. Good for you. Annoying for me, but good for you." Jo huffed. "But just know, if this book tanks, it's because you denied the world my cat-whispering origin story."

Raven smirked. "I'll take that risk."

"All right. Go be brilliant. I expect an update when you're less 'busy.'"

"I'll call you later." She tossed her phone back into her bag.

Hmm. Boundaries actually worked. A tiny win in a sea of chaos.

But the feeling didn't last.

A sour taste crept up the back of Raven's throat, hot and bitter. She swallowed hard, pressing a fist against her mouth as if that could keep it all down—the truth, the panic, the nausea climbing its way up.

Her fingers fumbled through her bag until they closed around the Tums bottle. She poured out two chalky tablets and forced herself to chew.

Breathe. Swallow. Don't lose it.

But the words on the screen didn't change.

And neither did the sickening weight pressing against her.

"Sweetheart, you need some water?" A soft voice floated from across the aisle.

Raven looked up, blinking back tears that threatened again. An older woman's face lit with a gentle smile, revealing a few wrinkles around her bright blue eyes. Her silvery blonde hair was styled into a neat bob. She held out a small, bottled water.

"I'm fine."

The woman gave her a knowing look. "No, you're not. But that's okay. No one ever *really* is."

"It's . . . family stuff."

"Ah." The woman nodded. "Family's never simple."

Raven managed a weak laugh.

"I understand. For years, my ex-husband and I couldn't be in the same room without it turning into a scene. And our kids? Let's just say conflict runs in the family. My son and daughter didn't speak for a year. Holidays were a logistical nightmare."

She let out a quick laugh. "But things change. I'm on my way to see all of them now. Even my ex's new wife. Who would've thought?"

"What changed?" Raven said.

"My son had a baby. First granddaughter. Suddenly, we all realized we'd missed too much already. Now here we are, on our way to see this little bundle of joy." She flashed Raven the wallpaper on her phone, a sweet baby in a pink dress. "Do we still bicker? Of course. Do I roll my eyes every time my ex-husband opens his mouth? You bet. But God gave us something to rally around."

"That sounds good and all, but I'm not sure the same thing applies to my situation."

The woman smiled. "Sometimes we're so busy being angry or hurt that we miss the path right in front of us. Lord knows I've walked a few wrong paths in my life."

There was something about the woman, something kind in her eyes, that made Raven pause.

She didn't usually open up to strangers, but this time, she felt a nudge. "What if the path is a complete mess?"

The woman nodded. "Any time I start to question things, I think of Psalm 16. God pokes and prods, but He gets us moving in the right direction. Even when we don't see it yet."

Raven gave a polite smile before she faced the window. Maybe. But how could any of this be the path she was supposed to follow?

Beyond the window, the landscape blurred into streaks of muted color, but her mind drifted somewhere else—somewhere forgotten.

A laugh echoed in her memory, deep and full of life. Her father's. She remembered the way he'd spin her in circles, her tiny hands gripping his as the world tilted around them, laughing until they were dizzy.

"One more time, Daddy! One more!"

And he always would. One more. And then another.

She squeezed her eyes shut and let out a shaky breath.

Her fingers hovered over the keys of her laptop. She opened her notes and started typing:

Family isn't perfect. It's messy, complicated, and sometimes broken beyond repair. But love is a choice. It's showing up when no one else does. Maybe God's path isn't meant to be clear. Maybe it's meant to hurt, tug, rip apart everything until there's only one thing you can do. Get on your knees and surrender.

The train rocked beneath her. She typed faster, spilling out everything—the path she'd walked, the memories she clung to, the truth she wasn't ready to face but knew she had to.

Did it matter if he wasn't her biological father?

No.

Love made him her dad.

And nothing could take that away. Not even the truth. Whatever that looked like.

Cole gritted his teeth as he cleared the chaos of the Holland Tunnel. He had no idea where to go. The second he spotted a Shell gas station, he veered off, parked, and jumped out for air.

Nerves buzzed in his arm. His pulse pounded. Heat crawled under his skin.

She'd left.

Just like that. Chose a train over him. Eight hours with strangers instead of five more minutes with him.

He dropped his forehead against his fist on the truck bed. He should've stopped her. Said something. Anything. But what could fix it?

He checked his phone. Nothing.

Her words echoed.

You avoid everything.

She didn't get it. Didn't know what it meant to make choices that haunted you. Didn't understand pressure that crushed you if you paused for one second.

You hold back until it's too late. And then someone else pays for it.

He slammed his hand against the truck. A woman getting gas stared. He didn't care.

Anger uncoiled in his chest, but there was nowhere for it to go.

Deep breath.

He looked around and got back in the driver's seat. What was he trying to prove?

And the truth of it hit. Raven. Preach. Even years ago with Emily.

How many times had he refused to act or face things?

His frustration shifted. He let out a slow breath. Maybe Raven was right.

That thought sank into him. He flexed his fingers around the steering wheel, staring at the gas station lights.

He threw the truck into drive. By the time he hit the turnpike, he knew where he was headed. Where he should have gone first.

Brigadier General William C. Doyle Veterans Memorial Cemetery.

He had an hour to wrestle with it. An hour of replaying every decision, every moment he should've made a different call.

By the time the turnoff for the cemetery came into view, one thought settled heavier than the rest. This wasn't about him. Preach deserved more than silence.

Cole pulled in, cut the engine, and stepped out into the cold. He shut the door with more force than necessary. It had been a long time. Too long. How he remembered where to go floored him, since the funeral blurred in his mind.

The cold bit into his jacket. His boots crunched over fallen leaves. Headstones stretched in rows. And then he saw it.

SPC MICHAEL "PREACH" RAMIREZ
UNITED STATES ARMY
75TH RANGER REGIMENT
BRONZE STAR – PURPLE HEART
DEC 12, 1999 – JUN 14, 2025

He stopped.

His breath was ragged, but he got hold of it. He shoved his hands into his pockets, staring at the stone.

"I should've come sooner."

A lump formed in his throat, but he swallowed it.

"I don't know why I'm here." He shook his head. "You deserved better. You were always better than the rest of us." He let out a quick laugh. "You'd probably tell me to stop standing here talking to a headstone like an idiot."

Thick silence settled around him.

He shifted his weight again, rubbing the back of his neck. "I stopped by your parents' place. You weren't kidding about your mom's cooking. That pie . . ." He looked at the ground. "I—I don't know what I'm supposed to say."

His throat tightened.

"I'm sorry, Preach."

Wind through the trees filled the silence.

He swallowed hard, his eyes locked on his best friend's name carved into stone. "I don't have the answers, man. I never did. I kept thinking if I worked harder, tried harder, I'd figure it out. Make sense of it. But the more I tried, the more I felt like I was losing something." He looked down. "Maybe I was losing myself."

His fists tightened in his pockets.

He lifted his eyes toward the gray sky. "I don't know what comes next. I don't know how to fix this. But I know I can't keep carrying it. I can't keep trying to be something I'm not. Without the Army, I don't know what I'm supposed to do."

His breath came out in a slow drag. He blinked hard, eyes burning.

"You'd probably tell me to trust God." He huffed a short laugh. "Wish that came as easy for me as it did for you."

The wind stirred around him. For the first time in a long time the silence didn't crush him. His hands unclenched.

He touched the top of the headstone. "I miss you, man."

Pinching the inside corners of his eyes, he pivoted. He stood straight, brought his hand to his brow, and gave a clean salute. No words. Just respect. Then he dropped his arm and turned back to the truck.

Once inside, he took a moment to sit. To think. He opened his center console for a napkin, and there it was, Preach's journal. That worn leather, creased at the edges. He'd had this thing for months but never brought himself to read it. Never wanted to face whatever was inside. Not until Mr. Ramirez put it in his hands.

He flipped it open to a random page. Scanning the familiar scrawl, he stopped at a line.

Doc carries everyone else's baggage and doesn't realize until it buries him. Father, show him Your grace. Help him to know that Your grace is enough to establish him.

His chest tightened.

Underneath, scribbled in dark ink:

For by grace you have been saved through faith, and that not of yourselves; it is the gift of God, not of works, lest anyone should boast. Ephesians 2:8-9

Cole let out a slow breath, his fingers tightening around the journal.

His vision blurred.

The weight of those words cracked something he hadn't realized he'd been clinging to. All this time, he had been trying to carry something that had never been his. For years, he had done everything in his power to be enough, to fix things, to make up for the things he couldn't change. He wasn't in control. And maybe . . . that was the point.

He set the journal on the front seat, but didn't move. Just sat there, letting the thought dig in. He wasn't sure if it was something he should carry or let go.

His phone vibrated against the dash. Tick.

"Talk to me."

"Good news, Doc. I found your missing link."

Cole straightened in his seat. "I can definitely use some good news."

"First, that paternity test is faker than a two-dollar Rolex at a street market. Tampered with, chain of custody compromised, the works. The whole thing was rigged. Rigged worse than the 1876 election!" Tick launched into it, barely pausing for breath. "Hayes versus Tilden, man! Rutherford B. Hayes, our nineteenth president, stole that election through backroom deals and shady compromises. One minute Tilden's winning, the next—boom—Hayes—"

"Tick! I don't need a history lesson."

"The paternity test was tampered with. The ex-wife submitted it. Oh, and get this: the lawyer who signed off on it? Sketchier than an MRE labeled 'meat surprise.'"

Cole gripped the wheel. "What does that mean?"

"It means your boy Jeffrey Cunningham isn't some jerk who disappeared. He pulled a Houdini—changed his name to Jeffrey Carter to get out from under the mess the ex dragged him into. That Jersey address I gave you? That's his real house. J.C. Nevermore is Jeffrey Carter and he lives at 196 Woodward Ave, Jersey City."

"You're sure?"

"As sure as I am that pineapple does not belong on pizza. It's him, Doc. All the dots connect. I pulled Carter's DNA from his military records—don't ask how, call it magic. Then I cross-referenced it with a little something I, uh, borrowed from a consumer database."

"You hacked her DNA from 23andMe, didn't you?"

"Pfft, please. That's amateur hour. I was way more subtle. Used some hospital data—they're terrible at cybersecurity. But maybe cross-referenced it to be sure . . . anyway, the point is, it's a match! 50.3% shared DNA. Carter's her father, no question."

"So, you're saying you have proof Raven's mom orchestrated this?"

"Bingo." Tick whistled. "Margaret Sullivan's got a track record uglier than a busted Humvee. This isn't her first rodeo with bending the truth. Make sure you tell Raven I didn't crawl through my usual fifty dark web rabbit holes to find this. Nope. I went to one—the most secure, clean-ish one I know—because this is special. For her."

"She's not exactly speaking to me right now."

"Well, you've got the golden ticket here. Don't stand outside the chocolate factory moping about it."

"I'll figure it out. Thanks, man."

"Don't make me crawl out of my bunker and fix it for you. I'm not great with people. Too much blinking."

Cole ended the call. Before making any moves, he had a thought. He dropped his head, a move he hadn't done in a long time.

God please, help me to do the right thing here. In Jesus' name.

He scrolled to Raven's name in his phone, hovering over the call button. She might not want to see him. Might still be furious. But she deserved to know the truth. After multiple rings her voicemail picked up.

"Look, I know you don't want to talk to me," Cole said. "I understand, but Tick found proof, real proof. It's about your father. It changes everything. Just . . . call me."

He let the phone drop onto the passenger seat. He'd done his part, hadn't he? Put the ball in her court. If she wanted to ignore him, that was her choice.

Maybe he should leave it at that.

It was probably better. Him out of it. Out of her way.

But what if she thought he didn't care? That he'd let her chase this truth alone like everyone else had? What if she believed she wasn't worth the fight?

If he went to that address, if he stepped in, there was no going back. Part of him wanted to head home and leave it alone. Let her deal with it. Let her decide.

Then he remembered her face. The look when she walked away.

No.

He couldn't leave her in the dark. Not again.

He texted Tick to send him the address.

A few seconds later, his screen lit up with a message.

And just like that, he had one destination.

One chance to start showing up.

CHAPTER 17

As the train hissed to a stop, Raven jerked upright. Her neck screamed in protest. She bumped her laptop and it glowed like a spotlight in the dim car. She logged back in, and the open document showed an endless stream of W's lining the page.

"Perfect." She groaned and deleted them before wiping a line of drool from her cheek. She checked the time. 8:46 p.m. She rubbed the kink out of her neck, then shut the laptop.

How long had she been out?

She stuffed her laptop into her bag and checked her phone.

> Zoe: R U alive?

> Raven: Barely, getting ready to step out now.

Another buzz.

> Nina: I hope you had a wonderful trip, darling. We're by the entrance.

> Raven: Thank you. I'll be out soon.

We? Maybe Zoe's dad drove. Nina preferred to avoid city traffic.

She followed the flow of people off the train, thumbing through unread texts—four from Zoe. And one from Cole.

> Cole: I have more information from Tick. If you want the truth, it's yours. If you don't want to hear it from me, I can give you Tick's number. Please don't ignore this, Raven. You deserve to know. I'm sorry.

Her thumb hovered. Her pulse jumped.

If you want the truth.

She read it again.

She stepped off the train and towed the line along the platform.

She did want answers. But not like this. Not now. Not standing in the chill of the station while her heart still felt fractured and raw.

Maybe he meant well. Maybe. But it still hurt. She slid the phone into her pocket.

One thing at a time.

When she stepped off the platform, Nina came into view.

"Hey, you." Nina pulled Raven into a hug so tight, tears threatened to fall. She hadn't realized how much she'd needed this. "We missed you. You okay?"

Raven nodded against her shoulder.

Nina pulled back, studying her face with a gentle but knowing look. "Zoe's waiting at the car, double parked. She said I could have first dibs."

"Zoe? But what about the conference in Boston? I thought she'd be there until tomorrow."

"She skipped the last sessions. She wanted to be here."

The cool air nipped at her face as they crossed the street. Her mind spun, still raw from everything that had happened—the canceled signing, the fight with Cole, the crushing weight of disappointment. But as they rounded the corner, Zoe pushed off her SUV and walked over.

"About time. I was starting to think you were ghosting us."

Before Raven could respond, Zoe wrapped her in a tight hug, nearly knocking the air out of her.

Raven stiffened, but then her hands clutched Zoe's jacket. The dam inside her cracked, and she let it out.

Zoe pulled back. "Whoa. Don't start crying or you'll make me cry and I can't have mascara running all down my face."

A quick laugh slipped out, and Raven wiped her eyes with her sleeve. "I'm fine."

"Yeah, sure. And I'm the Queen of England."

Raven laughed again, but her chest ached in that bittersweet way. For all of Zoe's sharp edges and chaotic energy, she was here. She always had been—through every heartbreak, every late-night phone call, and every moment Raven wanted to fall apart.

"Come on, let's get out of here before my mom cries too. I can't handle both of you sobbing while I'm trying to navigate Liberty Avenue."

Nina sniffled behind them. "I'm not crying. But don't tempt me."

They piled into the SUV, Zoe at the helm. Nina insisted Raven sit upfront. The drive through Pittsburgh was quiet for a Friday night.

"You know, I've been in a similar place as you Rae," Nina said.

"Here we go." Zoe rolled her eyes.

"What? I'm just saying I know what it's like to feel like everything is a mess."

Zoe groaned. "If this turns into one of those motivational speeches, just warn me so I can turn up the radio."

"Oh, shush." Nina swatted the air at Zoe.

Raven twisted in her seat to face Nina. "You mean with family?"

"Sure. But also with love. I almost sabotaged everything with Patrick. Didn't trust him. Or myself. But I got a second chance and took it. I told him the truth."

"What happened?" Raven said.

"I couldn't keep running. So, I told him I loved him. Scariest words I ever said. But he was scared, too."

Raven looked down at her ring, twisting it.

"Sometimes God shows you just enough of the path to get you curious. But you must take the next step, even if you can't see where it leads."

By the time they pulled up to her building, Raven felt lighter. Not whole. But grounded. Zoe stepped out and gave her a hug. She offered to stay, but Raven needed time alone.

The next morning, light spilled across her face. She blinked, caught between sleep and waking. For a moment, nothing. Then everything rushed back.

Her father. Not her father. Her mother. The truth—or something like it.

And Cole.

She wasn't ready to think about him yet. She pulled the blanket tighter around herself. An emptiness washed over her. She inhaled, and let it settle.

What would Gram say if she were here?

Had she kept this secret too? Or had she just believed the same lie Raven had?

A fresh ache twisted through her chest.

It didn't matter. Either way, Gram was gone, and Raven couldn't ask her. Couldn't sit at the kitchen table with her, listening to her wisdom that somehow made everything seem bearable.

Raven exhaled, pressing her palm against her chest as if she could calm the storm inside.

It wasn't gone.

But she wasn't shoving it down, either.

She let herself feel it.

After a little while, she stood and stretched, then walked to the kitchen to make coffee. Cole crept into her mind again. His voice, his steady eyes, the way he carried burdens he never revealed—it all lingered, pulling her back to every moment they'd shared the last few days.

And then the sting came back.

After she grabbed a cup, she walked to her desk. She couldn't let go of him. She shook her head, letting out a sharp breath.

Focus.

She plugged in the power cord and turned on her laptop. The chaotic sprawl of notes she'd typed yesterday stared back at her—raw and messy, but alive.

She skimmed the lines. Scattered thoughts became threads. Slivers of emotions wove themselves into ideas, blurring into something different.

Her fingers hovered over the keyboard. Then they moved.

The first sentence came slow, her breath catching as it appeared on the screen. Another followed. She'd never started without some kind of outline, but she didn't think about the words. They flowed out of her. Each keystroke pulled out bits of herself she hadn't dared touch in months. The messy notes transformed, becoming the bones of a backstory. A character took shape—not fully formed, but enough to move her fingers faster.

Loss. Resilience. Hope.

She poured it all out. The words seemed like they'd been waiting. Like they'd needed this moment to breathe. The kind of story she'd been afraid to write.

Until now.

Cole parked at the curb in front of Jeffrey Carter's house at 196 Woodward Avenue, Jersey City. The beige duplex looked silent on Jeffrey Carter's side. Curtains drawn. Driveway empty. A woman in galoshes tended a garden bed next door. Cole stepped onto the porch, scanned the window. No movement. The window slats looked dark. Empty.

The woman squinted while looking at him. "Can I help you?"

He gave a calm nod, hands in his jacket pockets. "Yes, ma'am. I'm looking for Jeffrey Carter."

The woman straightened, trowel in hand. "You're not one of those creeps selling fake roofing repairs and then robbing folks blind, are you? Because I'll have you know I've got pepper spray and a good aim."

"No, ma'am." He tugged out his dog tags. "Just here for someone who deserves answers."

Her expression softened, though she didn't let go of the trowel. "Jeff's a good man. Keeps to himself."

"Do you know when he'll be back?"

She studied him. "Far as I know, he was supposed to be back today. Heard him mention something about a flight, but I don't keep track of his schedule."

Cole nodded. Maybe he'd missed a flight.

"If you're lying, I'll call my son. He's an officer for the JCPD."

"That won't be necessary ma'am. Thank you for your help."

She muttered something about strangers as she turned back to her flowers.

Cole returned to his truck but didn't leave. He could've hit a hotel, found a gym, ran drills. But he needed to figure out his next move. He was running out of time.

Twelve days.

His final eval loomed. Twelve days to prove to the PEB he was still fit for duty.

And yet . . . here he was.

Not in Georgia. Not training. Not focused on what should be the only thing that mattered. Instead, parked across from the house of a man who'd walked away from his daughter and never looked back. His hands flexed on the wheel.

He should leave. Focus on the next twelve days. On his body and making sure the Army didn't cut him loose for good.

But, he stayed.

That night, he crashed in the cab. Stiff neck but decent sleep. Better than he'd had in weeks. The house stayed dark.

Day two, he returned from a gas station run with coffee and jerky, then parked again. Still, nothing at the house. No movement. No sign of life.

By midday, he pulled out the file he'd printed that morning at a nearby FedEx. Inside was everything Tick had uncovered—emails, old records, even a DNA match confirming what Raven had suspected all along.

But even with the proof, it wouldn't mean anything if he didn't get it in the hands of Jeffrey Carter.

As the second night settled in, Cole flipped open Preach's journal. Back to the same page and re-read the verse from Ephesians 2.

For by grace you have been saved through faith, and that not of yourselves; it is the gift of God, not of works, lest anyone should boast.

The words hit like a round straight to the vest. Preach had believed that with everything in him. That grace wasn't something to be earned. Maybe control wasn't the answer.

Cole exhaled, pressing his hand to his forehead. Control had kept him alive, kept his men alive. But maybe he had it wrong.

Cole bowed his head. "God, I don't know what I'm doing. Help me stop trying to earn what You already gave. Show me how to give it, too. Especially to Raven. In Jesus' name."

Morning of day three. Same routine. Coffee. Jerky. Patience. The hours stretched as he waited, neighborhood life passing by—a dog barking, a mail carrier making rounds.

Then, movement.

A blue SUV eased into the driveway. Cole straightened, watching as a man stepped out. Tall, broad shoulders, graying hair, just like in the photo Tick had sent.

Jeffrey Carter, Raven's father.

Cole grabbed the folder and stepped out. Mr. Carter walked up the porch steps, stopped at the door, and pulled out his key. Cole took the porch steps slow and measured. Jeffrey Carter might be a civilian now, but Cole knew a former soldier when he saw one. Even if thirty years had passed since he had served.

"Excuse me. Jeffrey Carter?"

Mr. Carter turned around, unhurried but sharp. "Who's asking?"

"Cole Walker. I need to talk to you . . . about your daughter."

A pause.

"I don't have a daughter." He turned.

Cole stepped forward. "Please. I'm not here for trouble, sir. I'm here for her."

Mr. Carter hesitated.

Through the cracked open door, a picture hung on the wall—a girl with dark hair and a grin Raven had never lost.

"Come inside."

Cole stepped into the modest living room.

Mr. Carter motioned toward the couch, but he remained standing, arms crossed over his chest. "Who are you and why are you here?"

"I'm a close friend of your daughter, Raven."

Mr. Carter didn't react.

Cole cleared his throat. "She's been wondering about you for a long time."

"Look, I don't know what you expect to get from me or how you found your way here. But I'm not her father."

Cole leaned forward, holding up the folder. "Yes, sir, you are. This is proof. The falsified paternity test, DNA match, and the records showing what her mother did."

Mr. Carter grabbed the folder and flipped it open. "How?"

"I have a friend that finds information."

Silence hung. Mr. Carter sat on the worn recliner opposite Cole. His eyes drifted past Cole to the picture of young Raven with her big brown eyes.

"I made many mistakes. But Margaret . . . I lost everything because of her."

Cole stayed quiet.

"That test." Mr. Carter's voice broke. "It killed me. Finding out she wasn't mine . . . but it didn't . . . I loved her anyway." He looked away, his hands clenched. "But after I saw that Margaret wouldn't stop. I didn't want to drag Raven into it. I thought it was better that way. That she deserved someone better." He dragged a hand down his face. "I knew. God help me, I knew in my heart. I should've tried harder. Especially after I got that letter from her. She was probably confused and—"

"Sir, she never wrote you any letters."

Tears welled in his eyes, but he blinked them back. "How is she?"

"Stronger than she knows. Brave. Stubborn."

"I don't know if I can face her." Mr. Carter swallowed.

"She deserves the truth, sir. Not later, not someday when you figure out whether or not you can handle it. She deserves it now."

A pause lingered between them. Mr. Carter's fingers tapped against the folder, his eyes dropping to the floor.

"I'll . . . think about it."

"With all due respect sir, don't let her suffer for your mistakes. She deserves the truth and should be given the choice of who she lets in her life." Cole stood. "I'm headed back to Elkwood, Pennsylvania. If you want to see her, you're welcome to ride with me."

He held out his hand for a shake. Mr. Carter stood and took it. Then he pulled Cole into a hug.

"Thank you." Mr. Carter pulled back.

Cole gave him a nod and pointed to the envelope. "Her address and phone number are in there. I won't push you, but I hope you'll use them."

Mr. Carter held the envelope like it was something fragile.

Cole paused at the door. "You don't have to have the perfect words, sir. Just be willing to show up."

Cole stepped outside, giving the man space to choose.

Should he say more? No. Raven wouldn't want him to force it. Cole had done what he could. The rest was up to Mr. Carter.

As he pulled away, he glanced at the house in the rearview mirror.

God, help him do the right thing.

CHAPTER 18

RAVEN LEANED BACK IN her chair, staring at the blinking cursor. *Chapter Four: Deprogramming Fear*, finished. She'd finally broken past the wall that kept her circling Chapter Three. And ironically, she had boundaries to thank for it.

Again, boundaries. Who knew they actually worked? Not that she'd planned on setting a boundary, it just kind of came out. And Jo respected it, with the exception of an email on Thursday at 6 a.m. about including a final monologue like in *The Lion King*. But for Jo, that was restraint.

If only Mom responded to boundaries that well.

Her eyes flicked to the clock. Almost 5 p.m.

Nine days since she'd last seen Cole. Nine days of silence. No calls. No messages beyond that one she couldn't bring herself to answer. But he lingered in the corners of her mind, sneaking into her day. She told herself it was for the best, that walking away had been the right call. But deep down, the words rang hollow.

She told herself it was better this way. But why did she keep glancing at his contact in her phone? Why had she driven by his house twice telling herself she was taking the long way home?

Even if she stopped, what would she say?

No, this was better. It had to be.

She tucked a loose strand of hair behind her ear and shut her laptop. She'd learned to be content with eating leftovers, hammering away at her half-formed story while ignoring Mom's passive-aggressive text messages.

Her phone buzzed on the desk.

Zoe: Can I swing by after work? I've got something for you.

Raven: Sure. What is it?

Zoe: You'll see.

Ten minutes later, the door swung open before Raven turned the handle. Zoe stood in her entryway, her face unusually serious.

"What's with the look?" Raven stepped back.

Zoe held a large yellow envelope. "Cole stopped by the shop today. He wanted me to give you this. Said he didn't want to overstep, but you needed to see it."

Raven stared at the envelope, her pulse racing. "What else did he say?"

"Nothing much." Zoe shrugged. She dropped onto the couch and folded her legs beneath her. "He's lucky I talked to him at all."

Raven took the envelope, hands shaking. She sat on the edge of the couch. Her thumb grazed the brass fastener.

"Well?" Zoe said.

With a breath, Raven opened it.

She pulled out a short stack of papers. The first page was a letter addressed to her. She unclipped it from the rest and read.

Raven,

I hope you're doing well. I've been thinking about you, about everything, and I wanted to say a few things. First, I'm sorry. For keeping the truth from you and for hurting you. I thought I was protecting you, but I see now that you were right. I was trying to protect myself. You deserve better. I also want to thank you for always being there for me, even when you didn't know it. Your words, your letters, your friendship, they pulled me through the hardest moments of my life. You gave me hope when I didn't have any left. I respect your need for space. If that's what you want, I won't push. But I wanted you to have the truth. You'll see in the paperwork here that the paternity test was a lie. Your father is J.C. Nevermore, just like you thought. He changed his name to Jeffrey Carter. His information is in there, along with the proof that Tick found. You finally have the answers you deserve.

Cole

Her hands trembled as she folded the letter back up.

"What did it say?" Zoe said.

"He . . . he's sorry. And that the paternity test was fake."

Zoe's eyes widened. "Wait, what? He found proof?"

Raven barely heard her. She sifted through the thin stack of papers and saw a DNA report. She skimmed the bolded lines. The room spun.

Zoe leaned in. "What is that?"

"It's . . . It's real." Raven's voice cracked. "He *is* my father."

Raven sank back into the couch. Her mind swirled. As she tucked the papers back into the envelope, something else caught her eye—another page, yellowed and worn. She carefully unfolded it.

It read:

When the clouds are gray and heavy,
And your heart feels cold and small,
Remember that the sun will shine,
Even after the rain will fall.
You're strong, you're brave, you're one of a kind,

A hero in every way.
So even when the dark feels close,
I know you'll find the day.
Don't forget, Cole, heroes never give up! You're my hero. Always.

–Rae

Tears blurred her vision. "He kept this? I can't believe it."

"What is it?" Zoe craned her neck.

Raven held it close to her chest. "It's something I gave him a long time ago. I wrote it after—" Her voice faltered, remembering when Emily had almost drowned. "He never told me he still had it."

"Let me get this straight. He found your dad and gave you this . . . and you're sitting here like a statue? What are you gonna do?"

Raven shook her head. "I don't know."

Zoe leaned back and crossed her arms. "Girl, if you think this man doesn't love you after that . . . I don't even know what to tell you. Do you know how many ex-boyfriends have kept anything I've given them? Zero. Zilch."

Raven laughed. It felt good to laugh, to feel something other than that twisting knot of confusion. Raven stared at the letter, the report, and the worn poem, feeling like the ground had shifted beneath her. Every ounce of logic in her brain screamed for her to keep that envelope buried in a drawer somewhere out of sight. But a soft voice in the back of her mind nagged at her to let it in.

To let *love* in.

Later that night, after Zoe left, Raven sat cross-legged on her bed, Cole's letter resting beside her. She stared at her Bible on the dresser. She thought of that woman on the train. And about what Nina said.

Sometimes God shows you just enough of the path to get you curious. But you must take the next step, even if you can't see where it leads.

Raven reached for the Bible and flipped through the pages until she found Psalm 16. She read, then stopped at verse 11.

> *You make known to me the path of life; in your presence there is fullness of joy; at your right hand are pleasures forevermore.*

Forevermore.

Tears slipped down Raven's cheeks as she pressed a hand to her mouth.

It wasn't just about her father, or Cole, or the pieces of herself she'd been trying to fit back together. Maybe God had wanted her to walk this path all along.

Maybe she didn't need all the answers to move forward.

Cole tightened his wrist wraps, exhaling hard as he eyed the barbell. One more set. He rolled out his shoulder, shook out his hands. Just like before. Like always.

He adjusted his grip and lifted. The bar dipped lower, muscles burning as he pressed it back up. He had it. He could still do this.

Halfway up, pain shot down his forearm. His right hand buckled.

"Got it." His spotter grabbed the bar and racked it.

Cole sat up fast, wiping sweat from his brow. His right hand trembled. He reached for his water bottle.

"Still fighting gravity, huh?"

Sergeant Hank Johnson walked over, arms crossed.

Cole smirked. "Hey sarge. Just a bad set."

Hank stepped closer. "That what you're planning to tell the PEB tomorrow?"

"I'll be ready."

"You sure?"

Cole stood and stretched out his shoulder. "Are you checking my form or here for a pep talk?"

Hank leaned against the rack. "Just wondering what you plan to do if this eval doesn't go your way."

"And what makes you think it won't?"

Hank gave him a knowing look.

Cole reached for the bar again. "Not looking past the uniform yet."

"Maybe you should. Got a buddy in South Carolina. Runs a program at the VA, and they're looking for counselors. Someone like you. Someone who's been in the fire and knows how to talk guys down."

Cole let out a humorless laugh. "I'm not the 'talk about your feelings' type, sarge."

"Yeah? How many guys have you kept from going under by letting them sound off?"

Cole shook his head. "Not interested."

"You've been keeping guys in the fight just by being the guy who listens." He clapped him once on the shoulder. "Don't throw it away, Doc."

Cole clenched his jaw. He wasn't throwing anything away. He was fighting for it. Even if it meant coming back to Columbus, Georgia. The place that was supposed to be home.

After Hank walked off, Cole grabbed his bag and left. He drove a few miles back to his apartment in Benning Park. As he walked inside the place, darkness swallowed him. Silence pressed in. He flipped on the light. Bare walls. A sagging couch. A kitchen counter cluttered with unopened mail and half-empty protein containers. The place was as lifeless as he felt—a holding cell between deployments.

He exhaled as he crossed the room. His duffel sat in the corner, half-packed. He swigged from his water bottle.

How many days had ended like this? Just him, a too-quiet apartment, and the ghosts in his head.

Too many.

This was never a home. It was a place where he slept and kept his gear. Temporary.

But Elkwood?

He pushed the thought away.

He passed the small bookshelf in the living room—the one with all the fragments of his old life. Deployment photos. Commendation letters. He pulled out a framed picture and ran his thumb over the glass. Him and Preach, arms slung over each other, grinning like they were invincible.

They *had* been invincible. Until they weren't.

A tightness coiled in his chest, spreading fast.

His pulse hammered.

His knuckles turned white on the frame as the edges of the photo blurred.

The room shrank.

His lungs stalled, caught between inhale and exhale. Not again.

Five things you can see.

The thought came unwilled. Raven's voice slipped through the static.

He forced his mind to focus. The framed picture in his hands. The old duffel by the door. The stack of unopened mail. The clock on the wall. The empty mug on the table.

He exhaled.

Four things you can hear.

The hum of the fridge. A car passing outside. The distant murmur of a TV in another apartment. His own heartbeat, slowing.

His fingers loosened on the frame. The tightness in his chest ebbed.

He didn't make it through the full list. Didn't need to. Not this time.

Raven's voice still echoed in his head.

Remind your body it's safe.

Safe.

He let out a breath and rubbed his hands over his face.

He set the picture down and reached for his old medical field guide. He flipped through the pages, stopping on a section about residual trauma in combat medics.

Prolonged nerve damage can cause loss of fine motor control, affecting grip strength and response time.

His jaw tightened.

Reflexes may diminish, leading to increased risk in high-stakes environments.

If he were the medic examining himself, would he clear himself for combat?

No.

The answer hit like a gut punch.

If another soldier walked into the barracks with the same issues—severe damage in his trigger hand, muscle weakness, irregular heart rhythm, flashbacks, delayed reflexes—Cole wouldn't just recommend leave or discharge, he'd fight for it. For the better of the soldier. Because that soldier wouldn't only be a liability. He'd get himself killed. Or worse, he'd get someone else killed.

He ran a hand down his face, exhaling hard.

What was he fighting for?

He'd spent so much time clinging to the Army, he never stopped to ask if he even wanted it anymore. And maybe that was why he couldn't stop thinking about Raven. She had seen it first.

Cole set the book on the table. He thought about what Hank had said.

You've been keeping guys in the fight just by being the guy who listens.

Maybe Hank was right. Maybe Cole wasn't done fighting.

But maybe it was time to fight for something else.

The clock ticked past 10 a.m. as Raven finished getting dressed for a quick grocery run. For two days, Cole's letter had burrowed into her mind. Maybe she was done with life-altering manila envelopes for a while.

Her phone buzzed.

Mom: I don't know what you and Gladys are trying to pull, but you won't win.

As if she knew half of it. Raven didn't want to put Mom out of the house, and still had no idea how she would tell her. Raven sighed, shoving her phone into her purse.

Tomorrow. She'll deal with it tomorrow.

Bigger things for today.

Like the truth about her father. The paternity test hadn't mattered as much as she'd thought. Sure, the proof that Jeffrey Cunningham, or Carter, was her father solidified a longing in her heart. But she'd loved him her entire life, and she'd continue to love him. Whether or not he wanted to see her was irrelevant. She'd go to him, at least to see him one last time. Even though it stung, the piece of her heart reserved for him held laughter and stories and memories that she'd clung to in hard moments. The love he'd shown her helped her recognize it in others. In Gram, Zoe, Nina . . . and Cole.

Cole had never made her feel like she was too much or not enough. He never flinched at her insecurities, never treated her like she was broken. He simply was there, a loyal, unwavering friend.

Friend.

Raven pulled her coat tight around her shoulders. That worn poem he had kept all these years. Silly words scrawled by a ten-year-old girl trying to make her best friend feel better. She hadn't thought about it. Yet, he had.

That realization pressed into her chest with quiet force. Cole hadn't just held onto the poem.

He held onto *her*.

Through every rejection, every betrayal, every moment she felt invisible or unwanted, Cole had been there in the background. No grand gestures. No empty promises. Just a quiet, steady presence.

And she'd been too blind to see it.

That heavy truth settled over her. Maybe him not saying I love you back didn't matter. Maybe it wasn't the worst thing. Maybe their friendship wasn't destroyed. But how could she trust him?

Raven closed her eyes for a moment, gripping the strap of her bag. The truth about her father mattered, yes. But what mattered more was seeing the people who had always loved her—the ones who never asked her to change, never abandoned her when things got messy.

And Cole had been at the center of that all along.

Time to stop running from it.

She slipped on her shoes and grabbed her keys. Right as she turned the doorknob, a knock startled her.

She froze. Cole? No, her neighbor. It had to be her neighbor. The woman forgot her keys at least once a week.

Raven swung the door open, her tone halfway teasing. "What'd you forget this—"

The words died on her lips.

A man stood there in a long brown peacoat. Lines on his face carved around his eyes and mouth, and a short grayish-brown beard framed his jaw. But it was his eyes—deep, dark brown and soft—that made Raven's heart drop.

Her breath caught. "Dad?"

CHAPTER 19

Raven stood in the doorway, staring at the man she hadn't seen since she was seven years old. Her father. She sucked in a sharp breath as she looked into his wide, glassy eyes. He smiled, faint and tentative. A worn leather satchel hung across his chest.

"Raven."

A flutter startled her at the sound of him saying her name. She'd imagined this moment so many times—what he would look like, what she would say, how she would feel. But now, all those thoughts scattered like dried leaves in the wind.

She cleared her throat. "Hi."

He stepped back as if to give her space. "I should've called first. I didn't mean to—"

"No, it's . . . it's okay." She swallowed hard, her grip tightening on the doorframe.

His smile wavered, and for a moment, he looked so much like the man in her faded memories. The man who twirled her around the living room and read her Dr. Seuss.

"I've thought about this moment every day for the past twenty-two years. And I told myself I'd be strong, but . . . I just—"

Before he could finish, Raven stepped forward and wrapped her arms around his neck. His arms closed around her, strong and desperate. He squeezed like he never wanted to let go. She melted into the embrace, tears spilling over and soaking into his shoulder.

"I've missed you so much, Little Bird." His voice cracked as he cradled her head with one hand. "I thought I was doing what was best for you. But I was wrong."

She invited him in. The silences stretched at first, awkward and unsure. But slowly, they faded. She made coffee, and they sat in the living room, two steaming mugs between them. For the first time, she could ask him about things that had haunted her for years. A dozen questions slushed forward, but where should she start?

Her fingers curled around her mug as she sank into the armchair. "Do you ever think about how different life would've been if you hadn't left?"

His lips pressed into a thin line.

She winced. "Okay, wow. That was blunt. Sorry."

He huffed out a soft laugh. "No, it sounded honest. You have every right to ask me whatever you want."

She nodded, but as she searched for the right words, something sharp and old and unshakable rose to the surface. Never seeing him again after that last fight with Mom. Never knowing if he'd fought for her at all. And the sting of second grade. The way she'd beamed with pride, telling the class her dad was an author—only to hear the snickers, the whispers.

Daddy-Daydream.

She could still hear it. The way they'd sung it like a taunt, like she'd made him up. Like she was the foolish little girl who clung to a ghost.

And maybe, in a way, she had been.

"If you loved me . . . why didn't you ever come back?"

He hesitated, rubbing a hand over his jaw.

"I waited for years but got nothing." She looked at him—the man she'd spent a lifetime wondering about.

He didn't answer right away. Instead, he reached into his bag and pulled out a bundle of envelopes, worn and rubber-banded together. He handed them to her.

"What's this?" She kept her voice even, but her hands trembled as she took them.

"These are yours."

She stared at the stack. Torn edges. Yellowed corners. Some crisp, unopened.

Her breath caught. Her name was on them in his handwriting. She removed the rubber bands.

"You sent these?"

"I tried."

The top envelope had "Return to sender" written in bright blue ink.

"I never knew," she said.

His jaw flexed. "I know."

The air thickened, pressing on her.

He leaned forward, his voice low. "I wrote you for years. Birthdays, Christmas, random Tuesdays when I missed you. I kept trying."

She blinked back tears, staring at the letters. The proof of him, of the validation she never received. She flipped through them and noticed one addressed to him. The paper felt different. She flipped it over and—

Her blood ran cold.

It was from *her*. Only, she never wrote it.

Her fingers trembled as she pulled out the letter and scanned the lines. The handwriting was messy, cold, short. The first sentence said:

Please stop writing. I don't want to hear from you.

Her voice trembled. "I didn't write this."

He nodded. "I know that now."

Tears blurred her vision as her grip tightened. "My mother did this. She stole you from me."

He rested his hand on her back.

She clung to the letter. Her mind spun, trying to reconcile what she had believed her entire life with the truth now sitting in front of her. "I don't understand."

"I sent child support every month. Like clockwork. I never stopped. I wanted to make sure you were taken care of. But then she pushed for more. Not legally—just pressuring me. And I pushed back, saying I wanted partial custody. That's when she insisted on the paternity test. I didn't realize what she was doing until I heard from my publisher."

"Your publisher?"

"She told them I was a deadbeat dad, that I was refusing to support you. That they should cut my contract, or she'd go to the press. All while she was cashing the checks."

Raven covered her mouth with her hand. But she wasn't surprised.

"That's when it hit me. She wasn't just angry, she was playing me. She figured I'd pay her off to keep her quiet." His voice dropped. "I confronted her. Told her I was done playing games. That I'd take her to court if I had to. Then she pulled the paternity test."

Raven stared at him, trying to piece it together. "You believed her?"

"I didn't know what to believe. But I kept writing. I couldn't let you go. I hoped you'd find the stories. You loved mysteries, and I had to get to you somehow."

Something still and fragile hovered between them. A lump formed in her throat. She glanced toward her bookshelf at the entire Shadows of Hawthorn series she'd read countless times. His books. His words had found a way to weave into her life. And now, for the first time, she wondered if she had spent her whole life chasing clues about him without realizing it. She wanted to be angry, but she believed him.

She wiped her eyes. "I did get one of your letters. Gram saved it. Left it for me after she passed."

He looked at her with something close to awe.

"I don't know why she didn't give it to me sooner, but after I read it, I started digging. Linked the dedications to your signature in the letter." Then it hit her.

Her father showed up *here*. Not the other way around.

"Did you know I was looking for you? How did you find me?"

"When your friend came by the house, he—"

"My friend?"

"I was skeptical at first. Then Cole told me about you two going on this trip, how you got my letter and connected the dots to J.C. Nevermore. I knew you'd figure it out, someday. You were always so clever, and sharp as a tack."

She squinted, trying to process what he had said.

Cole went to see him?

His brows came together. "Wait . . . you didn't know?"

No. She absolutely had *not* known.

Her father exhaled, shaking his head. "I thought you knew all of this. The way Cole talked, I thought he had told you."

"I didn't know he came to see you." Why would he go there? And why didn't he tell her in his note?

"You didn't know but you still opened your door to me?"

"Well, to be fair I thought you were my neighbor." She flashed a half smile. "But what should I have done, slammed it in your face?"

"I wouldn't have blamed you if you did. There have been a lot of misunderstandings over the years, and it tore me apart not to be in your life. I made so many mistakes. And you have every reason to shut me out. But here you are, with open arms." His thumb and forefinger dug into the corners of his eyes.

She nodded, emotion catching in her throat. "I buried every good memory after you left. It was too hard to keep you alive in my life when it felt like you had died, and part of me died, too. But then Gram died. And your words ignited that part of me. When I thought you weren't my biological father, it devastated me. But even then, I realized it didn't matter. I couldn't let others steal my joy any longer. You're the only father I've ever known, other than God. And I love you, Dad."

Dad. The word trembled on her lips, strange and unfamiliar—but it felt right.

He moved to the edge of the couch and put his hands on hers. "I love you too."

For a moment, they sat like that, father and daughter reunited after years lost. Her heart felt full and fractured all at once.

With a shaky breath, he straightened his posture. "I can't believe how grown-up you are. All the birthdays I've missed, and I don't have anything to give you."

She let out a short chuckle. "What did you want to show up with, balloons and a cake?"

"No. But, I thought about wearing a T-shirt that says 'World's Okayest Dad.'"

She laughed, wiping her eyes. "That would've broken the ice."

He sipped his coffee. "Seems like Cole cares about you."

"Yeah, we've been friends for a long time."

"Friends, huh? He tracked me down. Nearly chewed me out. Then told me you deserved the choice to know me after learning the truth."

She stared at her cup, heart skipping. "That's just Cole. He's . . . protective."

"Protective." He crossed one leg over the other and leaned back. "He made me see that I couldn't keep running from this. That man's got guts and I respect that. He even offered to drive me here himself."

She let out a breath, trying not to focus on the way her heart leapt at every mention of Cole.

Later that evening, Dad left to check into a nearby hotel. Raven sat on the couch, staring at her phone. She'd just spent an hour updating Zoe, replaying every detail of one of the best moments of her life. Zoe had to jump off to take care of a customer. But now, one thought refused to yield.

Cole did this. He put the pieces together. He brought her father back into her life.

And she'd pushed him away. She dragged her hands through her hair, fingers gripping at the roots.

Her phone buzzed and she answered.

"Sorry, that took a minute. But you will not believe what just happened." Zoe laughed. "This guy came in asking if we have books on pet psychic readings. I told him I can predict that his cat is judging him."

Raven's mind spun. She wasn't sure why she hadn't said it out loud earlier.

"It was Cole."

"Huh?" Zoe said.

"Cole went to my dad. He's the reason all this happened."

Everything clicked into place all at once.

"Okay . . . you told me that already. He's earned some points back for sure."

Raven shot to her feet. "I gotta go. I have to see him."

"Yes! Run. I'll be on standby if you need me."

Raven grabbed her coat and keys. The path became clear. Clearer than anything in her life. The weight of it settled heavy and impossible to ignore.

She bolted for the door, then paused at the mirror in her entryway.

At Your right hand are pleasures forevermore.

Forevermore. That one word had guided this entire journey. A word from her heavenly Father, taking her on a path without her realizing it. This time, there wasn't silence. Instead, a quiet peace.

A tingling sensation came over her. God *had* been with her. Even when she'd thought He'd abandoned her, too.

"Alright. If this is what You want, let's go. Please guide me, Jesus."

She rushed out the door.

Stars sparkled above as she started the car.

Her mind raced.

What if she was too late?

That wasn't the point. Cole had shown her what love looked like. Real, messy, sacrificial love.

And she had to tell him how much it meant to her.

How much *he* means to her.

After speeding through the twists and turns of Silver Creek Lane, Raven parked outside the Walker house, heart pounding. She didn't see his truck. Maybe she could wait. She got out of the car and walked toward the back porch.

Now she felt stupid. What was she doing?

Just as her foot hit the top step, the door opened.

Emily poked her head out, a blanket draped over her tiny frame. "Raven?"

"Uh, hi." Her palms sweat despite the thirty-degree weather.

"Do you want to come in?"

Raven hesitated, then stepped inside. Emily motioned her to sit on the couch, but Raven stood, fidgeting with her coat. "I don't mean to barge in like this."

"You're not barging. You're always welcome here." Emily leaned against the doorway to the kitchen, pulling the blanket together at her chest. "I'm guessing you're here to see Cole."

Raven nodded.

"I'm sorry, but he went back to Georgia. Said he had something to take care of."

Back to Georgia?

Her stomach dropped. No—He said his final evaluation was coming up—that had to be it.

If he passed . . . if they reinstated him . . .

"When did he leave?"

"Two days ago, I think. He didn't say much before he left," Emily said.

Two days ago? That had to be after he'd dropped off the envelope to Zoe.

Raven thanked her and left.

Back home, she stared at her phone. She tapped on Cole's name and called, but got voicemail. She closed her eyes as that impersonal pre-recorded message filled her ears.

She hung up before the beep.

That was it, then.

She'd waited too long.

Sliding to the floor from the edge of her bed, she pressed her hands to her face.

Cole was gone. And she didn't know if he was ever coming back.

The evaluation had gone as well as Cole could've hoped. No fight. No last-ditch effort to prove he was still a soldier. He'd walked in, answered their questions, and when the discharge papers were handed to him, he signed. It was time. Time to stop gripping the past so tightly and to finally trust God with what came next.

Now, as Cole pulled into the driveway, the familiar white bag of Primanti Bros. sat in the passenger seat. If anything said "home," it was the smell of fries and cheesesteak filling the cab of his truck.

He cut the engine, grabbed the bag, and headed toward the house. The motion light flicked on before he reached the steps.

Emily's eyes widened when he opened the door. "You're back?"

Cole smirked, lifting the bag. "Got hungry."

Emily folded her arms. "You drove all the way from Georgia because you got hungry?"

He brushed past her and set the food on the counter. "They don't have Primanti's down there."

"I thought you had to get back to work. What's going on?"

"I don't want to get into it right now. Just, want to eat my sandwich in peace. Deal?"

Cole opened the cupboard and grabbed a plate. He unwrapped the sandwich.

She turned to face the TV. "Raven was here."

He stopped mid bite. "When?"

"She came over hours ago."

"Why didn't you call me?"

Emily raised her eyebrows. "I tried, but it went straight to voicemail. Plus, you said you were going back to Georgia. How was I supposed to know you weren't staying?"

Cole pushed a hand through his hair, already moving back toward the door.

"She looked like she had something to say, like she was upset," Emily said.

That was all he needed to hear.

He grabbed his keys.

"Where are you going?"

Cole shot her a look.

She smirked. "Does that mean I can have your sandwich?"

He was already half out the door.

The drive to Raven's place passed in a blur. His chest ached with each mile.

What had happened? Had he made things worse? Was it her dad?

When he pulled up outside her apartment, he paused, eyeing the soft glow in her window. 10:43 p.m. She was still up.

He climbed out and knocked, heart pounding.

Raven opened the door wearing his old Army PT sweatshirt. Her hair tied up in a messy bun and her eyes looked red and puffy. Those beautiful eyes. She stared at him, unreadable, one hand gripping the door like she might slam it shut any second.

Oh, he needed to hold her. Tell her.

"Cole?" She stood in the doorway and wiped her eyes with her sleeve.

He swallowed.

Raven stepped back, holding the door open. "What are you doing here? I thought you left for Georgia."

"I did. But I'm back."

"Back? They didn't honor the appeal?"

He hesitated. "I accepted the discharge."

Her lips parted, but she said nothing.

"I could've fought it. Pushed for the appeal. But I realized I was fighting for the wrong thing. It was time to let go."

She didn't move.

"I've spent my adult life as a soldier. It's all I know. But maybe it's not all I have to be. Turns out, I enjoy helping guys get back on track. Hank mentioned something about counseling, but who knows?"

A flicker of something passed through her eyes. Hope, maybe. He'd wished she said something. Anything.

"So, I thought I'd look into what's available here. In Pittsburgh."

Silence. The kind that stretched a little too long.

"Of course," Raven said. "Of course, you come back here, all calm, dropping life-altering decisions like it's no big deal."

This was not how he pictured this going.

"No. I can't do this." She yanked her hair tie free as she stepped inside her apartment. He followed behind her and closed the door.

She spun to face him. "You went to my dad. Fixed something I didn't know needed fixing. You do things like that, and . . ."

"Rae, I'm sorry—"

She grabbed her hair with both hands. "I love you, okay?"

His world stopped.

She groaned, throwing her hands up. "You make it impossible not to! You drive me insane with all your noble, self-sacrificing, emotionally stunted Army medic vibe. I told you once, and you ran. And now you're here, on my doorstep, and I have no idea what you want. But I need you to know. I can't help it. I love you more than a friend, and I know that sounds super high-school, but it's true. And there it is."

Her voice trembled, but she stood her ground.

And that was enough.

He stepped forward, grabbed her face, and kissed her.

Not slow. Not gentle. Just real. Raw. Everything he'd been afraid to say poured out in that one moment.

For a second, he thought she'd push him away. But she pulled him closer. Her soft lips felt as if they'd been made just for him. All the noise in his head fell silent with her in his arms—like everything had finally clicked into place.

She pulled back, breath shaky.

"I love you, Rae. I knew it from the first time I saw you in those ridiculous yellow shoes. That's why it never worked with Sofia, or anyone else for that matter. Because deep down it was always you. I'm sorry it's taken me so long to say it."

She grabbed his jacket, yanked him down, and kissed him again.

Time slowed. She held onto him. A tremor ran through her fingers, matching the one in his chest. It wrecked him and put him back together all at once.

He pulled her closer. She fit like she'd been his missing piece, and he hadn't even known until now. Pressed against him, she silenced every scar and every shadow he'd carried.

When they finally broke apart, she rested her forehead against his, breath warm against his skin. Neither of them moved.

"If you ghost me again, I'm going to hunt you down." She smiled.

He tightened his arms around her. "I'm not going anywhere."

CHAPTER 20

RAVEN STOOD AT THE sink, rinsing out her coffee mug as sunlight filtered through the thin curtains. She'd slept more than four hours last night for the first time in months. The morning felt quieter than usual, like the world was holding its breath.

She couldn't stop thinking about the way Cole had kissed her—the warmth of his hands, the honesty in his voice.

I love you, Rae.

The confession had torn through her, leaving something raw in its place. Vulnerability had scared her, but with him she'd felt seen. Loving Cole felt as natural as breathing, but the fear of things going wrong started creeping in.

What if he ran again? What if she wasn't enough for him?

Her mug slipped, clanging against the sink. Water splashed up her arms. She winced, reaching for a towel.

She wished Gram were here.

Gram would be stitching in her chair with morning news in the background saying something like, "Finally, you two came to your senses."

Tears pricked Raven's eyes, but she welcomed them. Something made her feel like Gram was close, and she didn't want to shut her out by pushing down every feeling. That hadn't worked for most of Raven's life. Those feelings resurfaced in worse ways. Today, she chose to embrace them.

She walked into her room and pulled on a cream chenille sweater for work. It paired well with her favorite jeans. She glanced at her Bible sitting on the dresser, still open to Psalm 16.

Fullness of joy.

That was what she felt. But not because two decades of feelings had surfaced. Or because her father was in her life again. But that God *had* been with her, even when she'd doubted and pushed Him away.

"Thank you, Father, for not leaving me. For guiding me and blessing me."

Tears pricked again, but she wiped them free.

She walked back into the kitchen and shut off the coffee pot just as a knock sounded at the door. Zoe wasn't up this early, and Cole had already texted from the gym. Curious, she peeked through the peephole.

Her stomach dropped.

Mom.

Raven opened the door. Mom stood there, face tight and arms folded.

"Hi Mom. Is everything okay?"

"Don't play innocent." She pushed past Raven inside. "I just got off the phone with some lawyer named Whitaker who says we have no standing in the probate case. That the house was already transferred."

Raven shut the door calmly behind her.

Mom turned around. "Did you know about this? You knew and said nothing while I was working to get things moving, didn't you?"

"By getting things moving do you mean Tim filing a delay motion claiming Gram wasn't of sound mind when she wrote the will?" Raven kept her voice calm and unshakable.

"She wasn't well. That senile old bag!"

"You know that's not true. But that doesn't matter to you, does it. All you want is the money. You couldn't care less who you hurt in the process."

Mom paced in a tight circle. "This is unbelievable. After everything I've dealt with, I'm being boxed out of my house by my own daughter."

"It's not your house."

Mom whirled around, eyes blazing. "Excuse me?"

"Gram left it to *me*. Because she knew I would protect it. Protect her memory. Not sell it for a quick payout."

"This is outrageous. You think because—"

"I'm not doing this with you." Raven straightened her spine. "The house is mine. Legally. And I'm not selling it."

Mom scoffed. "Are you going to kick out your own mother?"

"No, of course not. But here's what's going to happen." Raven kept her tone even, though her stomach churned. "You're not going to push me around anymore. If you try to challenge the will, I'll take you to court. And if you tamper with anything on the property, I'll press charges."

Mom's eyes widened.

"I didn't want this fight," Raven kept her voice low. "But I'm not afraid of it."

Silence sharpened around them.

"You'll regret this." Mom charged toward the door, slamming it behind her.

Raven exhaled a huge breath. For the first time, her mother's words didn't crush her. They didn't burrow under her skin or twist into self-doubt.

They meant nothing.

And that felt like freedom. It was her house. Her life.

Raven knew this was not the last of Mom's antics. But she'd face whatever came next head-on. She wasn't that scared little girl anymore.

And she never would be again.

The hum of fluorescent lights filled the small office. Cole kept his posture straight and his hands rested on his lap waiting. He adjusted the cuffs of his dark green service jacket, the brass buttons catching the light. The uniform felt strange now, but he'd manage.

The woman across the desk studied his paperwork, brow furrowed. She looked up, her glasses slipping down her nose.

"Sergeant Walker, I have to say, your experience is impressive. Ten years, five tours, and senior combat medic training—most people don't walk in here with a résumé like that."

"Thank you, ma'am."

She set the papers down and folded her hands. "Sergeant Johnson spoke highly of you in his recommendation. Said you're dependable and level-headed. Someone who gets the job done. That's the kind of person we need."

The mention of Hank stirred gratitude. But it also made Cole wonder if Hank had oversold him.

"This position is a significant change from combat," the woman said. "Helping veterans transition, guiding them through civilian life. It's meaningful work, but not easy. Are you ready for that?"

The weight of the question settled over him like lead. Was he?

He thought of the countless nights wrestling with his own pain, the way he'd pushed through for others with barely anything left to give.

"I know what it's like to feel lost. To need someone to tell you it's okay to take a step forward, even when everything in you says it's not. If I can be that person for someone else . . ." He paused. "Then it's worth it."

She nodded, seemingly satisfied with his answer. She glanced at his file and tapped a pen against the folder.

"One more thing. You mentioned you've been in counseling. Do you think that affects your ability to take this on?"

Cole hadn't hidden it, but he also hadn't expected it to come up.

He drew in a breath. "It doesn't affect my ability to do the job. But I'd be lying if I said I had it all figured out. I still have work to do."

She waited. Patient. Expectant.

He swallowed hard. "Maybe that's a good thing."

For a second, something flickered in her expression. Approval, maybe. Hard to tell.

"It is." She closed the file. "We'll be in touch soon."

He stood and shook her hand.

Cole stepped out into the cool, city air, his shoulders tight. He walked down a maze of stairwells to level 4 of the parking garage.

The interview had gone well. Better than he expected. But how could he help others face their pain when he was still walking into therapy rooms trying not to break?

Was this the next step? Even if it wasn't, he needed to move forward.

He reached his truck and leaned against the side, his breath fogging into the air. Preach's journal came to mind. One word echoed louder than the rest.

Grace.

Could grace be for him?

He closed his eyes. Memories flashed—blood, smoke, the stillness of death. His fears. The things he'd seen . . . and wished he hadn't. He carried it all. Every failure. Every horror. Like it was his to bear alone.

Could grace cover that?

Maybe it already had.

He'd spent his life trying to fix things, to be strong enough, fast enough, smart enough to keep people alive. But he had limits. And he could either keep pretending he had control over the things that haunted him, or he could let go. He'd never know unless he kept surrendering.

Not just once or in desperate moments. Every day. Every step.

He wasn't fixed, by any means. But lighter. Maybe that was grace. Not a clean slate. But a strength that held him up when his own failed. Maybe that ache he couldn't name wasn't just pain, it was mercy, rewriting the wreckage one breath at a time.

Not erasing it. But walking with him through it.

Cole climbed into the truck. A strange calm came over him.

Time to see the woman he loved.

Cole stopped home to change out of his greens. He ran downstairs, stomach growling at the smell of Mom's chili. He sent a quick text to Hank, thanking him for the recommendation. When he looked up, both his sister and Mom were staring at him, arms crossed.

"Who were you texting?" Emily said.

"None of your business." He tucked the phone into his pocket. "Hey Mom, I don't need a bowl. I'm going out."

"Oh my gosh. It was Raven wasn't it." Emily clapped her hands. "You're taking her out on a date, aren't you? Please tell me it's not another one of those 'we're just two pals enjoying dinner' things."

He smirked.

"Whatever. I'll call her myself. Don't worry Mom. I'll fill you in, too." Emily pointed a piece of her breadstick at him. "Don't screw this up."

Mom stirred the chili. "Emily, enough with the commentary." Then she turned to Cole, her expression shifting to something softer but no less serious. "If this is a date, you open doors. Be respectful. Compliment her hair. Be a gentleman."

"I always am." He kissed her cheek.

"Your strength holding up? Any chest pain?"

"I'm fine."

She raised an eyebrow. "Grip?"

He flexed his hand in response.

She nodded. "Glad to see you made a move. Raven's a good one."

He hesitated at the door, her words lingering. Then he shook his head, smiling as he left.

Cole pulled into the Stop n' Shop on his way to Raven's apartment. He went straight to the floral section. No hesitation. He already knew what he was looking for—sunflowers.

On the drive to Raven's, Cole thought about the many times his family had thrown out advice he didn't need. But Mom was right. And being with Raven was something he hadn't deserved. Something that God had made possible, despite his numerous mistakes.

He had cared about her for a long time, but this? This was different. The kind of different that could either light up his world or shake it to the core. Maybe both. And he'd take it, as long as she stood next to him.

He parked in front of her apartment, grabbed the sunflowers, and knocked. The door swung open, and there she was—hair down, soft waves brushing her shoulders, somehow looking more beautiful than ever.

"You ready for some ribs?" He held out the flowers. "This time without forks."

A smile tugged at her lips as she looked at the flowers. "Are these for me?"

"Nah, they're for your neighbor. Thought I'd start building goodwill."

Raven laughed, the sound sinking into him.

"What she needs is an extra set of keys, but I'm sure these will brighten her day." She smelled the bouquet. "Sunflowers. My favorite."

He offered his hand. "Shall we?"

She slipped her hand into his, and they walked to the truck.

He opened the passenger door. "After you."

She turned, her eyes catching the glow of the dashboard light. "So . . . is this an official date?"

Cole grinned. "Depends. If it is, do I have to make a reservation and wear cologne?"

She tilted her head. "Might not hurt."

He chuckled, shaking his head. "Not sure I can handle the pressure."

"Sunflowers earned you points. But I don't know, Walker, you might have to step up your game."

Without thinking, he leaned in, fingers grazing her cheek as he kissed her. When he pulled back, her eyes stayed closed for a second longer.

"That a good start?"

She opened her eyes and smiled. "Definitely a good start."

CHAPTER 21

November 4th

30th Birthday Reflections

The last few weeks have been surreal. In moments of stillness, gratitude overflows like a river breaking free of its banks. One month ago, I was sure I'd be alone forever. Not just because of my past, but because I believed I wasn't worth fighting for. But God saw me differently. He kept His promise. He never left me, guiding me step by step on the path to a new life. A life full of hope and joy I never saw coming. And along that path He led me to love—from my best friend.

Cole's deep laugh echoes in my mind as I write this. We're taking it slow, savoring the moments. But I want to kiss him all the time. He's lighter now, like he's finally letting go of the weight he carried for years. We used to find ways to laugh through the hard things, like my mom's chaos and Emily's hospital stays. It was how we survived. But that friendship anchored us. It still does. I love the amazing man he is and the one he's becoming. And he loves me. He sees me, really sees me, and loves every part.

What surprises me most is that we're still us. Still laughing, still leaning on each other. Only now there's something deeper, steadier. The kind of love that makes me believe in forevermore. The one God made possible. Tonight isn't just about celebrating my birthday.

It's about celebrating the hope I'd thought was lost, the love I never expected, and the life I'm finally stepping into.

Raven closed her journal and slid her pen into the side pocket. She glanced at her phone.

"Oh my gosh, it's already eight o'clock."

She grabbed her coat and smoothed down the silky fabric of her red dress. The airy material sparkled when the light hit it a certain way, and it flowed perfectly for twirling on the dance floor. Something a little fancier tonight for a change.

Her heart fluttered as she heard Cole's truck. She made a quick stop at the mirror, adjusting her scarf before opening the door. There he stood, tall and dapper as ever in his black peacoat, steel-toed boots, and dark jeans. A faint whiff of his cologne made her pulse quicken. That mix of sandalwood and mahogany was her kryptonite every single time.

"You ready, birthday girl? Wow."

"Wow good or wow like too much sparkle?"

"Definitely wow good." He stepped back, his eyes giving her that slow once-over that sent heat rushing to her face. "Like, I might need a minute to remember how breathing works good."

"Oh, you're laying it on thick tonight." She stepped toward him.

He leaned down, giving her a quick kiss. "Happy birthday."

The words rippled low and velvety against her lips, sending little sparks down her spine. He pulled her closer.

For a moment the teasing smile on his face vanished, replaced by something more sincere. A look that told her she wasn't the only one who thought this love was nothing short of a miracle. She cleared her throat and looked away. She still hadn't quite learned how to react when he'd looked at her that way.

"Well, if we stand here any longer, I'm going to freeze to death in this dress. And you're going to have to carry a sparkly popsicle to dinner."

He chuckled as he escorted her to the truck and opened the door for her. "I don't know, I think you could pull off being a popsicle. Red's your color."

She climbed into the truck, making sure not to snag her dress on her way up. Cole closed the door with that quiet confidence he carried about him.

He climbed into the driver's seat, then stopped to look at her. "Alright, I have to make a quick stop first." He flexed his right hand into a fist, then opened it, as if it had fallen asleep.

"Are you okay?"

"Yeah, it'll pass." He grabbed her hand and kissed it.

As he drove into town, he reached over to hold her hand. They pulled onto Main Street. Instead of heading to Luigi's, Cole turned toward the town center. Ten minutes later, he parked in the lot near the bookshop.

He hopped out and rounded the truck to open her door. "C'mon."

Where were they going?

Raven adjusted the scarf around her neck, her breath curling into the crisp air as she stepped down from the truck. Elkwood's town center had already started dressing itself up for Christmas—twinkling lights wrapped around lamp posts, red bows adorning storefront windows. She looked up, her focus lingering on the clear, starry sky. She glanced at Cole as he joined her on the sidewalk, her gloved hand slipping into his.

She turned to face him. "What are we doing here? I thought we were going to Luigi's."

"You'll see. Just trust me."

"Trusting you is a pretty big ask." She winked.

They stepped into the bookshop—and a chorus of voices rang out.

"Surprise!"

Raven froze, her mouth dropping open. Zoe and Nina held a tray of cupcakes with sparklers while Zoe's dad Patrick towered behind them. Cole's parents, Emily, and Emily's boyfriend waved from a table stacked with gifts. And, at the center of it all, stood her dad, arms open wide.

"Happy birthday, Little Bird." His glassy eyes softened, and she dove into his embrace.

Tears welled in her eyes. "I thought you had a conference in New Orleans."

"I couldn't miss this." Dad kissed her cheek and stepped back.

She wiped her eyes with a small napkin. "How did you all do this?"

"Cole planned it." Zoe walked up and put her arm around Raven. "*We* made it amazing." Zoe let go and walked to the refreshment table.

Raven faced Cole. "You did this?"

"Figured it'd be nice to celebrate with your family."

She blinked back more tears and reached for his hand, giving it a squeeze. "Thank you."

Gratitude swelled in her chest, thick and unexpected.

Behind them, Zoe clinked her glass to catch attention. "Rae! Tell everyone about the editor thing."

Raven's eyes widened as heat crept up her cheeks. "It's not that big of a deal."

"I knew she'd say that." Zoe shot a grin at Nina. "Didn't I tell you she'd say that?" She raised her glass. "Okay, then it's up to me. I'm going to make a toast to my best friend on her thirtieth birthday who has just talked with an editor at Random House.

And—plot twist—the editor wants Raven to send a proposal for her new story idea. P.S., thanks, Mom, for the connection."

A round of cheers and applause broke out. Raven smiled through her blush. Dad beamed like his heart might burst, eyes misty.

"I talked to her about the story I've been working on," Raven said. "She said they're interested in a proposal. But only if I get it to her by next week. No pressure."

Cole laced his fingers through hers. He gave her hand a gentle squeeze.

Zoe tapped her glass with a fork. "Okay, now for the good stuff. Raven, you are the best, most thoughtful, capable person I know. You haven't had it easy. But your strength inspires me, and I think I can speak for everyone in this room when I say that you make all of our lives better just by being you. So, here's to you, our favorite bookworm and soon to be bestselling author. I hope all your dreams come true. I love you."

Raven's heart thudded, soft and full. For once, she didn't shrink from the attention—she let Zoe's words wrap around her like warmth.

Tears pooled in Zoe's eyes. "Okay, okay, I'm getting all mushy now. And if you don't send that proposal, I *will* lock you in a room with coffee until you do. That's how much I believe in you. Cheers!"

"Cheers!" everyone echoed, glasses clinking around the room.

Raven laughed, swiping her own tears away. "Thanks Zo. I love you, too."

After they ate the most amazing chicken parmesan and shared many laughs, Raven stood near the window, watching the streetlights glow against the quiet night. She folded her arms against her chest, her heart both full and aching.

Behind her, Cole's parents were deep in conversation with Nina and Dad. Across the room, Zoe and Emily danced barefoot to an Anne Wilson tune while nibbling on second helpings of dessert, laughter spilling between them like music of its own.

It was everything she never thought she'd have—people, warmth, home. And still, part of her felt like it was missing.

"You okay?" Cole came up behind her.

"I'm thinking about Gram. She would've loved this."

He stepped closer, wrapping an arm around her shoulders. "She's here in spirit. And I know she's proud of you."

A tear slipped down her cheek. "I miss her. Especially now, when things feel . . . hopeful again."

She leaned into him, her head resting against his shoulder. He kissed her head.

The room buzzed around them with laughter, the clink of glasses, and the low hum of country music. But for Raven, it had all blurred into a distant hum. All she could see was Cole. The warmth of the moment spread through her chest.

She turned to face him. "When I'm with you . . . I feel like I can do anything."

He pulled her closer. "You don't need me to be brave. That's all you. But if being with me helps you finally see how extraordinary you are . . . then I'll spend forever reminding you."

She cupped his face. "I love you."

"I love you, too."

He leaned down and pressed his lips to hers in one gentle, grand movement. Soft and sure, the kiss sent shivers down her spine, even amidst the whistling and cheers behind them.

For the first time in her life, Raven felt whole. Like she belonged right where she stood. God had taken her on this path, and a whisper in her heart reassured that wherever the road ahead might lead, she could have pleasures, forevermore.

FREE GIFT

If this story touched your heart and you're ready for more in the Renewed Hearts Series don't miss Nina's story—download the exclusive free novella now! Just scan the QR code below to get your free ebook.

Love in Pages reveals the story behind Nina's resilience and the love that changes her future.

LETTER TO THE READER

Thank you so much for reading this story! I hope you could escape into an entertaining (and maybe emotional but in a good way) experience that reflects God's love. If you enjoyed the story, would you mind doing me one favor? Head to the product page and leave an honest review. Just a few words to let others know how the story made you feel. But please keep it spoiler-free so everyone can enjoy the full ride.

When reading about Raven and Cole's struggles, did something tug at your heart? Do you often feel like you're too broken to love, or too far gone to experience God's grace?

These characters may be fictional, but they're drawn from real struggles that we face in this world. Brokenness, abuse, rejection, abandonment, guilt, shame, fear, loneliness, and feeling not worthy of God's love.

I've struggled with that most of my life . . . not feeling good enough to pray to Jesus because of the horrific mistakes I've made. I remember being in my twenties, living carelessly and keeping Jesus on the sidelines. I had a red-letter Bible stuffed into a drawer. One day when I finally opened it, I fell to my knees reading Jesus' words, bawling because I didn't feel worthy to keep going.

I spent years believing I wasn't good enough for Jesus, buried under shame. Convinced my mistakes disqualified me from grace.

But that's the lie Satan wants us to believe, because if we're looking at our failures, we're not looking at God.

The truth? None of us are worthy, but Jesus saved us anyway. Not because we cleaned ourselves up first, but because we couldn't.

Jesus, fully God and fully Man, lived a sinless life, died in our place, and rose again to break every chain—shame, guilt, fear, addiction, abandonment—you name it. Whatever you're carrying, He already defeated it at the cross. You can trust Him to take that burden from you. Asking for His help doesn't have to be pretty, just real. Honest and raw.

If you've ever felt too broken or that grace isn't for you, you're not alone. I've been there. But friend, brokenness isn't the end of your story. Jesus rewrites it with grace.

We are complete in Jesus.

With Jesus, you don't have to earn anything, just come to Him. Trust Him as your Savior and Lord. He'll take care of the rest. God loves you and Jesus died for you, whether or not you ever accept it.

> For God so loved the world that He gave His only begotten Son, that whoever believes in Him should not perish but have everlasting life. For God did not send His Son into the world to condemn the world, but that the world through Him might be saved.
>
> John 3:16-17, NKJV

I'm not trying to preach (okay, maybe a little). But not from a place of judgment. I've carried the same shame. I've walked the same road of wondering if I was too far gone.

Jesus wants you to know that you have a wonderful purpose. You are a beautiful, intelligent, charismatic person that God has created in His own image.

If you want to share your story, or just need some encouragement, reach out to me anytime at kjw@kellyjowilson.com.

I'm listening.

Warm blessings to you,

ABOUT THE AUTHOR

Kelly Jo Wilson writes Christian romance filled with grace, redemption, and the healing power of love. Drawing from her work as a nurse, she weaves heartfelt stories of second chances and restored hope. When she's not writing, Kelly is cherishing life in the woods with her husband, two spirited boys, and a snuggly Rottweiler. She believes hot cocoa tastes best in a Christmas mug, Hallmark movies count as research, and that Jesus is the Master of plot twists. Kelly hosts The Christian Romance Podcast where she chats with Christian romance authors about faith, fiction, and the heart behind happily-ever-after stories.

Join Kelly's free email newsletter at KellyJoWilson.com

ACKNOWLEDGEMENTS

This book is the fruit of a journey I never walked alone. The support, prayers, and encouragement of a beautiful community have been a surprising and cherished blessing. Truly, where God guides, He provides.

First, to my Lord and Savior Jesus Christ, thank You for not only Your sacrifice for me, but for walking beside me. You've guided every step, every word, and every bold move. From career shifts to creative leaps, You've sustained me and my family through the hard and the sweet. I've learned (many times the hard way) that when I try to steer on my own, it gets messy fast. Thank You for never giving up on me.

To my husband Matt (my boy in blue), you're the most handsome and brilliant brainstorming partner a girl could ask for. This book would still be idea fragments without your patience, problem-solving, and support. You're my best friend. I love being your wife.

To my boys, you are my entire universe. Jacob, you're my hype man and creative sidekick, always cheering me on with your amazing heart and imagination. Nathaniel, you bring the laughs and hugs at all the right times. Seeing you both grow reminds me everyday of God's grace. You inspire me to keep dreaming big and trusting God.

To my sister Melissa, you're the heartbeat of my creative world. My muse, my cheerleader, and my reality check when I need it. I hope to thrill you with every word.

To my mom, your unwavering encouragement and constant support have been a guiding light in every season of my life. Thank you for being my cheerleader, my anchor, and a beautiful example of quiet strength. I couldn't have done this without you.

To my dad, thank you for faithfully planting God's Word in my heart. Your wisdom and encouragement have shaped who I am. I'm forever grateful for your steady faith and the way you've taught me to walk in truth.

To my family and friends, thank you for accepting my characters as real people and giving them honorary seats at our Thanksgiving dinner table. Your love and support mean everything.

To my sweet Lily girl (my rottie), thank you for being my writing buddy on many early mornings.

To my critique partners Amanda Trumpower, Becca Wierwille, and Laurie Christine, thank you for your wisdom, encouragement, and for always being there to catch my wild ideas, no matter the hour. I'm so grateful for your hearts and your friendship.

To my writer's group members Jon Shuerger, Kristin Flanagan, and Chris Pierce, you are a fantastic band of word-loving creatives, and I'm grateful for your brilliance and inspiration.

To my wonderful beta readers Jessica Baker, Ashlyn Sanders, Kelly Wickham, Kristin Flanagan, Christina Menhennett, Dana Barrett, and Jonathan Shuerger, your thoughtful feedback and insight helped shape this story into what it is. I'm so thankful for the way you shared your time and your hearts.

To my incredible editors Lisa Jordan, Natalie Hanemann, and Becca Wierwille, thank you for your honest feedback and for helping me weave this story together with clarity, grace, and so much heart. Your expertise has made all the difference.

To Thomas Umstattd Jr., thank you for being my publishing guru and marketing coach. You've pushed me to define my target reader and craft the story she reaches for when Netflix disappoints.

To my Novel Marketing Mastermind Group, your encouragement and feedback have turned this publishing journey into a roller coaster we're all riding together, white knuckles, laughter, and all. Thanks for clutching the handlebar with me.

To the incredible team at Novel Academy and My Book Therapy, thank you for your wisdom and solid storytelling tools you've poured into me and others. Your teaching has been the foundation of my writing life, and I'm so thankful to be learning from the best.

To the My Book Therapy huddle group members Wendy, Lee-Ann, Laura, and Kelly, thank you for the sisterhood, support, and all the laughter we've shared on this wild, wonderful romance-writing journey.

To my friend Lauren, thank you for skillfully covering my gray hairs when helping me brainstorm.

Special thanks to my Kickstarter backers, your belief in this story and your early support made this dream possible. I'm so grateful you took a chance on me. I could not have done this without you. Thank you!

Here's the list of backers in order of when they backed: Lee Anne Womack, C.J. Milacci, Laurie Christine, Giselle, Amanda Trumpower, Josiah DeGraaf, J.A. Webb, Becca Wierwille, Marguerite G, Kathy Brasby, Ani, Melissa, Beth, Jonathan, Mark Warady, Camy Tang, Rick Tester, Gayle Veitenheimer, Thomas Umstattd Jr., Raymond Keith, Kristin Flanagan, Rebecca Reed, Valerie Jo, Jamie Foley, Heather Wilson, CK, Jeroen, Christy S, Rita Sartori, Kylee Weidner, Laura Longo, Leann Wilson, Glenda M Shaw, Stephanie De Luna & Chloé Fasano, Lora Alston, Rebekah, Chris, AJ Elliot, Theresa, Pamela Hart, Kristyn Brendle, Morgan G., Carrie Turansky, E.R. Paskey, and all those who chose to remain anonymous. You are truly a gift and I'm so grateful for you.

www.ingramcontent.com/pod-product-compliance
Lightning Source LLC
Chambersburg PA
CBHW061230310726
48971CB00007B/2010